CW01395692

Jessica Huntley

JINX

Kim
I hope you enjoy reading Jinx.
Thank you for your support.
Jessica
x

Huntley

First published in 2023
Copyright © Jessica Huntley 2023
Jessica Huntley has asserted her right under the Copyright,
Designs and Patents Act 1988 to be identified as the author of
the work.
This is a work of fiction. Unless otherwise indicated, all the
names, characters, businesses, places, events and incidents in
this book are either the product of the author's imagination or
used in a fictitious manner. Any resemblance to actual persons,
living or dead, or actual events is purely coincidental.
All rights reserved. No part of this publication may be
reproduced, transmitted, or copied by any means (electronic,
mechanical, photocopying, or otherwise) without the prior
permission of the author.
ISBN: 978-1-7397697-5-8
First edition
Website: www.jessicahuntleyauthor.com
Cover Design: Getcovers
Edited by: Jennifer Kay Davies
Proofread by: Julia Slack

About Jessica Huntley

Jessica wrote her first book at age six. Between the ages of ten and eighteen, she had written ten full-length fiction novels as a hobby in her spare time between school and work.

At age eighteen, she left her hobby behind and joined the British Army as an Intelligence Analyst where she spent the next four and a half years as a soldier. She attempted to write more novels but was never able to finish them.

Jessica later left the Army and became a mature student at Southampton Solent University and studied Fitness and Personal Training, which later became her career. She still enjoys keeping fit and exercising daily.

She is now a wife and a stay-at-home mum to a crazy toddler and lives in Newbury. During the first national lockdown of 2020, she signed up on a whim to a novel writing course, and the rest is history. Her love of writing came flooding back, and she managed to write and finish her debut novel, The Darkness Within Ourselves, inspired by her love of horror and thriller novels. She has also finished writing the My ... Self trilogy, completed a Level 3 Diploma in Editing and Proofreading and has worked with four other authors on a collaborative horror novel entitled The Summoning.

She is now working on a new novel in her spare time, reads every day (thrillers...obviously) and is also a Thriller Ambassador for Tandem Collective.

Other books by Jessica Huntley

The Darkness Series
The Darkness Within Ourselves

My ... Self Series
My Dark Self
My True Self
My Real Self

Standalone Thrillers

Jinx

Writing in collaboration with other authors
The Summoning
HorrorScope: A Zodiac Anthology

Acknowledgements

This book has been a long time in the making. I wrote the original version when I was a teenager, and it was only a year ago that I revisited the characters and decided to use my own life experience in the Army to add a different twist on the normal crime thriller.

First of all, my thanks go to my sister Alice and my best friend Katie, who always support me with my writing and are always willing to read my books. They've both said that this is my best book yet, so here's hoping that's true!

Thank you to my husband Scott, who helped me with the Army terminology to ensure I remembered everything correctly and helped me format the formal letters within the book. He also told me stories of his time in Afghanistan and told me what it was like over there (as I was pulled off my tour due to my broken hip).

I had six amazing beta readers for Jinx, who helped me adjust some storylines as well as add in some new ones, so a massive thank you to Jamie Taylor, Aimee Johnson, Lucy George, Dawn O'Toole, Becca Bramall, and Sam Mouat.

A huge thank you, as ever, to my amazing editor, Jennifer Davies, who always ensures my writing is shown at its best.

Thank you to my lovely friend, Julia Slack, who proofread the book for me and picked up some pesky missing commas!

Thank you to my writing buddies, Amanda Jaeger, and Mariétte Whitcomb, who kept me accountable every day when I had a deadline to stick too when writing this book. Even messaging my word count for the day was enough to keep me focussed, so I was able to complete it in time to send to my editor. An extra thanks goes to Amanda for helping me with the blurb.

Thank you to my son Logan, who tried his best to distract me at every opportunity! One day I'll be able to show you what I've accomplished, and I hope you'll be proud of how many books I've written while also being your mummy.

I also tried something different with this book by reaching out to some of my favourite thriller authors for a short quote to go on the cover and to use for book promotion. Thank you to S.Graham, Mariétte Whitcomb and Amanda Jaeger, Abigail Osborne, Julia Slack and J.Taylor for taking the time to read Jinx. I'm so happy that you all enjoyed it.

Lastly, I want to thank my readers. Without you, there would be no point in me writing because without you, there would be no story.

Connect with Jessica Huntley

Find and connect with me online via the following platforms.

Sign up to my email list via my website to be notified of future books and receive a twice-monthly author newsletter www.jessicahuntleyauthor.com

Follow me on Facebook: Jessica Huntley - Author - @jessica.reading.writing

Follow me on Instagram: @jessica_reading_writing

Follow me on Twitter: @jess_read_write

Follow me on TikTok: @jessica_reading_writing

Follow me on Goodreads: jessica_reading_writing

This book is dedicated to ...

All the serving soldiers who risk their lives every day.

To all those who are different and are judged because of it.

To any serving soldier who has suffered sexual harassment
and abuse for whatever reason.

To all those who have lost their lives, limbs and parts of
themselves.

To those who keep going no matter what ...

... This is for you.

Trigger Warnings

Attempted suicide
Abortion/Unable to conceive children
PTSD/Depression/Panic attacks
Murder/Death of a loved one
Graphic injury detail
Sexual harassment

Chapter One
Then

Helmand Province, Afghanistan, July 2009

The heat is bone-shatteringly exhausting; each time I inhale it burns my throat and nostrils, and I dread taking my next breath. It never lets up, continuing its relentless tirade of abuse, day in and day out, each day worse than the last.

I knew it was going to be tough out here. It's not like I was expecting it to be chilly and refreshing (it's Afghanistan for fuck's sake), but I also wasn't expecting it to be like living in Hell's basement, where the fire gets hotter every damn day, stoked by Satan himself. I'd prepared for this tour, trained for months on end, but the shocking reality of the heat, the terrain, the sheer amount of energy it takes to even remain standing is, at times, gradually eating away at my soul, one day, one hour, one soul-sucking minute at a time. I already feel physically and emotionally drained and I've only been out here for two months, yet it feels like an eternity.

My tired and overheated brain can barely remember what my mum and younger sister look like. I bet Zoe has already grown another foot taller. That teenager is going to end up towering over me at the rate she's growing. At five feet six inches I guess I'm of an average height, but she's destined to reach six feet for sure.

Even the days roll into one – what day *is* it?

Time appears to be non-existent in this wasteland. Every day is practically the same and I don't get a single day off, but I do get a late start on a Sunday. That's the only way I remember what day it is, when I'm told by my sergeant to be in at 10:00 hours instead of 07:00.

All that matters is my job. I show up when I'm supposed to, do what I'm told and never question it, not ever. That's the stark reality of being a British soldier on a six-month operational tour and I know that; it's why I signed up to join the Army four years ago.

Four years ... it feels like forty.

Four months to go, Aimee ...

'Price! Stop daydreaming about your next fucking shag and finish checking these fucking Snatches.' The rough voice of Sergeant Miller booms across the golden sand towards me.

'Yes, Sergeant!'

I snap out of my daydream of laying on a beach in Florida, sipping a cool cocktail, and focus on the job at hand, checking the oil levels, the tyre pressures and all the other things we're taught to do when first-parading a vehicle. The only thing that matters right now is ensuring the two vehicles, both Snatch Land Rovers, are fuelled and ready to embark on the short trip across the sand to a neighbouring camp. The supplies that need to be transported have already been loaded into the back of each of them so it's merely a matter of finishing my checks.

But the fucking heat ...

It might have been somewhat tolerable were it not for the extra thirty-plus kilos of kit I'm constantly carrying – body armour, webbing, rifle, ammo, day-sack, helmet – they all add up and, on my small frame of little more than fifty kilos, it's often over half of my body weight. And that's just the normal kit I have to carry. Of course, I don't wear full body armour all the time on camp, only when the force protection state is raised, or I venture off camp on a vehicle move, or to visit another camp, but more often than not I do always have to wear some form of protection, which is needed, especially when the threat of an exploding bomb is imminent.

On my very first night here one exploded right outside of camp, which rattled my insides so much I felt sick. The ground shook so violently that I could barely stand. I'd experienced controlled explosions during my training, but it was nothing like the real thing. After that night I realised just how dangerous this job was and told myself that I needed to be more *switched on*, as Sergeant Miller liked to say.

The straps on the webbing dig into my skin whenever I move, my desert camouflage uniform sticking to my sweaty skin. Staying hydrated in this climate is an absolute must and I already learned that the hard way upon first arriving here. Within a week I went down with dehydration and heat exhaustion, having not realised just how much water I needed to drink in order to remain healthy and fit. The usual two litres a day doesn't apply here; a minimum of five litres is required, which would be fairly doable, but here the water is warm, stale and tastes like it's been left out in the sun too long, so I often gag while swallowing it down.

Four months to go …

I rummage around for the set of dog tags I keep stored away in my left inside jacket pocket. They aren't mine (those are around my neck). They belong to Daffy, my grandfather. He gave them to me as a good luck charm and told me they'd keep me safe. I often squeeze them, feel the cool metal between my fingers for a few seconds when I'm feeling particularly down or homesick. It helps.

'All done, Sergeant,' I say, readjusting my webbing for the fifteenth time. The extra weight on my hips is almost unbearable. It's times like these when I curse my slender frame, which holds very little body fat to protect against the heavy armour grinding across my joints. At the end of every long day, when I can finally remove the issued kit, I'll often find a new bruise or laceration on my skin, reminding me how fragile my body truly is.

'Good. Go and find Jones, will you? He's late. Probably taking a nervous shit.'

I inwardly groan, ensuring Sergeant Miller doesn't see my less-than-enthusiastic reaction. Sergeant Miller is probably the toughest guy I've met in the Army to date. He's also one of the scariest men I've ever met and his voice could quite possibly wake the dead. He shaves his head (or maybe he's going prematurely bald, but I would never dare question him about it for fear of instant death) and his stare can pierce steel. He once glared at me for doing something wrong and I honestly thought I would spontaneously combust.

I leave the vehicles and go in search of Jones.

His first name is Thomas ... yes, he's called Tom Jones, but god forbid anyone ever calling him that to his face. He'd probably break their nose. He's known as Jones to everyone, even his civilian mates. I don't like him and I'm pretty sure the feeling is mutual. He's one of those male soldiers who believe women shouldn't be in the Army and he makes no qualms about spreading his point of view to anyone who'll listen. Basically, he's a sexist dickhead. He always gives me such a hard time, belittling my every move, but luckily I can hold my own most of the time so I gladly return the favour. I know very well that the percentage of female soldiers in the British Army is less than ten so it isn't new to me to come across sexism. Even Sergeant Miller muttered a few swear words upon being introduced to me, his latest junior member of the team. There's also something else about Jones that I don't like but, try as I might, I can't quite put my finger on what it is that bothers me so much. Maybe it's just his arrogant, stupid face.

Shielding my brown eyes from the scorching sun, I scan the area behind the main tent, but everyone looks the same in their desert-coloured combats, helmets and boots, and every single body I see is male. I've only seen one other female soldier so far and that had been in the medical tent when I'd woken up after passing out from heat exhaustion. I'm sure there are many female soldiers around but, generally, I'm the only one. It's a lonely life sometimes as a woman in a man's world.

I readjust my helmet, silently cursing my long brown hair which I have to constantly keep in a neat bun at the back of my neck; too high up my head and my helmet doesn't sit right and too far down my neck it gets caught in my uniform collar. I envy the men in the Army sometimes. At least they don't have to worry about their hair. Back in Phase 2 training I paid to have blonde highlights, thinking nothing of it, and when my instructor saw them he told me to take them out and then I was disciplined. Apparently, as a woman you have to ask permission to have your hair coloured and, if you happen to have short hair, you have to ask permission to grow it too.

I stick my head through the gap in the tent; a hot waft of stale air greets me. If it's at all possible, the tents appear to be hotter inside than they are outside. Yesterday, it had reached a scorching forty degrees inside the tent, whereas the outside area had only been a balmy thirty-eight. More often than not the air conditioning packs up and it takes days before it's fixed; that is, if you're lucky enough to work in a tent fitted with air conditioning.

Upon seeing the tent empty, I walk around to the back where the toilet block is located. It's never a pleasant experience using them at the best of times, but add in the extreme temperatures, a less-than-adequate diet and poor cleaning facilities, and it's fucking insufferable. The smell often floats around the camp, catching soldiers out suddenly, making us gag; it all depends on which way the wind is blowing and the time of day. If only I could walk around holding my breath. Heaving my rifle sling further up my shoulder I approach the stinking toilets whilst doing just that.

'Jones?' I call out. 'You in there?'

Without warning the flimsy wooden door flings open and Jones emerges, still doing up his flies. He's had to take all his kit in with him and there's never enough room to set it all down, nor is there often enough time to take it all off, so it's usually a case of deciding whether to hold it or go through the laborious task of taking your kit off.

Annoyingly, Jones is actually quite good-looking in a rugged sort of way. Short hair, chiselled jaw, strong arms and perfectly straight, white teeth. Jones grins when he sees me as my eyes automatically flick to his crotch.

'Sorry Price, wouldn't be right to fuck you in one of these shit holes ... even you deserve better than that ... or maybe you don't.' He winks at me as he fastens the chin strap on his helmet.

I roll my eyes. 'Charming,' I mutter. 'Sergeant says hurry the fuck up. We're leaving soon.'

'Yeah, all right, don't get all hormonal on me. Keep your panties on.'

'My panties are very much on, thank you very much.'

Jones stops in front of me and looks me up and down, cracking a thin smile. 'I bet they are. How long's it been? Did you get laid before you came out here? Wait … of course you did. When's your R 'n' R? Bet you're counting down the days till you can get someone to lick your—'

'Jones! Price! Stop fucking about and get in the damn Snatch! We're leaving in two!' Sergeant Miller is using his loud-enough-to-wake-the-dead voice, which means he isn't messing around.

'Yes, Sergeant!' we shout together.

'Jinx!' exclaims Jones, then pauses when I don't respond. 'You didn't say *jinx*.'

'So?'

'Don't you know anything? Now you've doomed us all, Price.'

'I highly doubt that.' I turn and begin marching back the way I came before he has a chance to speak back to me. I'm not a superstitious person. I was born on a Friday the 13th for crying out loud, so I think I'm beyond all that nonsense. Although, Daffy did say that if I ever lost his dog tags then I'd be jinxed forever … but maybe he was just joking.

Yeah, I'm sure he was joking.

I am not looking forward to spending several mind-numbing hours trapped inside a metal box with Jones. I'd rather be trapped inside the toilet block during the hottest part of the day with no air hole.

The noise from the engine is deafening, which, to be honest, suits me just fine because that way I can't hear the conversation going on between Jones and Sergeant Miller in the front seats. It's probably full of rude remarks and sick jokes that I rarely understand. As usual, I've been sentenced to sit in the back with the kit we're transporting. It's mostly electronic equipment and spare vehicle parts. As part of the Royal Logistics Corps my unit is responsible for ensuring all the surrounding camps are fully equipped, whether it be with general stores, engine parts or food and water supplies. At the lowly rank of Private I'm on the bottom rung of the ladder, something I'm reminded of on a daily basis; hence why I'm squashed into the back of the Snatch while Jones and Sergeant Miller get to sit on relatively comfortable padded seats at the front. However, even the padding does very little to protect against the terrible suspension. Jones is a private too, but he's a man, so obviously gets to sit in the front.

We're travelling in a convoy of two. Whenever we have to do vehicle moves no less than two vehicles are used. It's a safety measure. Our routes are always mapped out and we're constantly in radio contact with each other. Myself, Jones and Sergeant Miller are in the front Land Rover and two other members from our team, Phillips and Jenkins, are in the second.

While I'm being thrown about and wedged against boxes, I cast my mind back to two and a half months ago while I'd still been training for this deployment. Back then, my focus had been solely on my job and nothing else had mattered. I'd even missed Zoe's thirteenth birthday party because I'd had to attend a range day to ensure my Annual Personal Weapons

Test was up to date. I don't think she's forgiven me for that yet.

Then, three days later, two small red lines had appeared on the stick in my shaking hands and my whole life had turned upside down in a matter of seconds. Even then, my mind was focussed on my job and I'd had to make a quick decision about what path I wanted my life to take; did I want to serve my country, or become a mum at the age of twenty-two?

Here I am ...

I hadn't told anyone, not my mum, not my Commanding Officer, not anyone. If they'd found out then I'd have been pulled off this tour whether I'd decided to keep it or not. So I'd had it taken care of quickly and quietly and had turned up for the next part of my training two days later, a little sore, but convinced I'd made the right decision.

I'm still convinced ...

A large pothole puts an end to my daydream as my helmet crashes into the roof of the Snatch. My head spins and I see stars.

'You all right back there, Price?' shouts Sergeant Miller.

'Yes, Sergeant!'

'Atta girl!'

I swear under my breath as I straighten myself up on the hard seat. My webbing and day-sack are wedged beside me, but my rifle is lying across my lap. Its metal protrusions keep digging into my thighs.

'How much longer?' I yell, my throat dry and sore. I reach for my water bottle and take a swig just as the Snatch hits another pothole; the water spills across my lap. 'Fuck!'

'What's the matter, Price? Your ovaries shaking loose?' shouts Jones as he laughs.

I ignore his blatant sexist joke and retort without missing a beat, 'Nope, how about your balls?'

'Ha! My balls are still very much attached, Price.'

'Shame,' I mutter.

'Not far now!' shouts Sergeant Miller. 'Had to take a longer route cos of the Taliban in the area, but the route's all planned. You never know when—' Sergeant Miller never gets the chance to finish his sentence.

A massive explosion erupts like a volcano from underneath the vehicle.

The Snatch hurtles into the air as if it were a tin can.

It's all over in a matter of seconds.

I'm crushed against the force of the boxes in the back as the vehicle comes to an abrupt halt, landing on its roof.

My ears ring, my head swims with visions of blood and fire ... and then nothing ...

Chapter Two
Now

An almighty bang jolted Aimee awake, her eyes flinging open. She clenched the covers as she sat up in bed, her body tense, already in fight or flight mode despite the early hour. Heart pounding, she leaned back and sighed as she realised the noise had emanated from next door again and hadn't been the room erupting in an explosion. She wished her neighbour wouldn't slam his door so loud in the mornings. It was every single morning and it was becoming tiresome, especially since he had lived there for over four years. It didn't help that her entire flat shuddered whenever he slammed his doors. Even the lampshade above her bed shook, threatening to come crashing down on her; maybe one day it would.

Another bang, louder this time, like an explosion.

Aimee was catapulted back to the metal coffin, flipped upside down and pinned underneath the heavy boxes. She yelped and covered her face with her trembling hands, shaking her head side to side as she said 'no, no, no' over and over.

'Stop it!' she shouted through her fingers, which she dug further into her face. She stopped at the sting of pain as one of her longer fingernails pierced her fragile skin. Bringing her hands away, she stared down at them. They were filthy and covered in thick blood … Aimee closed her eyes and began to take deep breaths, like her therapist had instructed her to do so many times.

Breathe in through the nose for a count of three, hold for three and breathe out for three.

Repeat.

Breathe in through the nose, hold, out through the nose.

Repeat.

Aimee's heart rate gradually returned to a relatively normal rhythm. When she opened her eyes she was no longer trapped inside the burning vehicle and her hands weren't covered in blood. She was safe; perfectly safe.

Except she wasn't.

Not really.

She hadn't truly felt safe for the past twelve years.

Her bed was damp. Her excessive sweating had become an almost nightly occurrence. It was always the same nightmare.

Sighing loudly, Aimee threw back the covers and began to strip the bed. She heard the squeak of Darth's hamster wheel coming from the living room down the hall. That little terror had been at it all night, but the sound never bothered her. It was reassuring to know that someone (albeit a hamster) was awake while she was asleep, or at least trying to sleep. He was sort of like her tiny protector.

Bed stripped, Aimee padded down the hall, entered the kitchen diner and stuffed the damp bed sheets in the washing machine, adding washing powder and turning it on. She then flicked on the coffee machine, a present from her mum last year. It whirred to life and began brewing the magical liquid that would hopefully instil her with some much needed energy. No matter how long she slept it was never enough, like her tank was always running on fumes. She imagined that must be what it was like for parents with small children ... A solid lump caught in her throat at the thought, which she quickly swallowed down.

'Morning, Darthy Girl,' Aimee cooed as she dropped a few nuggets through the bars of the cage into the tiny bowl. The smooth black and white rodent stopped running, her nose twitched from side to side for a few seconds and then she continued her never-ending quest. 'Don't you ever get tired of running in place and going nowhere?'

Darth Vader didn't answer; she was a flatmate of very few words.

Aimee sighed deeply as she straightened up. 'Time for coffee. I don't know if you remember, but today's a very important day for me. It's okay that you didn't get me flowers or anything, I understand. I mean, you have important things to do as well ...' Aimee tailed off and suppressed a laugh as she walked back to the kitchen area.

Her flat was fairly small, comprising a double bedroom, a lounge area which was open-plan, located next to the kitchen diner, and a bathroom, but it had been brand new when she'd bought it about eleven years ago and it was still in excellent condition, despite the walls being thin enough to hear doors slamming in the flat next to hers. Her mum had thought her impulsive when she'd told her she bought it without even looking around, but that was who she was; she was impulsive and always had been.

She'd been impulsive when she'd signed up to join the Army at age eighteen.

She'd been impulsive when she'd terminated her pregnancy within a day of finding out.

She'd definitely been impulsive when she'd agreed to marry a man she'd only met months before when she was at her most vulnerable.

And then, of course, she'd been impulsive when, two days before they were due to get married, she'd called off the wedding.

It was her one redeeming quality ... or was it her one astronomical flaw?

Her coffee poured and cooling, Aimee took a quick shower, setting the water to cold, her preferred temperature in the mornings. She squeezed the remaining dribbles of shower gel onto her sponge and began running it lightly across her scarred body. The red puckered lines of skin across her arms, chest and thighs were a constant reminder of her near-death experience; an array of ugly companions. She hated them; hated the way they criss-crossed her body as if they were a decoration, despised the fact that no matter how much Bio Oil she rubbed into them they never faded. They were just there, and would be, always and forever, as a symbol of what she'd given up to be on that tour, a reminder of the terrible choice she'd had to make ...

Aimee shook her head to quell any further horrific visions forming as she turned the shower off. The sound of running water was immediately replaced by a shrill ringing.

'Dammit!'

Aimee wrestled with her towel, securing it around her chest as she sprinted across the corridor to her bedroom. She reached for her mobile, which should have been where she'd left it last night, on the small table by her bed, but it wasn't there. Aimee stopped, attempting to kick-start her foggy morning brain. She could hear it, as clear as day ... but why wasn't it on her side table? Aimee followed the shrill noise and finally found it resting on her dressing table on the opposite side of the room.

'Hello?' she answered in a somewhat aggravated and breathless tone.

'Jesus, it took you thirteen rings to answer your phone … what's wrong?'

'Nothing's wrong. My phone wasn't where I left it and also I was in the shower.'

'With?'

'With myself.'

'Right. Got it.'

'No! Not like …' Aimee smiled as she shook her head, any frustration dissipating upon hearing her best friend's voice. 'What's up, Dot?'

'Okay, so basically I need your opinion on what to wear tonight. It's a first date with this really hot chick who's way out of my league and I'm really nervous and I always hate being nervous cos I get this weird sweaty top lip, and then my pits start to sweat and then I look like a complete sweaty idiot who doesn't know how to string a sentence together.' Dot's words all rolled into one and were spoken at the speed of light, but Aimee had become accustomed to her speech pattern so she was able to easily decipher her code.

'But you never get nervous on dates?'

'Exactly, which must mean I really like her, right?'

'Yeah, I guess so. Okay, well I finish work at five tonight so pop over any time after that.'

'Got it, thanks. Oh … and I may raid your wardrobe, although your taste in clothes is somewhat lacking, but wouldn't hurt to check. Bye!' Dot hung up before Aimee had a chance to say goodbye.

Aimee dropped her phone on the bed and got dressed for work, choosing a pair of black fitted trousers and a black and white striped shirt that she left open at the collar, just enough to show a hint of cleavage, but not enough to see the dull scar across the top of her left breast. She slipped on a pair of comfortable work shoes, went into the kitchen and slurped her now cooled coffee while watching Darth, who was still hard at work running a marathon in her immoveable wheel.

Aimee had never told Dot this, not directly, but Dot, along with her other best friend Cindy, had saved her life eleven years ago when they'd first met. One chance encounter at a bar had completely redirected Aimee's path in life and, instead of ending it all, she'd accepted the kindness of two strangers who turned out to be her future best friends.

Her eyes glazed over as she leaned against the kitchen counter. She was trying not to dwell on the importance of today and the fact that by the end of it she'd know if she was ready to progress to the next stage of the application process in becoming a police officer. Today, she'd hopefully receive her competency interview results.

She placed her empty mug in the sink, grabbed her bag and phone and scanned the immediate area in case she'd forgotten anything. Nothing jumped out at her so she slung the bag over her shoulder, said a quick goodbye to Darth and headed out the door, bumping straight into Nathan, the door-slamming neighbour.

Chapter Three
Then

Helmand Province, Afghanistan, July 2009

There's blood in my mouth and lots of it; that's the first sensation I'm aware of, and the second is the intense wall of heat that surrounds me. I think I only blacked out for a second or two after the Snatch landed upside down. My hearing's impaired; all I can make out is a crackling sound, like wood burning on a cold winter's night, except it isn't cold outside and the fire isn't neatly encapsulated inside a metal stove ... it's inside this metal coffin and it's getting hotter and more vicious and out of control by the second. My ears are also ringing and everything around me is hazy, as if I'm looking at life through dirty glass.

I shout, but my voice is drowned out by the billowing of the flames encircling the vehicle. My throat burns from the thick plumes of smoke coming from the engine area. I gulp down a mouthful of my own blood; I must have bitten my tongue upon impact. My hands are violently shaking and covered in dirt and vivid red blood.

Whose blood is this? Is it mine?

'Sergeant!' I cough. 'Jones!'

A sharp, severe pain shoots through my head like a direct laser beam and a shrill, high-pitched shriek echoes around the metal enclosure.

.Fuck ... I need to get out, but everything is upside down and I have no idea where I am or which way will lead me to safety.

'Sergeant!' Screams of panic choke me as tears fill my eyes, but then I stop, remembering my military training.

Stay calm. Assess the situation. Get help.

Breathe ... you can do this.

That's when I remember the second vehicle in the convoy. They'll come and rescue me soon. They'll have seen the Snatch explode and will be radioing for help right now. It will all be okay.

The unmistakable sound of gunfire erupts around me and my hope of rescue flickers out like a candle flame at the end of its life. The gunfire rattles the metal can as bullets riddle the sides with tiny holes. I duck and cover my head as more gunfire explodes like fireworks from somewhere outside. I hear shouting, but it sounds very far away. Our convoy is under attack and I have no idea where my rifle is because it was flung from my grasp when the vehicle hit the ground.

Stay calm. Assess the situation. Get help.

I repeat the mantra inside my head as I scramble to right myself and somehow manage to get on all fours. I'm still wearing my body armour and helmet, but they are suffocating me; the strap of my helmet digging into my throat. Fuck knows where the rest of my kit is.

The flames are growing higher; smoke is filling the vehicle, sucking out all the oxygen, but I can just about glimpse a murky ray of sunlight ahead of me so that's the direction I head in. I scramble over boxes and debris until eventually arriving at the front of the vehicle; the scene that meets my eyes is one I know I'll remember for the rest of my life.

Sergeant Miller is crumpled in a heap, upside down and motionless, blood running down his face in miniature rivers, soaking his uniform. The entire front section of the vehicle is embedded in his body, almost severing him into two pieces.

I clamp a hand over my mouth to muffle my scream.

I've seen photos and videos of these types of injuries during training. Back then, I'd scoffed and thought nothing of it, never really taking it seriously, but nothing could have ever prepared me for the gravity and horror of this situation. There's so much blood, so many ... mangled body parts. I can see slimy intestine and what looks like a large slab of meat. I immediately retch and vomit up the contents of my stomach.

Even though the image of Sergeant Miller is horrifying to behold I can't look away, but I have to ... I manage to tear my eyes off him and turn to Jones who's half hanging out of the open window, not moving. I can't see any major injuries on him from my vantage point, so there's a chance he's still alive.

I claw my way through the twisted metal until I'm in the front seats, or what's left of them. The windscreen of the Snatch has been blown away, tiny shards of glass covering the area like hailstones, so I pull myself through and out into the open air, coughing violently from the black smoke.

That's when I realise the gunfire has stopped. I hadn't even noticed. I know there's enemy nearby, but I don't know which direction the attack originally came from. The shouting has stopped too ... and that can't be a good thing.

I scour my surroundings, checking for signs of further danger, but I can't see anything but sand and sky for miles. I crawl towards the edge of the vehicle and spot the second vehicle about fifty feet behind. It hasn't been destroyed by an explosion, but it's riddled with bullet holes and there are two dead bodies lying beside it; the other two members of the team.

Stay calm. Assess the situation. Get help.

I take a deep breath, attempting to quell the panic that's rising. I'm alone in the middle of nowhere, surrounded by the enemy. They may have left the area thinking everyone is dead, or they may be hiding somewhere close by, waiting to attack again. I don't know if the other members of the team had managed to radio for help before they'd been killed.

I need to get help. It's up to me now.

Over the sound of the crackling fire I hear a weak groan behind me ...

Jones!

I scramble to my feet, but immediately collapse when my legs erupt in pain. I can't think about my own injuries now. I scream as I drag myself back to the side of the vehicle to the passenger door where Jones is hanging lifelessly, blood and sand covering his face.

'Jones! Jones!'

I grab hold of his body armour and pull, but he doesn't shift, not even an inch. I reckon he weighs in excess of seventy-five kilos and with his kit on top he is probably nearing one hundred kilos in total. I weigh a mere fifty-five, but I've never let my small size stop me before. I've taken part in exercises where I've had to drag a casualty that was double my weight over one hundred feet in distance, but Jones is in an awkward position and it looks as if his legs are trapped somehow inside the vehicle.

I try again, this time bracing my right foot against the side of the vehicle for extra leverage. I heave on the dead weight, leaning back as far as I can ...

The body moves ... ever so slightly.

Again, I pull, shouting out as loud as I can through sheer effort, putting my whole bodyweight into it. Jones's body finally begins to shift until I'm able to drag him out of the burning vehicle and onto the ground.

'Jones!' I scream. 'Jones! Wake up you fucking dickhead! Wake up! Don't you dare die on me.'

Sweat is pouring from my body, joined by trickles of blood, which makes my hands slippery. I have no idea where it's all coming from. I lose grip and stumble backwards onto the hot ground, all of my energy completely depleted, as Jones lands on top of me with a heavy thud, but I can't stop … Jones is bleeding … badly.

That's when I realise the bottom half of his left leg is hanging off, dark red blood pooling around the decapitated limb, soaking into the sand.

'Fuck!'

I hurry to retrieve my personal first-aid pack from my left pocket, yank it open and find the combat-applied tourniquet. My hands are shaking so badly I can barely control them as I hastily apply the tourniquet above the injury, which should help stem the blood flow, but without immediate help I know he doesn't have long.

I check his breathing and quickly conduct a full body search for any further serious injuries, but there are none that I can see, bar a few cuts and contusions, which I can attend to once I've radioed for help.

Jones groans again, but otherwise remains unconscious.

My next problem to tackle is finding a working radio. The one located in this vehicle is destroyed, so I need to get to the second vehicle.

I perform another quick scan of the area and then hobble out from behind the Snatch, my focus on the task ahead. I ignore the blinding pain in my legs and collapse as I reach the second vehicle. One of the bodies has the radio still in his hand, probably halfway through requesting a rescue. I grab it and hold it to my mouth, my voice trembling as I speak.

'Hello Zero, this is Alpha-One. Contact. Over.'

There's static and a short pause. 'Hello Alpha-One, this is Zero. Acknowledged contact. Send 9-Liner. Over.'

'Fuck!' I shout as my brain struggles to recall how to actually send one.

I reach into one of my pockets, emptying everything out, and grab my 9-Liner card, scanning it quickly to refresh my memory of the information I need to send. I try to not hyperventilate as I rattle off my approximate location, the number of casualties and their priorities, the current situation regarding the enemy and the pickup zone details.

'9-Liner received. Medevac estimated in ten minutes. Over.'

'Acknowledged medevac … Alpha-One … Out.'

I breathe a sigh of relief as I drop the radio. I check for a pulse on each of the bodies, but I know they're already dead. I leave them and hobble back across to the burning vehicle. I drag Jones a bit further away from the intense heat and collapse next to him. He stirs slightly.

'Jones,' I say as I shake him gently. 'Jones … wake up. I can't give you anything for the pain, but please just try and stay conscious.' Jones groans again, mumbling incoherently. 'If you survive this, you better start being fucking nicer to me,' I mutter.

I begin to dress his gaping wound with a supplied compression bandage. The blood has stopped flowing out of his leg. There's no way his leg can be saved, even I know that, but at least he'll be alive. I just hope that the medical evacuation team arrives soon. How long's it been since I radioed them?

After I've done everything I can for Jones I turn and look at the burning vehicle. The flames have engulfed it and Sergeant Miller is merely a blackened corpse. I blink back tears, watching the flames crackle and dance. I know in my heart that I made the right decision by leaving him. He was dead when I found him, but at least I've saved Jones ... for now.

I then realise I haven't checked the extent of my own injuries.

Before I have the chance another huge explosion catapults me backwards.

I land with a heavy thump and am met by darkness once more.

Chapter Four
Now

'Oh god, I'm so sorry Nathan, I didn't see you there.' Aimee blushed as she stepped away from the most gorgeous man she'd ever laid her eyes on. Whenever she saw him in passing her stomach performed mini somersaults and her face burned. It was an annoying trait of hers, her body so easily would give away her innermost desires and thoughts.

'No worries, Aimee. It's always a pleasure bumping into you,' he said with a dazzling smile. She reckoned he must work in the model industry with teeth as straight as his and his year-round tan. He always wore designer clothes too, expertly tailored to emphasise every muscle in his body. Despite having lived next-door to Nathan for four years she didn't actually know a lot about him. He was oddly mysterious, which was very intriguing, but he didn't always have time to stop for a chat. This morning, however, he appeared happy to engage in conversation.

Aimee blinked several times and plastered on a happy smile. 'Off to work?'

'Yes, bright and early. Sorry about the door banging by the way. The wind caught it.'

'Of course. No problem. I didn't even hear it,' Aimee lied. He may have been gorgeous, but the door-slamming was becoming his most infuriating trait.

'Great. Listen ... ah ... are you doing anything tomorrow night?'

'No. I mean, well, yes, actually ... I sometimes box on a Friday night.' She wasn't sure why she lied. Friday nights were usually set aside for a girl's night with Cindy and Dot, but the lie had slipped out before she'd had a chance to correct herself.

Nathan tilted his head to the side. 'You … box? As in … punching people?'

'Yeah,' she replied with a hint of a laugh, slightly embarrassed. She was used to the odd looks people would give her when she admitted that a petite woman, such as herself, enjoyed punching the crap out of a punching bag (or whoever agreed to get in the practice ring with her). It was the same look they'd given her when she used to tell people she was in the Army. "You? Really? You're in the Army? You don't look like a soldier." Then they'd usually act slightly weird and awkward and mutter an excuse to leave. Eventually she'd stopped telling people, especially men who asked her out, because the second she told them she was a soldier they'd suddenly find their shoes extremely interesting and would cut the conversation short, almost as if they were intimidated by her.

The same thing was happening now.

Nathan looked as if he'd been backed into a corner by a hungry wolf and was desperately trying to find a clear escape route. He scratched his neck and glanced around nervously. 'Ah, well, in that case, never mind.'

Aimee inwardly groaned. The one time she'd actually managed to talk to him and she'd scared him off within a minute. 'Why, what were you going to suggest?' Maybe she could save the situation somehow …

'Uh … nothing, I mean … I was going to ask if you wanted to come to a new bar that's opening tomorrow night. It's supposed to be pretty good. They serve cocktails in teacups …' As soon as the words were out of his mouth Nathan blushed and stifled a laugh, running his left hand through his perfectly styled black hair. 'Actually, it sounds pretty lame, doesn't it?'

Aimee squeezed her lips together to stop herself from properly laughing. 'No ... it sounds ... interesting.'

'It's just that I'm part of the promotional team for the bar. The owner wants me to go and I'll have my picture taken. I'll post it on all my socials and hopefully drum up a bit of buzz for the place.'

Aimee fought the urge to screw her nose up at his use of *socials* as a noun. She rarely used social media. She was on Facebook, but that was it and her profile was set to private and she only had about a dozen or so friends.

'To be honest, Nathan, I appreciate the offer, but bars aren't really my ... cup of tea.' Another lie, but she couldn't help herself at the obvious joke.

Nathan held her gaze for several seconds and then they burst out laughing at the same time.

'That was a really good one,' he finally said when he brought his laughter under control. 'You're really funny.'

'Clearly you've caught me on a good day,' answered Aimee with a shrug of her shoulders, although she did applaud herself for her quick wit.

'Well ... what *is* your cup of tea?'

'Boxing.'

Nathan scratched the side of his cheek. 'Right ... I don't think my manager would be happy if I turned up for work with a black eye.'

'Are you a model?' She had to ask. The man was pretty much a stranger; maybe it was about time that changed.

'Sort of,' he replied.

'Sort of?'

'I tell you what … how about one night you come and watch me … work.' Nathan dipped into the tight back pocket of his jeans and produced a business card, holding it out for her between two fingers.

Aimee took it slowly, her eyebrows raised as she saw the title heading. 'You're a stripper?'

Nathan beamed his pearly whites at her. 'Not what you were expecting?'

'I'm just shocked at the fact I've lived next door to you for the past four years and I'm only now finding out you're a stripper.'

'You never asked.'

Aimee shrugged her shoulders; he had her there. She'd never once gone out of her way to speak to him directly, always passing him in the hallway with merely a smile, but then he had never made an effort either. They'd exchanged a few pleasantries over the years, but he often had an attractive woman with him, usually blonde and over six feet tall without heels. It was enough to intimidate Aimee. He was way out of her league.

'What do you do?' Nathan finally asked after a few beats of silence.

'I work in a police station.'

'You're a cop?'

'No, I'm an Evidential Property Officer, but I'm hoping to hear whether or not I've passed my competency interview soon so I can progress my application to becoming a police officer.'

Nathan arched a perfectly manicured eyebrow. 'Wow … that's … cool. So you're training to be a cop and you box …

should I be worried?' His cute smile told her he wasn't concerned, but possibly flirting with her.

Aimee found herself blushing again. This would usually be the time she'd reveal she had also been a British soldier, trained to shoot a rifle and stab an enemy in the heart, but she feared that information might send him running, like it did with all the other civilian men she told. 'No need to worry,' she said with a smile. 'I'm not dangerous.'

'Can I call you?'

'Huh?'

'Maybe we can go out another day when you're not busy punching people.'

Aimee gulped, the wind knocked out of her. 'Um … sure, I guess.'

'So, can I have your number? I know you only live next door, but …' Nathan trailed off as he held out his mobile for her to take it, which she did and quickly entered her number before handing it back to him, her hands trembling slightly. Nathan nodded. 'I'll call you.' And then he walked down the corridor away from her and jogged down the stairs without a backwards glance.

Aimee stood still with her mouth open. What the hell had just happened? She'd barely stepped two feet from her door and already had a prospect of a date from a beautiful man … a stripper, none the less. She hadn't been asked out on a date since … god, it was so long ago. She was thirty-four and had only been on one proper first date, but it had gone well. In fact, it had gone so well that he'd ended up proposing to her only a few months later …

'Did the stripper finally ask you out?'

Aimee glanced over her shoulder as she spied Mrs Leamington hovering in the doorway to her flat on the opposite side of the hallway. She was the second neighbour to Aimee on the third floor, but Aimee never heard her doors slamming.

The old woman was dressed in a knee-length fuchsia dressing gown, pink fluffy slippers and pink hair rollers were dotted randomly over her grey hair; Aimee rarely saw her wearing anything else. Mrs Leamington was one of those nosey neighbours who assumed it was her God-given right to know the life story of everyone who lived in the building. Aimee tried to keep her life as private as possible, but Mrs Leamington somehow managed to find out the details anyway, despite Aimee never revealing them. She sometimes wondered if the old woman could see and hear through solid walls.

'No, he was just saying hi,' Aimee said with a forced, friendly smile. She wasn't sure how much of the conversation had been heard.

Mrs Leamington narrowed her eyes. 'I heard everything, dear. There's no point in denying it.'

'Ah …' Aimee stopped and glanced around nervously, wishing the floor would swallow her whole. 'Well … I better get to work.'

'You'll have to let me know how you get on with your police officer application. I've got my fingers crossed for you.'

'Sure. Thank you.'

'And you'll have to let me know when you're going to see him do his stripper routine. I'd love to come and watch.'

'Uh … sure.'

'And you'll have to give me all the gossip on that murder case. You must get all the juicy details working in a police station.'

Aimee stopped beside her and frowned. 'Uh … what murder case?'

'Haven't you seen the news this morning?'

'No, not yet.'

'Ah, well, apparently there was a brutal murder last night only a few roads over from here. Pamela, from my water aerobics class, lives right across the street. She was woken up by loud sirens and noises and there were loads of police outside the bar where it happened. The press haven't released any proper details yet, but they did say that the victim was male and he died because he was stabbed. Isn't that awful? An actual stabbing, right in our neighbourhood. You will tell me what details you find out later, won't you?'

Aimee sucked in a breath. 'I don't have access to the details of ongoing cases and I wouldn't be able to tell you anyway.'

'Of course.' Mrs Leamington stepped closer and gave her a wink before smiling. 'I wouldn't want you to get in trouble or anything, dear.' Another wink. 'You run along now … Oh … make sure you stop by after work. I have another stack of newspapers for you.'

'Thanks, I will. Have a good day.'

'And you, dear.'

Aimee watched as the old woman closed the door to her flat. She rolled her eyes. When she'd first bought Darth two years ago, Mrs Leamington had offered to save all of her old newspapers to line the bottom of the cage. At the time Aimee had accepted and thought nothing more of it, but that small gesture had opened the door enough to make Mrs Leamington assume they were life-long friends, despite the forty-year age gap. She knew all about Fred, her dead husband and the fact that they used to swing with other couples when they were younger. Mrs Leamington delighted in telling everyone who'd listen her life story in excruciating detail. It wasn't even particularly exciting, bar the swinging. Aimee assumed that Mrs Leamington liked to live vicariously through her, although even she had to admit that her life wasn't exactly thrilling either, not anymore.

Aimee jogged down the stairs two at a time and began her ten-minute walking commute to Golding Police Station.

Chapter Five
Then

Camp Bastion Hospital, Afghanistan, July 2009

A sharp beeping noise pierces my body, every inch, every crevice. It drills into my skin, forcing me to the surface of my consciousness. There's nowhere to hide; I have to open my eyes, but they really hurt and I silently scream in protest as I peel my lids open, blinking rapidly at the bright light that's being shined directly into one eyeball at a time.

'Private Price, can you hear me? Focus on my voice. You've been injured in an IED explosion. You're at Camp Bastion Hospital. Can you hear me?'

I hear the words, spoken in a husky male voice, but they make no sense. They're jumbled together like an unsolved jigsaw puzzle, not one word in the correct order.

Something isn't right ...

Fuck ... I can't breathe ...

I can't breathe!

My lungs forget how to inhale as a horrendous pain floods my body from the top of my head down to my toes.

I'm on fire.

My skin is crackling.

I can smell it sizzling, and I'm hot – I'm so fucking hot.

I attempt to suck in the searing air, desperate for the sweet relief of oxygen to sooth my burning lungs, but there is none. It's vanished from the room, taking with it my once calm exterior. I frantically grab the forearm of the man hovering above me as panic and fear rattles through my body. I scream, but no sound escapes my lips as my arms and legs thrash in every direction. My right fist makes contact with something soft yet firm and I hear a snap and a yelp.

'Get the mask on her!' Again, I hear the words, but don't understand them. Numerous pairs of strong hands start pinning me down, grabbing me, forcing me into the hard surface I'm lying on.

Where the fuck am I?

An oxygen mask is shoved over my nose and mouth and held there with a great deal of force ...

And breathe ...

'Private Price, I need you to calm down. You're hyperventilating. The oxygen mask will help, but you have to let it. Look at me. Focus on me. Focus on my voice. My name is ...' I listen as the man above speaks to me, softly and calmly, his voice as smooth as silk. He has a nice face, his skin dark and flawless. Rough hands are still grabbing me and holding me down, but I try and ignore them as I watch the man's mouth open and close. The words still make no sense ...

'IED ... explosion ... injured ... died ... hospital ...'

It's a dream; it has to be. I can't have been involved in an explosion ...

That had been a dream, hadn't it?

'Private Price? Stay with me ... Stay with ... She's haemorrhaging ... She's—'

I don't hear anything else as I slip quietly into unconsciousness once again, revelling in the fact that the pain has finally left my body and I'm free. The concerned face of the handsome Army doctor is the last thing I remember.

Chapter Six
Now

Aimee had lived either in or around Woking her entire life. Her mum lived on the outskirts of the town in a rural village and that was where Aimee had grown up. She'd briefly moved to Guildford to attend university where she started studying Criminology, but had quickly retreated back to Woking upon dropping out of the course after less than a year. She'd then – at a loss as to what to do with her life and after Daffy, her grandfather, had told her she couldn't just sit around and do nothing – walked into her nearest Army Careers Centre and signed up on the spot. Her mum had laughed at her when she'd broken the shocking news. Zoe had high-fived her and cheered, too immature back then to realise what being a soldier actually involved. Daffy, on the other hand, had given her a big hug and then proceeded to enthral and terrify her with his World War II stories, although she expected he'd left out a lot of the serious parts. His one piece of advice had been to always keep her feet dry because foot rot was extremely real and not something she wanted to experience.

Aimee cracked a small smile remembering that titbit of information. It had served her well over the years when she'd been patrolling in all sorts of weather conditions. She could put up with her uniform and kit being soaking wet. She could deal with being so cold her fingertips felt like they might drop off, but what she couldn't deal with was having cold and wet feet inside her boots. The squelching noise was something that sent shivers down her spine even now.

Looking up, squinting into the morning sunshine, Aimee ran her eyes over the large stainless steel Martian sculpture situated in Woking town centre, a homage to the H.G. Wells classic *The War of the Worlds*. At twenty-three feet tall it was hard to miss during her daily commute, its spindly legs only seven inches thick, towering above the public, threatening to come to life.

Golding Police Station was only another five-minute walk from the sculpture and, thanks to the two unexpected conversations in the hall, she was running slightly late. Aimee picked up the pace, almost immediately feeling the tightness in her hips and thighs. She rounded the corner and spied the large building opposite, its glass windows reflecting the light from the sun.

Stepping out into the road, she forgot to pause and check her surroundings as a cyclist zoomed past, shouting expletives at her. Aimee cursed herself, shaking her head, wondering what the hell was wrong with her this morning. Something had her on edge, feeling shaken ... Then she remembered ... she hadn't taken her anxiety medication last night.

'Fuck,' she muttered as she strolled towards her place of work. She looked up at the large gold letters stuck above the glass door, which read "Golding Police Station - Professionalism; Integrity; Courage; Compassion." Aimee wondered if she possessed any of those core values. Maybe she wasn't cut out to be a police officer after all, especially since she'd practically lied to everyone about—

'There you are!' A shrill voice erupted from somewhere in the reception area.

Aimee froze on the spot, but realising it was Cindy, she relaxed her shoulders and smiled. 'Sorry I'm late. I got stopped by two of my neighbours.'

'Get your tiny, pert butt over here and help me decide on whether you think Tony looks more like Chris Hemsworth or Chris Pratt today.' Cindy grabbed Aimee's arm and dragged her over to the main desk, manoeuvring themselves into a position where they could spy Detective Inspector Tony Fields through the glass doors of the back office.

Aimee squinted and bit her lip as if she was seriously considering her answer. 'I'd say he looks more like Hemsworth today. It's the shirt … Chris Pratt would never wear a shirt like that, not with a waistcoat over the top.'

'Yeah, you're right. Plus the stubble on his chin is very Hemsworth. Uh! Don't you just want him to rub his face all over you, so hard it causes a rash all over your body?'

Aimee quickly covered up a laugh with a cough. 'Oh Cindy … how long's it been since you've been on a date?'

Cindy straightened up and stared at Aimee with one hand on her hip. 'Excuse me, but Cindy Booker does not *date*.' The word was emphasised as if it were a dirty one. 'Cindy Booker does very well in the male department, thank you very much.' Aimee cocked one eyebrow, waiting for the final answer. Cindy blew out a breath and rolled her eyes. 'Fine! It's been two weeks, three days and … seventeen hours and … twenty-three minutes since I got laid.'

'You're such a man, you know that. Only a man would know down to the minute when their last shag was.'

'Do I look like a man to you?' Cindy proceeded to unbutton her pink blouse and thrust her ample breasts in Aimee's face, both women erupting into a fit of giggles, which caused the officer who was on duty at the front desk to turn and shush them.

Aimee and Cindy piled into the nearby empty office. Cindy was Aimee's other best friend, her work wife and also the office gossip. She changed the colour of her hair on a weekly basis (this week it was pink) and she kept in great shape by teaching Pole Fitness. She owned and ran a pole dance studio in town and only worked as an Evidential Property Officer here to make ends meet.

'Babe, you look like you haven't slept in a week. What's with the dark bags under your eyes? I can give you some cream for that.'

Aimee sighed and rubbed her neck, feeling the stiffness and knots under her skin. 'I've been having ... bad dreams again.'

'You still seeing your therapist?'

'Sort of ... I haven't been going as often as I should. I'm just not sure it's doing much good anymore.'

'You have long-term PTSD. It's not something you can get over after a couple of sessions.'

'I know that, but it's been twelve years. You'd think if I was going to recover I would have done so by now, right?' Aimee lowered her voice as she continued. 'I can't let anyone here find out about ... you know, what happened.'

Cindy cocked her head to the side. 'You mean about the fact you got blown up in Afghanistan twelve years ago, saved someone's life, earned a medal for bravery and now have PTSD?'

Aimee rolled her eyes. 'Yeah ... *that*.'

'Babe, they're gonna find out sooner or later. You've been here for over a decade. God knows how they haven't found out by now. Don't you think it's going to come up when they do the whole vetting procedure if you pass your officer assessment training, or when you go for your medical and they see the shit tonne of scars on your body or, I don't know, when you have to fire a gun and you can't cos you're scared of loud noises?'

Now Aimee turned defensive. 'I'm not scared of *every* loud noise.'

Cindy raised a perfectly manicured eyebrow at her best friend. 'I just worry about you, that's all. I love you, babe, and I don't like to see you suffering.'

Aimee hung her head slightly. 'I know, I'm sorry, but you know I hate talking about what happened.'

'Maybe that's half your problem. You should be proud! You saved a man's life and have a goddamn medal to prove it … If I were you I'd be wearing that dang thing everywhere I went. What's it called again?'

Aimee cracked a smile. 'It's a Military Cross … It would look good on you too.'

'Everything looks good on me, babe. Anyway, you heard about this murder that happened last night, right?'

'Only briefly. What happened?'

'I don't know anything other than what's on the news, but they're all having a briefing about it soon. Tony's the officer in charge of the case, but you know how tight-assed he can be—'

'You mean tight-lipped …'

'No, I mean tight-assed … Have you *seen* how tight his butt is looking today?' Cindy fanned herself with her hand while leaning back on a nearby desk. 'I reckon he must do squats in his office when no one's looking.'

'Would you just ask him out already?'

'Oh, please! I would *destroy* that man. If we shagged he'd be ruined for all other women, and I just can't do that to our gender. *You* should ask him out though. I can see you two going out.'

'No, thanks.'

'Babe!'

'I don't date men I work with.'

'You don't date at all.'

'Touché.'

'Besides, it's not like you work directly with him. He's a detective and you're not.'

'I still work in the same building.'

'But—'

'I learned my lesson years ago about dating men I work with.'

'But—'

'Ah! Stop.' Aimee held up her hand. 'I don't want to hear another word about me asking Tony out on a date. Not one word.'

'Not even one word?' The deep, rough voice of DI Fields made Aimee and Cindy spin around on the spot, their mouths gaped open in stunned horror.

Cindy recovered quicker than Aimee so she fluttered her long eyelashes at him and smiled, tossing her long pink hair over her shoulder. 'Sorry, *Detective*, didn't see you there, but feel free to sneak up behind me anytime.'

Aimee blushed and attempted to hide it by staring at the ceiling. DI Fields beamed his perfectly straight teeth at Cindy. 'You're a sexual harassment case just waiting to happen, you know that, Booker?'

'Don't you know it,' Cindy responded, not even pausing for breath. 'I love it when you call me by my last name.'

DI Fields smiled faintly and then quickly adopted his strict demeanour. 'Sorry ladies, but I'm going to have to ask that you exit the room. We're using this room for our briefing in five minutes.'

'Right, of course, Detective,' said Cindy as she saluted him.

DI Fields ignored her and turned his whole body towards Aimee, who had been hoping she'd turned invisible within the past minute. 'And Aimee … I actually do need to speak to you about something later. Could you come to my office at ten, after the briefing?'

Aimee's mouth turned as dry as a desert. 'Yes, of course, Detective. See you then.'

DI Fields nodded and stepped to the side so the women could leave the room. They scurried out as quickly as possible, then turned to watch as several officers entered the briefing room, all carrying cups of coffee and clipboards. Once the door was closed Cindy grabbed Aimee's arm and squeezed it so tight she let out a yelp.

'Ouch!'

'Babe!' Cindy shrieked.

Chapter Seven
Then

Camp Bastion Hospital, Afghanistan, July 2009

A cold numbness is spreading through my whole body. It's penetrating every fibre as it forces my previously unconscious mind to find its way back to the surface, back to the light. I wish I could bury myself again, retreat back into my mind so I don't have to face reality because it's too painful, too terrifying. The darkness is much safer. I feel protected by it, but my body is stubborn and it's slowly waking up whether I like it or not. The cold is now so painful that I'm struggling to breathe; something is restricting my breathing ...

Something is ... down my throat.

I gag; the overwhelming urge to breathe washes over me as my body fights the foreign object.

'Private Price, it's okay. Stay calm while I remove your intubater.'

I almost vomit as the tube slides up from the depths of my throat. I cough violently, gagging back bile, but at least I can now breathe, sucking in oxygen as rapidly as I can. Warm hands are on me, gently holding me down on the bed while I regain my composure. It takes several minutes until I'm able to take in my surroundings.

'Can you hear me?'

I blink several times, attempting to clear my blurry vision of the soldier in front of me. He's wearing the usual British Army uniform, but his attire also includes a flimsy light-green plastic apron and white medical gloves. On his right arm there's a large white patch with a red cross, signalling his association with the Royal Army Medical Corps. That's the first thing I notice; the second is that he has the kindest, darkest eyes I've ever seen and I immediately feel slightly less terrified.

'W-Where am I?' My throat burns with the effort of speaking, as if I haven't spoken in years.

'You're at Camp Bastion Hospital. I'm Sergeant James Daniels. Can you tell me your name?'

'P-Price.'

'Rank?'

'Private.'

'Number?'

'W1026915.' I rattle off my Army number easily, having committed it to memory back in basic training, something I know I'll never forget as long as I live. During basic training we were paraded in front of the Commanding Officer to recite our name, rank and number perfectly and if anyone stuttered for a second or forgot it then they'd have to do twenty push-ups, come back and do it again. You had to learn fast or do push-ups. It had been that simple.

'Good. I'll give you this, you have a decent punch. You broke my nurse's nose.'

I frown. 'I-I'm sorry.'

'It's okay. She'll be fine. Do you remember what happened ... Why you're here?'

I stare at him blankly for several seconds, taking in his dark complexion and black hair, and then slowly shake my head. 'I ... I'm having trouble remembering.'

'That's okay, it's perfectly normal. Your memories should return in time. Your helmet did a good job of protecting your head. You were involved in an IED explosion while on a routine vehicle manoeuvre. Do you remember who you were with?'

'I - I don't ...'

'I'm just trying to kick-start your brain into remembering, but it's okay if you don't know.'

I frown as I pull a tiny sliver of memory from the haze in my head. 'Jones ... and Sergeant Miller and two others, Phillips and Jenkins. They're all dead ... Wait ... Jones!' I sit bolt upright and grab the edges of the bed, but the intense pain flooding my body forces me back down. Sergeant Daniels places a hand on my shoulder as the numerous medical machines I'm hooked up to beep ferociously at the sudden change in my body statistics.

'Private Jones is alive ... all thanks to you. Your quick thinking and rapid response saved his life.'

'His leg ...'

'I'm afraid we couldn't save his leg, but he's alive.'

'Where is he?'

'He's in the room next door under sedation at the moment due to the pain. He's stable. Sergeant Miller, Lance Corporal Phillips and Private Jenkins were pronounced dead at the scene.'

I nod my understanding. I knew they were dead, so this doesn't come as a shock. 'There were two explosions ... and gunfire ... I remember bits ...'

'The fuel tank on the upturned vehicle eventually exploded, which caused you further significant damage. You have severe lacerations to your legs and arms. Your body armour did its job of protecting your vital organs, but a piece of shrapnel found its way through and you have a laceration across your chest. You'll be left with scars I'm afraid. You did lose a lot of blood from a piece of shrapnel that sliced through your left leg, which has caused some nerve damage, but with physiotherapy you should make a full recovery in time. You also have internal bleeding, but it's under control for now.' Sergeant Daniels lowered his head. 'You're lucky to be alive, Private.'

'T-Thank you for saving me, Sergeant,' I reply quietly.

Sergeant Daniels nods as he places his large hand over my own. 'Get some rest, Private ... That's an order.'

I force a smile and lean back against the soft pillow, but almost immediately lift it off again. 'My family ... have they been told?'

'They've been informed and, as soon as you're stable, you'll be medically evacuated back home to recover, but after that you'll be expected to attend the Military Rehabilitation Facility, as will Private Jones.'

'When can I see him?'

'I'll let you know when he's stable enough for visitors.'

I rest my head once more and close my eyes. I can still feel Sergeant Daniels's gentle, warm hand covering mine, even though he's already left the room. I breathe in as deeply as my injuries allow; my chest is tight, my body aches down to the core.

And I sleep.

Chapter Eight
Then - James

Camp Bastion Hospital, Afghanistan, July 2009

He could still feel her warm skin on his palm. He couldn't explain it; the tingling sensation he'd felt as he had touched her hand, but he liked it. James smiled as he finished writing his notes on her chart. She didn't need to be woken again to administer her medication for several hours, so for now he'd leave her in peace to sleep. God knows she needed it. He'd witnessed some awful injuries in his time as a medic, seen soldiers crazy with fear and shaking from shock, but the haunted look in her eyes had been one he knew he'd never forget. It hadn't been merely fear he'd seen in them; he wasn't sure what it was, but Private Price was likely to be a changed woman now. He didn't know what she was like before. All he knew was that he wanted to get to know her more, to know the woman who was likely to be changed forever.

Aimee ... that was her first name.

James discarded his gloves, washed his hands and put on new gloves before entering the next room. He needed to put Aimee out of his mind for a while, focus on his other patients, on his rounds and other jobs that needed doing during his eighteen-hour shift, but his mind kept reverting back to her, to her face, her eyes, that tingling sensation ...

What was that?

James approached the bed at the far end of the ward. A thin screen separated the bed from view, which he walked around and then faced the soldier who was lying down, completely motionless bar the small rise and fall of his chest. The son-of-a-bitch was lucky to even be alive and it was all thanks to ... Aimee ...

There she was again, slipping into his thoughts.

James checked the man's statistics on the screen beside him, double checked his bandages for any sign of infection. He hadn't woken up yet, not properly. He'd been semi-coherent when he'd arrived, mumbling gibberish, but had almost immediately been sedated and rushed to the operating theatre where his left leg had been amputated just below the knee. It had barely been attached anyway, only clinging on by a few tendons and strands of muscle. The bones had been severed completely.

Satisfied that he was stable, James walked out of the room and went to walk down the corridor to see his next patient, but his desire to see Aimee again pulled him back to the entrance of her room. He peered in, watching her for several seconds. He studied her face, the small cuts, the dark bruises, the thin, dry lips. She was a hero and the bravest person he'd ever met. He didn't know her background or what her favourite colour was, but he did know that he wanted to know everything about her. She was a shining beacon of light in his otherwise dreary life.

At twenty-eight years old he had barely begun his Army career and, up until this moment, it had been the only thing he'd cared about. His Army record was spotless, full of praise and recommendations from his superiors, all determined to see him promoted as soon as possible. James always went above and beyond for everyone. He worked those extra hours even if he wasn't supposed to, mentored the new junior doctors and nurses when they needed training, never said no to anyone. But now? All he could think about was the woman lying in front of him, covered in lacerations with that empty look in her eyes. He wanted to save her. He wanted to do everything possible to ensure she was happy, yet he had no idea why.

Chapter Nine
Now

A dull, thumping ache floated inside of her head, mainly behind her eye sockets. Aimee wished she could massage her brain, tell it to chill out, relax, but it always refused to cooperate. Her headache grew steadily as she unlocked the security gates to the property storeroom and switched on the lights, illuminating rows upon rows of plastic see-through boxes that were stored on grey metal shelves against all four walls. The lights in this room gave it an eerie vibe, but Aimee was used to spending a lot of time on her own here. Cindy worked with her too, but she was often out on jobs, delivering the stores and items to various locations whenever they were needed. Aimee, on the other hand, preferred to stay at the station and handle the paperwork and emails. Sometimes, when the work was slow, she sat and watched the lights flicker randomly, counting the seconds between each one. She turned on the computer and checked the phone for messages – there was one, so she pressed play and listened while she checked through today's to-do list on her online calendar.

'Hi Aimee, it's Sal from the Guildford branch. Any chance you can deliver the evidence box for case 2348A, dated the 17th of August 2020, today? I need it by this afternoon. Thanks. Bye.'

Aimee scribbled the case number down on her notebook and sighed heavily. Her mind kept focussing on DI Fields and what he wanted to speak to her about in his office later. What had he said exactly? Just that he wanted to speak to her about *something* ... and he'd overheard her and Cindy talking, but how much had he heard? Yes, he'd made it perfectly clear that he'd heard them talking about her asking him out on a date, but it wasn't that particular topic that had Aimee's pulse racing and her palms sweating. Merely seconds before they'd been talking about her PTSD and the medal she'd been awarded for bravery, something that no one in the building knew anything about, except for Cindy.

Aimee slumped in her chair and stared at the flickering lights, counting her breaths. She got to twenty-five and then decided that doing some work would at least take her mind off her meeting with DI Fields for a while.

She was wrong.

Ten o'clock arrived and Aimee had already been waiting outside the detective's office for five minutes. One thing the Army had taught her was punctuality and she was never less than five minutes early for anything ... Well, except for this morning, but that hadn't been entirely her fault.

At five minutes past ten DI Fields finally appeared from around the corner, holding a steaming cup of coffee and clutching a large notebook under one arm.

'Sorry I'm late. The briefing ran over a bit.'

'No problem, Detective.' Aimee felt a familiar lump form in her throat, catching a whiff of his cologne as he leaned past her to open his office door.

'Please ... after you,' he said, stepping to the side.

'Thank you.'

Aimee scurried into the warm office and glanced around, taking in the bare walls and low-key decoration; white walls, no plants, no picture frames, nothing. His desk was immaculately presented, his computer and accessories lined up in perfect symmetry. She'd known him for over a decade, but the man was a complete mystery to her. He rarely smiled, never showed any sort of emotion and didn't appear to have any sort of personality; at least, not at work. Aimee wondered what he was like in his personal life. She assumed he didn't have a family of his own because he basically lived at the police station, often sitting at his desk long into the night, pouring over case reports and answering emails.

DI Fields gestured to the nearby chair in front of his desk. 'Please, take a seat.'

Aimee sat without a word and folded her hands in her lap, attempting to hide the fact they were trembling. She wasn't sure whether it was her nerves or that she'd missed taking her medication last night. She watched as DI Fields drank from his cup and checked something on his computer. Eventually, he relaxed into his high-backed leather swivel chair and made eye contact with her, raising all the hairs on the back of her neck.

Flight or fight ...

'So,' he said with firm tone, 'have you seen the news this morning about the local murder?'

'No, I haven't. I'm sorry, I know you like everyone to be up on current events, but I didn't have the chance this morning.'

DI Fields held up his hand. 'That's okay, I mean, it only happened last night so it's pretty damn current. I don't expect you to know the details yet, I was just curious. However, I've been up all night since it happened and we already have a prime suspect.'

Aimee raised her eyebrows. 'Already? That's quick work, Detective.'

'Thank you. Yes, well, obviously we haven't officially arrested him yet, but my team has been doing some background research on the suspect and something rather interesting has come to light. I thought it best that I speak to you directly about it before we proceed with his interview.'

Aimee sat up a little straighter and adjusted her position on the hard chair. 'Okay.' She had no idea where he was going with this, but something in his tone of voice had her feeling ... uncomfortable.

'Does the name Thomas Jones mean anything to you, Aimee?'

Her heartbeat pounded not only in her chest, but in her ears; the pain in her head was so intense she feared her brain was going to explode from behind her eyeballs. The room swam in and out of focus as her mind conjured up vivid images of dragging a bloodied and disfigured body from a pile of burning wreckage. She smelled the smoke and the blood, felt the heat of the flames singeing her face, even tasted the dry sand in her mouth.

Oh god ... no ...

'Aimee? Aimee, are you all right?' The deep voice was hazy and distant, coming from somewhere in the room, but she couldn't pinpoint it. Where was she? 'Aimee?'

'D-Detective,' she stuttered. 'I'm sorry, I ... What was the name again?'

'Thomas Jones,' he repeated with a frown. 'Are you sure you're all right? You look as if you're about to pass out or puke.'

'I'm fine. It's just a bit hot in here.'

'Let me open a window.' DI Fields stood up and did just that. Aimee took the few moments his back was turned to suck in a deep breath and conduct her counting routine.

One ... two ... three ... four ... five ... breathe.

She felt the cool air tickle her face as DI Fields returned to his chair and watched her for several seconds. He was clearly waiting for her to answer. She had two choices: deny everything or tell the truth, and if she chose wrong then her reputation would be in tatters.

'Y-Yes,' she finally said. 'I think I recognise that name. I might have gone to school with him or worked with him in the past. Why?'

'He's our prime suspect in this murder.'

'I see ...' Aimee paused and opened her mouth to continue, but no words formed on her tongue so she closed her mouth again.

DI Fields leaned forwards in his chair. 'According to our background research team, Thomas Jones was a soldier in the British Army from July 2001 until the end of 2009 when he was then medically discharged due to being involved in an IED explosion in Afghanistan in July of that year. He was pulled from the wreckage by a comrade, but had to have his left leg amputated.' Aimee looked up when he stopped talking, expecting him to continue his story, but he didn't. He merely stared at her.

Aimee attempted to avoid his gaze by staring straight past him at the bare wall, but it was no use. She cracked. 'Okay, Detective. Yes, I knew him when I was in the Army.' There, she'd said it and now everyone would know about her previous career as a soldier and she'd be known as "The Army Girl".

'And you didn't think to mention the fact that you were a British soldier when you started working here eleven years ago?'

'No one ever asked.'

'Not even when you had to list your previous occupations on the application form?' Aimee bit her lip as he continued. 'What about the fact that you saved a man's life by pulling him from a burning vehicle and was awarded the … What was it … Military Cross and sustained severe injuries, spending time at a rehabilitation facility? You didn't think you should mention that either?' DI Fields stopped and inhaled deeply. It was the first time Aimee had seen him slightly rattled.

'You researched me too?'

'Well, we had no choice when we found out who'd pulled Thomas Jones from the vehicle. Why didn't you say anything? When you started working here that incident had happened less than a year before.'

'I don't like to talk about my past.'

'No shit.'

Aimee scratched the side of her neck and sighed. 'Look, okay, I'm sorry I didn't tell anyone about my previous career, but I honestly didn't think it was vital that the station know about it.'

DI Fields narrowed his eyes. 'You withheld information about yourself. Okay, so answer me this … What about when you began the application to become a police officer several months ago? You didn't think it would be vital for us to know then? You intentionally lied on your application form.'

Aimee remained silent as she slowly leaned forwards in her chair. Then she lowered her voice as she spoke. 'I'm sorry, Detective. I really am. I didn't think. I just wanted to put everything behind me and start afresh.'

'What are you hiding, Aimee?'

Aimee coughed, shocked by his direct question. 'Hiding? Nothing. I'm not hiding anything.'

'Why wouldn't you want people to know you're an ex-soldier and a hero?'

'I'm not a hero.'

'Heroine?'

'No, I'm ... I'm nothing. It was nothing. I was just doing my job, that's all. I'm sure anyone who found themselves in the same situation would have done the same thing.'

DI Fields tilted his head to the side. 'I beg to differ. I know a lot of blokes that wouldn't have been able to drag anyone out of a burning vehicle, let alone someone twice their size.'

Aimee lowered her gaze and stared at her fingers, which were still interlaced on her lap. She really needed a manicure. Dot would oblige if she asked her, which she rarely did because she never liked to ask for favours from anyone.

'Okay,' said DI Fields finally, stretching his arms up and leaning back in his chair as he linked his fingers behind his head, 'let's forget about the fact you kept your former career a secret for a second and focus on the fact that you know our prime suspect.'

At this Aimee looked up. 'I don't know him anymore. I haven't seen him in years, not since I left the rehabilitation facility.'

'Right, okay, but you *knew* him. How well did you know him?'

'What do you mean?'

'Were you ever romantically involved?'

Aimee screwed up her nose. 'No, of course not. The man was a sexist and a vile pig.'

DI Fields raised his eyebrows and smiled slightly. 'Okay … now we're getting somewhere.'

Chapter Ten
Then

Camp Bastion Hospital, Afghanistan, July 2009

I spend the next couple of days sleeping periodically, drifting in and out of time and consciousness. One minute the piercing bright sun is beaming through the grimy window next to me, and the next minute the blind is drawn and the lights are off, my hospital bed shrouded in shadows. The only time I really wake up is when Sergeant Daniels administers my pain medication or the nurse brings me some food, but I barely eat a bite, not because I don't have an appetite (and even if I did the hospital food is worse than the cookhouse grub), but because it's too much effort to chew and swallow. Every muscle in my body hurts; the painkillers are only taking the edge off, just enough so I don't pass out from the pain whenever I'm conscious enough to feel it.

I wake up from a particularly bad dream. I see fire and blood and dog tags and they keep swirling around me, getting closer and closer. As soon as a nurse walks into my room I ask her, 'Where are my personal items?'

'Everything you had on you I placed in a plastic bag ready for you to collect when you go home.'

'Dog tags. I need the set of dog tags that were in my pocket.'

The nurse frowns at me. 'Your tags are around your neck.'

'No, not *my* tags. I need my grandfather's tags. I kept them in my pocket for good luck.'

'I'm sorry, but I didn't see any other tags other than the ones around your neck. They must have been lost during the … I'm sorry.' She doesn't finish her sentence. She merely bows her head slightly and leaves the room.

They're gone. The dog tags that Daffy gave me to keep safe and bring me luck are gone. Am I jinxed now?

I blink back tears as I close my eyes. Sleep is calling my name and I must answer …

Eventually, after five days, I'm awake enough to have a coherent thought and the first thing I think about are the missing tags and the second thing is Sergeant Daniels. He has a kind smile and always pops his head round the door to check on me, even if he isn't on shift at the time. An odd fluttering sensation grips my stomach at the thought of seeing him each day. There's no doubt he's an attractive man; his dark skin and brilliant-white teeth make him even more dazzling to look at.

A day later he stops by my bed with a clipboard, a solemn frown on his face. 'I'm afraid I have some bad news.'

My heart plummets like a stone to the pit of my stomach as nausea begins to rise to the surface. 'Oh god.'

'Yes, I'm afraid, Private Price, that you and I won't be seeing each other anymore … This time next week you'll be on a flight home.'

'And that's bad news?'

'It is for me. You've become my favourite patient.' Sergeant Daniels doesn't elaborate any further. Instead, he winks at me and glances at the clipboard. 'By the way, Private Jones is awake and stable enough for a visitor if you'd still like to see him.'

I quickly disregard the possibility that Sergeant Daniels may have just flirted with me and instead nod enthusiastically even though my head explodes with pain seconds later. 'Yes, please!'

'Just a few minutes though, mind.'

'Of course ... Is he ... I mean, has he asked to see me?'

Sergeant Daniels sighs. 'I'm afraid not. He doesn't want to see anyone, but maybe he'll feel better if you pay him a visit.'

Somehow I don't think he will.

'Sergeant, can I ask you a strange question?'

'I love strange questions.'

'Do you believe in jinxes?'

He raises his eyebrows. 'No, I don't think I do. Why?'

'No reason.'

I lower my head as I peel back the thin bed sheets, gingerly manoeuvring my legs over the edge of the bed. Why does my body feel as if it's on fire? Sergeant Daniels pushes a nearby wheelchair closer to the bed, grasps my arm and helps me into it. I let out a gasp as a jolt of lightning shoots through my chest and travels down my leg.

'Don't worry, you're doing great,' assures Sergeant Daniels, 'but I'd advise against any contact sports for a while.'

I crack a small smile as he wheels me out of the room and down the short corridor into the next one. The air conditioning isn't doing a very good job of keeping the hospital cool, but it's a damn sight better than what I've been used to in the tents back on Camp Bastion. My skin is sticky with sweat; I long for a cool, refreshing shower, but that won't likely happen until I'm back home. There's no such thing as a cold shower here.

I still haven't been able to speak to my family directly and can only imagine what state my mum is in, constantly worrying and thinking the worst. She's probably telling the neighbours all sorts of horror stories, attempting to get sympathy.

A screen is pulled around the farthest bed in the room. I take a deep breath as it's drawn back, revealing Jones lying on the bed, hooked up to numerous beeping and whirring machines. His sunken, bruised eyes are closed; his breathing shallow. Several cuts criss-cross his face, giving him the hard, vicious look of a cage fighter. His right arm is in a plaster cast and secured inside a sling, which is strapped to his chest, and what's remaining of his left leg has a dressing over the stump, cut off just below the knee.

My stomach flips as I remember the blood ... so much blood ...

My hands had been drenched in it as I'd tried desperately to stem the flow with the tourniquet. It had done its job. He is alive; that's all that matters.

'Jones ... I have someone here to see you.' Sergeant Daniels pushes me closer to the edge of the bed and flicks on the brake. 'I'll be back in a few minutes.' Then he leaves.

Jones's eyes flicker open, but he doesn't turn his head to look at me. Instead, he stares at the ceiling, barely blinking.

'It's good to see you, Jones,' I say quietly.

I want to ask how he is, but I stop myself just in time because it's a stupid question to ask a man who's just lost his leg. I let out a long breath and slump my shoulders, already beginning to feel exhaustion creeping into them. My chest pounds and my head feels like it's not attached to my body, constantly spinning, despite my body remaining still.

'I'm going home soon so I wanted to see you before I left, but I think we'll be in the rehab facility together so we can help each other get through … you know … everything.'

Jones continues to stare blankly at the ceiling. He blinks once as his jaw clenches.

'Sergeant Daniels tells me you're doing great—'

'Don't … fucking … lie to me,' mutters Jones through gritted teeth.

I straighten up slightly. 'All I meant was that you're stable and out of danger now. I know it's going to be hard to adjust to—'

'You have no fucking idea, you fucking bitch. You should have left me there to die.'

'I couldn't leave you there. I saved your life, Jones.'

'You shouldn't have fucking bothered.'

'You'd have done the same for me.'

'No, I fucking wouldn't have.'

I frown as his hate-filled words pierce my heart. 'I don't believe you.'

Jones slowly turns his head until he's staring straight at me. He strains against the pain as he lifts his head off the pillow, leaning as close to me as his body will allow. 'I'd have left you there to fucking burn to death, you goddamn bitch. Because of you I have to live the rest of my life as a fucking cripple, with people feeling sorry for me. I never want to see your fucking face ever again.' He lowers his head, turning away from me so I can't see the tears forming in the corners of his eyes, but I do see them and I'll never forget the look on his face for as long as I live.

Sergeant Daniels pulls back the screen, breaking the tension. 'Everything good?'

I nod slowly, tears burning my eyes. 'Yes, thank you. Please can I go back to my bed now?'

'Of course, I need to change your dressings anyway.'

'Goodbye, Jones,' I say as I'm wheeled away, but he doesn't respond.

Chapter Eleven
Now

DI Fields rested his elbows on the desk as he leaned towards Aimee. 'Tell me about Thomas Jones. How well did you know him?'

Aimee shrugged and spoke from the heart. 'I didn't, not really. I met him while we were training for our tour of Afghan. The whole section had a few nights out before we deployed, but I never spoke to him properly. He didn't like the fact that I was going to be in his section. He didn't believe women should be in the Army, not out on tour anyway. He said we were weak and made fun of me when I couldn't make it up a hill carrying him on my back during one of our fitness training exercises. I basically avoided him as much as I could, but unfortunately that's hard to do when you're stuck in the same tent day in and day out.'

DI Fields nodded as he made a brief note on a pad of paper. 'Was he ever violent towards you?'

'No, never, not physically, but verbally … yes, very violent and extremely rude.' Aimee cringed as she remembered the barrage of names he used to call her, which had been enough to make her blood boil at the time.

'Did you ever make a formal complaint against him to your chain of command?' Aimee shook her head. 'Why not?'

'Because back then it was always classed as nothing but friendly *banter*. A lot of the time others joined in and laughed about it. Sometimes that's what it's like in the Army, especially as a woman. You have to have a thick skin, especially if you're a minority and don't fit in with the standard squaddie group. He'd always shrug it off and use the line *only joking*. If I reported it then it would have made the situation ten times worse. I learned to live with it.'

DI Fields frowned, tapping his pen on the desk in quick succession; each tap sent a jolt of uneasiness through Aimee's body. 'Was it only you he targeted? Do you think he singled you out at all?'

'No, he was like it with every woman he came across in the Army, but since I was the only woman around a lot of the time, I bore most of it.'

'Were there any men he verbally abused?'

'Not really. It was all banter and jokes with his male colleagues. No one took him seriously. He was just *Jones the Joker*. He was a good soldier. He passed every fitness test with flying colours, was never late, never talked back, always followed orders.'

DI Fields raised his eyebrows. 'And you?'

Aimee gulped. 'I admit I struggled with some of the fitness tests, especially when it came to carrying weight. In fact, I fractured my hip in basic training, but I still managed to pass the tab.'

'The tab?'

'It's a weighted march over a certain distance that needs to be completed in a certain amount of time. I was carrying fifteen kilos over eight miles, which needed to be completed in under two hours.'

'And you completed it with a broken hip?'

'It turned out to be only a stress fracture. It's a fairly common injury with female soldiers since they're expected to carry the same amount of weight as the men, despite weighing less. Not that I'm complaining. It's merely a fact.'

DI Fields scribbled more notes, barely looking up. 'So it's fair to say that Jones had an issue with female soldiers.'

'Yes.'

'What was he like when he found out you'd saved his life and pulled him from a burning vehicle?'

Aimee took a deep breath, recalling the memory that had haunted her vividly since the day it happened. It haunted her dreams; that look on his face. He hadn't been joking.

'To be completely honest, Detective, he was a complete dickhead even then. He blamed me for the fact that he'd have to live the rest of his life with one leg and told me I should've left him to die. He said if it had been the other way around he'd have left me to burn to death.'

DI Fields blew out a breath and snorted. 'Wow, what a wanker. Maybe you should've left him ... Sorry, I didn't mean that. What I meant was he should've been grateful to you.'

Aimee attempted to hide a smirk at his throw-away comment. 'Thank you, Detective.'

DI Fields cleared his throat, looking slightly awkward at the fact his professional shield had collapsed for a brief moment. 'I'll be interviewing him shortly. I don't usually conduct the interviews; that's normally a DC's job, but since this could be connected to you I want to monitor this case a little closer than normal. I'd like you to come with me when I interview him.' It wasn't a question, Aimee noted.

She raised her eyebrows. 'Me? Why? He made it perfectly clear he never wanted to see me again, and I'm more than happy to oblige him.'

'I believe it may persuade him to talk.'

'I highly doubt that, Detective. What's the real reason you want me to come along?'

'You don't miss anything, do you?' Aimee held her nerve and tongue while DI Fields shuffled the papers on his desk. 'It appears that not only do you know – sorry, *knew* – the suspect, but you also knew the victim.'

Aimee failed at holding back a gasp. 'Who?'

'His name was James Daniels. He was your doctor who treated you in Afghanistan, if I'm not mistaken.'

The little colour Aimee had left in her cheeks drained away as she saw black spots dance in front of her eyes. 'Oh god ...' She covered her mouth with her hand and fought back the bile that bubbled at the back of her throat.

'I think you and I have a lot more talking to do, don't you?'

Chapter Twelve
Then - Jones

Camp Bastion Hospital, Afghanistan, July 2009

The nurse with the badly broken nose has left the blinds open at the window to my left, so a scorching beam of sunlight is practically searing my eyeballs in their sockets, but I don't attempt to shield my face. I want the distraction. I don't even close my eyes, just allow the sunlight to blind me as I lie on the hard hospital bed. My body is broken; looking at the pathetic stump where the bottom half of my left leg used to be makes my stomach lurch.

It's gone ...

One second I had two legs and the next I only have one.

I don't remember much about what happened. There was an almighty roar and the Snatch flipped upside down. I heard the gunfire, which sounded like fireworks, and I heard my name being shouted. The memories I have are like small snippets of a movie, fading in and out of a scene, playing in slow motion. I remember landing with a thud on the ground, but have no idea how I got there. I do remember one thing, though ... Price ... Her face ... She was staring down at me and shouting, but not making any sound. In fact, after I landed on the ground there was no noise at all. It was eerily quiet.

I refuse to admit this to anyone ... but I was afraid at that moment, afraid it was the end of my miserable life. There was so much I wanted to do and at that exact moment I realised I'd wasted it. When I woke up I was in this fucking bed where I've stayed ever since. The longer I stare at the ceiling or the wall the angrier I become, as if a dark shadow is taking over my body. I hate Price for saving my life because it wasn't worth saving and now, thanks to having only one leg, it's not worth living. I'll never play football again, never run a marathon, never be able to live a normal life and it's all because of *her*. She should have left me to die.

She came to see me several hours ago and I could barely look her in the face. I didn't want to see her and I never want to see her again. I may have overstepped the line and hurt her fucking feelings, but I don't give a shit about her feelings. Why the fuck did she save me anyway? I'm pretty sure she hates me. Why would she save someone like me, who calls her names and treats her like shit? I admit it; I treat her badly, but it's only because …

No, fuck it.

Fuck her and her stupid bravery. What the hell was she thinking? If it had been me in her position I'd have got out of that Snatch as fast as possible, radioed for help and then checked for casualties, by which time she probably would have burned or bled to death. I'm a good soldier, but sometimes it's about making the right decision, and she made the wrong one. And one day she'll pay for her mistake. I can guarantee it.

Chapter Thirteen
Then

Camp Bastion Hospital, Afghanistan, July 2009

I'm waiting patiently in my wheelchair by the bed after being told that someone will come and transport me to the airfield where I'll then fly back, via various modes of air transport, to RAF Brize Norton and, finally, be transferred to Woking General Hospital to finish my recovery close to home. It's going to be a long journey back, one I hadn't been expecting to be making so soon. As it turns out, I was due to fly home for my R 'n' R, a two-week break in the middle of my six-month tour, in a week's time anyway, but now I'm returning home for good, injured, with a heavy black cloud of doubt and despair hovering over me. This was never part of the plan.

There's a dull ache inside me, deep down, which I know is the unmistakable feeling of guilt, gnawing away at my insides. I shouldn't be going home now; I still have four months left to serve in this hellhole. It's what I trained for months for. It's what I'd given up the chance to be a mum for. I hate the idea of being dependant on my family to look after me and who knows how long it'll be until I'm able to work again – if I'm ever able to go back to work as a soldier. My injuries are fairly severe, not as severe as Jones's, but Sergeant Daniels hasn't mentioned anything about being medically discharged yet, so there's still a chance I can continue my career once I'm fully recovered. It's all I have to cling on to at the moment.

'You okay, Price?' The gentle voice of Sergeant Daniels disrupts my thoughts, which have begun to turn slightly disturbing lately. I don't have any control over them.

I look up and smile. 'Yes, Sergeant.'

'Is it just me or are you not happy about going home?'

'It's just not the homecoming I had planned.'

'But you're a hero. Your family will be even more proud of you than I'm sure they already were before.'

'Sergeant Miller is dead. Phillips and Jenkins are dead. Jones lost his leg and now wishes he was dead and hates me. I'm no hero.'

My face falls and I look down, quickly wiping away a tear, not wanting a senior rank to see my vulnerability. Plus, I've always been told that as a woman in the Army it's seen as weakness to cry and it makes you look pathetic. I don't want people to think I'm weak, especially Sergeant Daniels.

He immediately rushes to my side and crouches down, placing a kind hand on my arm. 'Hey, you listen to me, Price. Don't you dare think that, not for one second. Miller was dead upon impact. Phillips and Jenkins were killed by enemy fire while you were trapped inside a burning vehicle. There was nothing you could have done to save them and you know that. Jones is a dickhead, but deep down he's thankful you saved his life. I can promise you that. It might take him a while to adjust, but one day he'll thank you for what you did.'

I stare down at his hand, which is still clutching my arm softly. His palm is warm against my skin but, despite this, my entire body is covered in goose bumps. I smile and, this time, allow my tears to slide down my cheeks. 'Thank you, Sergeant. Thank you for saving my life.'

Sergeant Daniels squeezes my arm in response as we hold eye contact. His eyes are dark, like molten chocolate. 'Well, it wasn't just me. I had a whole team behind me, but there is one positive thing that's come out of this.'

'And what's that?'

'I got to meet you.'

I hold his gaze as long as possible before I feel my cheeks burn, my stupid body giving away my feelings. I turn away, fighting back the urge to lean over and kiss him. It would be career suicide. I'm a junior rank and he's a senior. Granted, he looks to only be a few years older than me, six at most, but it's still a bad idea. I'm pretty certain that he'd wanted to do the same thing too.

'And I got to meet you too,' I say quietly.

Sergeant Daniels clears his throat, and I'm relieved the moment is terminated. 'I tell you what … I'm out of here in two months. By that time you should be at the rehab facility and well on your way to recovery. I'll stop by and check up on you … if that's okay with you.'

I nod. 'Yes, I'd like that very much.'

'So … I'll see you in two months then.'

'See you in two months, Sergeant.'

Sergeant Daniels smiles at my return to formality. He stands up. 'Goodbye … Aimee.' Before I can return his goodbye he leaves the room, leaving me feeling empty and alone.

Chapter Fourteen
Now

The walls were closing in; the air was being sucked from the room at an alarming speed. Aimee had endured many panic attacks over the years so knew precisely what the telltale signs were. Sometimes, she knew she was going to have one even before the symptoms started, but she'd never had an attack in front of a senior member of staff. No one here knew she suffered from anxiety. She needed help. She needed—

A loud knock interrupted the silence. She looked up at DI Fields to gauge his reaction, which was to frown and look past her at the door.

'Yes?' he said roughly.

Aimee heard the door open behind her and then the unmistakeable, high-pitched voice of her work wife. 'So sorry to disturb you, Detective, but I'm afraid I need to steal the lovely Aimee away for a minute or two. Something's come up regarding the … Polo Case … and only Aimee knows how to handle it.'

Aimee's cheeks flamed as she turned around in her chair and looked at Cindy, who tilted her head with a smile. They'd set up a fake case name years ago to be used only in an event of an emergency, such as chocolate doughnuts in the kitchen or an attractive witness being interviewed. This, however, was the first use of the ploy in an *actual* emergency.

'The Polo Case?' DI Fields didn't sound entirely convinced. 'What's that? I've never heard of it.'

'It's a case over in Guildford that I've been helping with. They wanted some evidence taken over as soon as possible this morning, but I haven't been able to get it sorted yet because I came straight to your office.' The lie waltzed off her tongue easily and effortlessly.

DI Fields raised an eyebrow at Aimee's sudden change of demeanour. 'Fine. Is an hour enough time to sort it out?'

'Yes, thank you, Detective.'

'We still have a lot to talk about, Aimee, including your interview assessment results.'

Aimee nodded quickly. 'I'll be as quick as I can.' She stood up and exited the room as calmly as she could, even though her body was in the early throes of losing control. Cindy grabbed her by the hand and, without saying a word, dragged her along the hall and into the women's toilets, slamming the door shut and locking it.

By the time she'd turned around Aimee was on all fours on the floor, hyperventilating. The swirling black and white floor tiles zoomed in and out of focus, her ribcage squeezing her internal organs tighter and tighter. She heard Cindy's voice somewhere in the background, felt her reassuring hand on her back gently stroking her. She closed her eyes in an attempt to stop her head from spinning, but instead of darkness she saw blood, lots of blood, and an enormous ball of fire that engulfed her like a wave. She screamed as she collapsed on the floor, covering her head with her hands to try and shield herself from the heat. Her friend gently rolled her into the recovery position and mopped her brow with a damp piece of tissue as she lay on the floor trembling, waiting for the attack to be over.

A few minutes later Aimee opened her eyes, blinking at the florescent strip lighting above her. During a severe panic attack she often lost all sense of reality and forgot where she was in space and time. She checked her hands for blood, but they were clean; the fire had abated also. There was no bright orange flame licking at her feet, no blood staining her hands. She turned and looked at Cindy who was holding out a small cup of water.

'What would I do without you?' she asked as she slowly pushed herself into a seated position. She crossed her legs and leaned against the nearest wall, taking several deep breaths before accepting the water and sipping it.

'Babe, I'm just glad I got there when I did, otherwise you'd be on Mr Tight-Ass's floor right now and not this lovely and clean … eww … Seriously, do the cleaners even come *in* here?' Cindy's lip curled as she glanced around the area.

Aimee smiled at her attempt at humour, glad of the distraction. 'Thank you so much for rescuing me. The Polo Case came in handy, for once. How did you know I was about to have a panic attack?'

'I didn't, but I think I know you well enough now to know when you need a timeout.'

Aimee nodded her head, which pounded in response. 'It's bad.'

'What happened? What did he want to talk to you about? Tell me everything.'

'He knows.'

'He knows?'

Aimee nodded her head again and took a sip of water. 'This murder that everyone's talking about … I know both the victim *and* the suspect.'

'What! Does Tony think you have something to do with it?'

'No, nothing like that. He's not accusing me of anything, not yet anyway. He basically said he's found out about my past career in the Army. The guy I pulled from the burning vehicle in Afghan, the guy I saved … he's the suspect. And the doctor who treated me is the victim.'

'Holy shit!'

'But what I can't get my head around is why either of them are here in Woking. They don't live here and I've heard nothing about either of them for eleven years. It makes no sense.'

'Maybe this is about you.'

Aimee frowned. 'But why would it be about me?'

'Babe, I dunno … but that's what Tony is probably thinking right now. The whole building is going to put two and two together when they see you working with Tony on this case and everyone is gonna be talking about it. You'll be like a celebrity!'

Aimee sighed as she rested her head on the cool wall. 'It's the last thing I want. I don't want attention. It's why I've kept everything a secret and now Tony's pissed that I've lied to the whole building for years.'

Cindy gave her hand a squeeze. 'I know it sucks, but it was all gonna come out sooner or later. You know that, right?'

'I know. Tony really wasn't happy I hadn't informed him and HR about my previous career. I honestly didn't think it would be that big of a deal, but now my application to become a police officer is in jeopardy. I just didn't think … I'm an idiot.'

'You're not an idiot, but I think now would be a good time to tell the truth about everything that happened. Are you sure you've told him everything?'

Aimee glanced at her friend and bit into her lip, hard enough to make it hurt. 'There's more.'

'Like what?'

'Like stuff I haven't even told you and Dot about.'

Cindy leaned over and gave Aimee a playful slap on the arm. 'What haven't you told me? It better be damn good.'

Chapter Fifteen
Then

Woking General Hospital, August 2009

I arrived at the hospital late last night, thoroughly exhausted and disorientated. I hadn't managed to sleep during the twenty-four-hour journey, not even with the vast amounts of medication floating around my system. I'd had a nurse accompany me (not the one whose nose I'd broken), who'd checked my vitals and administered pain medication at the appropriate times, but she'd barely spoken two words to me during the trip. I, however, hadn't minded the silence, although it did force my brain into over-thinking every tiny thought that entered it.

What if?

Those two seemingly insignificant words joined together to form one enormous, ominous question.

Woking General Hospital is, thankfully, a much more hospitable place in which to recover. It's early August now, hot and humid outside, but the rooms are the perfect temperature. There's no thin film of dust and sand covering every surface, no rush of hot air whenever a window is opened, but there is one thing that's missing and that's the kind, handsome face of Sergeant Daniels. I miss him already and I know I shouldn't because I've barely known him a week, but during that short time frame I felt calmer, knowing he was there looking after me.

I've already been checked over by the on-call doctor, but another enters my room and stands at the foot of the bed, flicking through some pages on his clipboard. His presence doesn't put my mind at ease, nor does he have a kind face.

'Hi, Aimee. My name's Doctor Parker. I'm the Head Gynaecologist here. I have a few questions for you, if you don't mind.'

'Uh ... sure.'

'When was your last period?'

I furrow my brow, not because I don't know the answer, but because I'm confused as to why he's asked me. 'Um ... before I went on tour. So ... late April, I think.'

The doctor looks up from his notes and arches one eyebrow. Why do I feel as if I'm being judged? This is precisely why I've never seen a male gynaecologist. 'What type of birth control are you on?' he asks me.

'I'm sorry, Doctor, but why is this important?'

'I'm just trying to figure out your history. I haven't been given your records from the Army yet, but there's something that doesn't quite add up.'

'Meaning what?'

'Meaning – forgive me for asking so bluntly – but were you, by any chance, pregnant while you were in Afghanistan?'

I stare at the doctor, barely blinking, barely breathing. Shit ... Should I tell him the truth or a version of the truth? Would it get me in trouble even now?

'I—' I begin, but the words I want to say get stuck in the back of my throat and I start to choke on them, coughing painfully as I attempt to calm myself down. Jesus ... why do I feel as if my own body is trying to kill me? What is this?

Doctor Parker sighs as he lowers his clipboard. 'Aimee … this is important. I don't have to put this on your Army medical records if you don't want me to, but I really need to know the truth so I know how to treat you and what to look out for.'

I reach for the plastic cup of water that's resting on the side table, but the water burns like fire as I swallow. 'I-I had an abortion … b-before I left. I didn't tell anyone …'

Doctor Parker nods his understanding, but I can see judgement behind his eyes. 'Okay, that's fine, thank you.' I'm slightly taken aback by his casual tone as he continues. 'However, I will need to run some more tests and conduct an ultrasound on your uterus to check a few things.'

'W-Why? What's going on?'

'It looks like your uterus may have been damaged in the explosion. I won't know how much damage has been sustained until I take a look. There's been a lot of internal bleeding, but it's hard to differentiate which of your organs are damaged unless we do a thorough examination. We may then need to do surgery, depending on the severity. Do you give your consent to continue?'

'I … I don't … um, yes, that's fine.'

Doctor Parker nods abruptly. 'I'll get you in for an ultrasound this afternoon.' And he leaves the room.

My mind is reeling as I attempt to take in everything he's just said. Doctor Parker has the worst bedside manner of any doctor I've ever met. I'm left with more questions than answers.

The termination had gone as smoothly as was to be expected. There'd been no complications or concerns and I'd been told that I was free to return to normal routine within a week (even though I actually went back to work after two days), but I hadn't had a period since then. That, however, was perfectly normal for my body, due to the change in routine, diet, lifestyle and the increase in physical activity I'd endured since being on tour. The same thing had happened when I'd gone through the fourteen weeks of basic training at the start of my career. My periods had just stopped, which, at the time, I'd been thankful for, as it was one less thing to worry about. No female soldier wants to be messing around with fucking tampons while living in a hole in the ground for a week with no access to sanitation.

But now a doctor is asking me all these questions and sounds concerned, despite his rude and abrupt persona. I close my eyes and say a silent prayer, hoping that the trauma I've been through hasn't ended my ability to have children.

I can't help but think *what if?*

There's those fucking two words again.

What if I hadn't had an abortion?

Have I given up my only chance of having children for a job that I am now in danger of losing?

'Aimee!' The piercing shriek of my mum's voice interrupts my morbid thoughts.

'Mum?' My eyes fly open, darting around anxiously for a glimpse of my family. There they are, racing towards me from the doorway, their eyes brimming with happy tears.

Zoe makes it to my bedside first and, without thinking, flings herself over me like a blanket. I wince at the rush of pain, but don't push the warm body of my younger sister away. In fact, I pull her closer and breathe in her floral scent. She loves wearing perfume and washing her hair with coconut shampoo. Even though it's only been a couple of months since I last saw her, she looks as if she's grown another two inches and she's had her hair cut shorter, into a stylish brown bob, complete with blue dip-dye ends. I ponder how big the argument was between her and Mum when she decided she wanted blue hair.

Mum arrives next, bending over me and planting numerous kisses on my head. She looks tired, but then I'm pretty sure all mums always look tired, even if they've had a full night's sleep. Mum is wearing her favourite grey cardigan that is fraying at the edges and has too many holes to be of any benefit against the elements. Why the hell is she wearing a cardigan in August? I've always thought my mum was weird and this just proves the case.

My grandfather, Daffy, stands at the foot of my bed and offers me a relieved smile, which I return. He squeezes my feet through the thin bed sheet in response. He leans on his cane as he watches the three of us embrace.

Apparently when I was three, I found it hard to say *granddad*. One day, he and I were watching Daffy Duck on the television and I starting shouting Daffy at him, so from then on that was my name for him. Zoe continued the name when she came along. It suits him. He's getting on in years now, but he never lets that slow him down. He still delights in tending to the garden and fixing things around the house. He lives with Mum and Zoe, after having a nasty fall a few years ago in the house he once shared with Granny.

'Oh, darling, you gave us such a scare. You'll never understand the horror of receiving a phone call saying your baby's been injured in the line of duty. I told you joining the Army was a bad idea. You only have to talk to your grandfather to know that ...' Mum flicks a quick glance in Daffy's direction before pulling Zoe away, relieving the weight on my chest. 'Give her some space Zoe! You're hurting her.'

'No, Mum, it's okay. Zoe, squeeze in next to me.' I shuffle over as far as I can on the bed and Zoe cuddles up next to me.

'Did you really get blown up?' she asks.

'Zoe!'

'It's just a question, Mum.'

I smile, stroking my sister's soft hair. 'Yeah ... I did.' I know Zoe will have a lot of questions, as most thirteen-year-olds do.

'Did it hurt?'

'At the time I didn't really feel anything. It hurts now, but I'll get better soon.'

'And you really saved a guy's life?'

'Yeah.'

'Wow, you're a hero! I mean, you've always been a hero to me, but now you're an actual, real-life hero. Will you get a medal and an award and everything?'

'I doubt it.'

Zoe screws up her nose. 'Well, you *should*. So are you coming home now? Will the Army kick you out cos you're injured? Will you get compensation?'

My head starts spinning again, wishing I knew the answers to all of her very important questions. My whole life and career has a big red question mark on it at the moment and I can barely see a day into the future, let alone weeks, months or years down the line. Maybe my career as a soldier is over.

What will I do now?

'Zoe, stop asking so many questions,' scolds Mum. 'Aimee is very delicate right now and she doesn't need you upsetting her.' I smile at her words; she hasn't changed. She still thinks of me as a little girl who needs her constant protection.

'Mum, it's fine. I don't know what's going to happen. I know that once I'm a bit better I can come home for a while, but then I'll need to go away again to a rehab facility to get stronger and do some physiotherapy and after that ... I don't know.'

'Well, if you ask me, I think you should leave the Army and get a regular, safe job ... like Mandy from down the road. She's a lovely girl and she works in the library.'

'For goodness sake Karen, Aimee doesn't want to work in a goddamn library,' mutters Daffy. 'Once we know what's going on, Aimee will decide what's best for her and we should stand by her decision.'

'What, like when you stood by her decision when she decided she wanted to be reckless and join the Army and then go and get herself blown up? Do you still stand by her decision, Dad? Because now you have a granddaughter who's been blown up and could have died. I hope you're happy!' I watch my mum break down in tears as she sinks into a nearby chair, covering her face with her hands.

Daffy glances at me and rolls his eyes; I stifle a giggle. I know it's not a particularly funny moment, but my mum has a tendency to overreact and loves nothing more than a dramatic moment.

'Mum, don't blame Daffy,' I say, 'It was my decision to join. I'm an adult, I can make my own decisions.'

'Hmmfff,' is the sound that escapes her lips.

'Anyway, I'm fine. I'll have a few scars and may need to have surgery, but otherwise—'

'Surgery? What surgery? Why do you need surgery?' snaps Mum, suddenly sitting up straight in the chair as if she's been electrocuted.

'I have some internal damage and—'

'Internal damage? Oh dear god … where's the doctor? I demand to speak to your doctor!' She leaps to her feet and storms out of the room, her footsteps echoing down the corridor. Zoe, Daffy and I watch her until she disappears from sight, and then collectively let out long sighs.

'You should have seen her when we got the call you'd been injured,' says Zoe. 'She practically told everyone who'd listen that you'd been killed by terrorists.'

I knew it.

Chapter Sixteen
Now

Aimee sighed. 'Okay, so I may have lied slightly when I said I hadn't been romantically involved with him.'

Cindy shook her head and held up her hand. 'Wait … you've lost me. Who have or haven't you been romantically involved with?'

'Jones.'

Cindy's mouth dropped open, her jaw hanging limp for several seconds. 'Wait … are you telling me that you slept with the guy you saved? When! I insist you tell me everything right now.' Cindy's voice had reached a new level of shrill, but she didn't sound shocked; she sounded excited, like this was a piece of juicy gossip.

'Okay … I'm about to tell you something and you can't tell anyone. Not even my mum knows.'

Cindy's eyes widened with pleasure, but she nodded quickly and firmly. 'Yes, yes, okay, I promise I won't tell a soul. Wait … what about Dot? I thought we told each other everything.'

Aimee sighed. 'Okay, maybe we can tell Dot later.'

'Okay, okay … What is it?'

Bang, bang, bang!

'Hey! Why's the door locked? I need a pee!'

'Fuck off!' shouted Cindy.

'Excuse me?' came the quick response.

'There's more than one ladies' room in this building!' added Cindy. She turned back to Aimee. 'Okay, go.'

Aimee closed her eyes as she spoke, too ashamed to look her best friend in the eye. 'I slept with Jones during our training for the tour. It was a random shag that I regret every single day. It happened in the back of a club and we did it up against a wall. Anyone could have walked by and seen us. I knew what a dickhead he was, but when I was drunk it didn't seem to matter as much. I just wanted a bit of fun … You've shagged someone you've hated, right?'

'Hell yeah, best sex I ever had.'

'Right … Well, as soon as it was over I instantly wished I could take it back because he told everyone that we'd done it right there and then. I was humiliated and angry, but I kept my mouth shut.'

'So … technically you didn't lie. You weren't romantically involved. You just had sex.'

Aimee shrugged. 'When you put it like that it makes me feel slightly better.'

Cindy nodded. 'Okay … so what about the victim? Who's this doctor guy then?'

'His name was James Daniels and he treated me in Afghanistan and saved my life. When his tour ended he came and found me and we sort of hit it off.'

Cindy cocked her head to one side. 'Wait … I remember you telling me about this, about some handsome black dude who swept you off your feet while you were recovering and then … holy shit!' Cindy covered her mouth with her hand to stifle a squeal. 'He's the guy you were supposed to marry!'

Aimee let out a long sigh. 'Yeah, he's the guy I dumped two days before our wedding. I hadn't seen him since and now he's possibly been killed by the guy I had a ridiculously hot one-night stand with and whose life I saved.'

'And you still don't think this case is all about you?'

'This was all supposed to be in the past.'

'Yeah, but you know what they say about the past … It often has a way of catching up with you.'

Chapter Seventeen
Then

Woking General Hospital, August 2009

Later that day I was scheduled for an ultrasound to assess the damage to my uterus. Unfortunately, it hadn't been good news and now, two days later, here I am in the recovery ward after undergoing a complete hysterectomy. Apparently, my uterus had ruptured (they'd used complicated medical terms which I didn't, and still don't, fully understand). That had caused severe internal bleeding and there hadn't been any way for the surgeon to repair it, so the safest option had been to remove my entire womb.

My mum had been horrified when she'd been told, screaming for a lawsuit, but I merely sat quietly and completely still, taking in the complexity and seriousness of the situation. The doctor, thankfully, didn't reveal the fact that I'd had an abortion only months before. It's my dark secret to keep and now I'll never have the opportunity to become pregnant again.

Sitting up in bed, numerous soft pillows behind me and a scratchy sheet covering my legs, I feel empty. The small television on the wall is on, playing a random game show, but my brain can't fathom anything beyond ... nothing. The space where my womb had once been throbs, not due to the trauma of the surgery, but because of the reality of what the empty space means. I allow the tears to fall, without wiping them away, until the ugly hospital gown I'm wearing is soaked all around my neck and chest.

My mum is snoozing in the chair beside the bed. My family have taken it in turns to stay with me, except for during the night when they are basically forced to go home. Daffy and Zoe will be arriving in about an hour to relieve Mum who, despite her constant nagging and complaining, had held my hand as I'd been put under for the surgery and had been there the moment I'd woken up, cooing over me like I was ten years old again when I'd had my tonsils out.

My mum has a lot of faults, but I can't fault her for always wanting what's best for her kids. Yes, Zoe and I have different dads, but Mum is our one true hero and is basically two parents in one, so I can forgive her for being overprotective (sometimes). I've never known who my dad is (apparently he was a one-night stand and when Mum told him about me he bailed and she hasn't seen or heard from him since) and Zoe has only met hers once when she was seven. It's safe to say that Daffy is our only male role model. He lost his wife (my Granny) just over four years ago and it had hit the family hard at the time. I hadn't even been able to be there, due to having only just started basic training, when she'd taken her final breath.

The Army always came first … but now it's taken everything away from me. *Everything*. How I wish I'd never walked into that recruitment office, never signed my life away on the dotted line, never taken the oath of allegiance and never given up the chance to be a mum for a stupid six-month trip to the goddamn desert.

'Excuse me … Aimee?' I hear the whispered voice of the ward nurse, but I don't respond. I don't want to speak to anyone. My mum stirs from sleep and sits up in her chair.

'Sorry to disturb you, Mrs Price, but these were just delivered for Aimee.'

'Oh! How lovely, thank you. Aimee, darling, look what's arrived for you.' I continue to stare at the TV screen even though nothing is making sense. 'I'm sure she's just feeling a bit groggy,' adds my mum.

The nurse smiles and leaves the room after handing a big bouquet of flowers, a box of chocolates and a card to my mum, who then places them on the side table. The flowers immediately brighten up the plain, colourless room with an array of yellows, pinks and purple blooms, all different shapes and sizes. The box of Thorntons chocolates is so big that it takes up almost the entire side table. My mum sits back down in her chair and opens the card. I listen as the envelope is torn open, and I don't care that she didn't ask my permission to open it, despite it not being addressed to her. I don't care who the card's from. I don't care about anything anymore.

'Oooh!' exclaims Mum. 'Who is James Daniels?' At the mention of his name I turn my head and watch as my mum reads the words inside the card out loud. '*Dear Aimee, I hope this isn't overstepping the line, but I just wanted to send you something to remind you that you're an incredible woman and the strongest, bravest soldier I know. Keep your head up and I promise I'll come and visit you soon. Take care. James Daniels. P.S. I hope you don't mind the informality.*' Mum looks up at me and raises her eyebrows. 'Who is this man? Why have you never mentioned him before?'

I sigh and get back to staring at the screen. 'He was the doctor who treated me in Afghan.'

'It sounds like he was a little more than just your doctor.'

'We … became friends.'

'Friends?'

'Yes, Mum, *friends*. Now will you leave it alone?'

My mum huffs as she places the card beside the flowers. 'Can you blame me, darling, for getting excited when a man gives you flowers? You've never had a proper boyfriend. You're twenty-two. For all I know you're still a virgin.'

I roll my eyes. 'Mum, please.'

'Well, how am I supposed to know if you are or not? You never tell me anything anymore. Ever since you ran away to join the Army you've become so distant and we don't have those long chats like we used to have. Remember? We used to stay up for hours and talk about nothing in particular, but I loved it because I felt like not only were we close as mother and daughter, but you were also my best friend too. I miss that …'

I turn my head again to look at Mum who is now staring out of the window with her arms folded across her chest, her eyes lowered. I must say I'm quite taken aback by her words because, for once, she actually sounds sincere.

'I'm sorry, Mum. I didn't mean to pull away from you.'

'It's okay, darling. I know the Army means a great deal to you. Your grandfather is right … you two are very similar. He lived for his career too. In fact, he nearly died in the war.'

My eyebrows shoot up into my forehead. 'He did? But he's never told me that.'

'He didn't want to scare you, darling. The last thing you'd have wanted to hear before joining the Army was horror stories from the war.'

'What happened?'

'I think that's a story that he should tell you, not me. Ask him sometime.'

I nod in agreement. 'For the record, Mum ... I'm not a virgin.'

My mum turns and cracks a smile. 'I didn't think you were, darling.'

I smile back. 'And James Daniels *is* just a friend.'

'Is he handsome?'

'Yeah ... very. He's also black.'

I watch as my mum attempts to badly conceal her shock. 'T-That's lovely ... I look forward to meeting him one day.'

I just smile to myself. It's not that my mum is racist, but I know that the thought of her daughter possibly dating a black Army doctor will be enough to send her head spinning.

I know there's a topic of conversation that my mum is avoiding. It will need to be spoken about one day: the fact that I can now never bear my own children. Mum had been young when she'd fallen pregnant with me, slightly younger than I am now and I know she always worries about me and Zoe getting pregnant too young. Now, however, that's a worry she doesn't have to think about with me, but I can already feel the guilt creeping up, growing by the second; the guilt that I'll never give my mum any biological grandchildren.

Chapter Eighteen
Now

Aimee took a deep breath and lightly knocked on the office door. The hour was over and it was time to face the no doubt awkward questions that DI Fields would have lined up. Now that the waves of nausea, dizziness and breathlessness had passed she was ready to face the consequences … just about. Cindy had helped her clean herself up and had given her a brief pep talk before exiting the bathroom where there'd been a line of confused and slightly pissed off women waiting outside with their legs crossed.

'Come in,' was the sharp response from DI Fields.

Aimee winced as she opened the door, then walked in and took a seat, immediately blurting out her speech, which she'd practiced earlier in the bathroom with Cindy for at least five minutes.

'Detective, before we get started again, I just want to apologise for keeping the truth from you. I hope you won't hold it against me and that I can still continue with my application to become a police officer. I'm hard-working, dedicated and want to prove to you that I'd be a valuable member of the team.'

Aimee rocketed her words at DI Fields, and he raised his eyebrows. She was more assertive than she'd been previously, more sure of herself.

'I'll need to speak with HR and the recruitment team about your application,' he said. 'For the record, you did pass your recent interview process, so you are eligible to continue to the next stage, depending on what they say when I tell them the truth.'

Aimee breathed a sigh of relief. She'd thought she'd messed her interview up when she'd been asked how she'd handle a disagreement between two drunk men twice her size. She had immediately thought of telling the interviewers about her real-life experience when she'd broken up a fist fight between two male soldiers while on a night out. At the time she'd been very drunk herself, but had somehow managed to pull one of them away from the other, punched him clear in the face, breaking his nose, and then tripped the other one up. By that time, more drunk reinforcements had arrived and everyone had had a good laugh, but Aimee hadn't thought it appropriate to tell them about that, so she coughed and gave them a more adequate description of how she would deal with it, ensuring she ticked all of the metaphorical boxes.

'Thank you, Detective,' she said.

'However, I can't guarantee that the recruitment team will agree to continue with your application once I've informed them about your lack of integrity, but I'll do my best to fight your corner. As you said, you're a decent worker, never late and always dependable. I'm sure as a solider you were the same. I can't say I know exactly what you went through back then, but, having been in a few hairy situations myself and been shot at a few times, I can sympathise with you.' At that point DI Fields appeared to lose his train of thought and paused for several seconds before continuing. 'Although, I must say, I don't know if I'd have had the courage to do what you did ...'

Aimee nodded and smiled, accepting his compliment, but there was something dark behind his eyes, something he wasn't saying. It made him appear more … human, as if there really was a man with feelings and baggage behind his usual strict personality. 'Thank you. I appreciate you giving me a second chance to prove myself.'

DI Fields shuffled some papers on his desk. 'So … no more hiding the truth?'

Aimee gulped. 'No.'

'Great … Now, on to business. Will you come with me to interview the suspect? As I said earlier, he's in custody at the moment, but we haven't charged him yet. We just need to interview him and get a feel for him. You can watch the interview to start with from behind the two-way mirror and, if he starts to act up, then we'll bring you in and hopefully it will make him nervous and more willing to talk.'

'But why? I don't see how that will help. It might make things worse.'

'Just trust me. You're an important person in this case, Aimee. You know the suspect and you knew the victim. That makes you my new favourite person right now.'

Aimee titled her head to one side. 'Lucky me.' Her casual, almost flirty tone surprised her, but DI Fields clearly hadn't noticed it.

'Unfortunately, it also makes you a possible target. Until we find out why James Daniels was killed we have to ensure that anyone connected to him is safe.'

'But I haven't seen him in years.'

'When was the last time you saw him?' DI Fields had his pen poised on his notebook again.

Aimee swallowed hard and felt her confident persona begin to slip again. Should she tell him the truth, that the last time she saw him was eleven years ago when she'd called off their wedding after a whirlwind romance, or twelve years ago when she'd left Afghanistan after he'd treated her injuries? DI Fields was waiting for an answer …

'I … I … The last time I saw him was when I was in Afghanistan in July 2009. He treated me for my injuries.' It was out of her mouth before she'd had a chance to properly think about it.

'And you never saw him again after that?'

'No.' She watched as DI Fields scribbled a few notes.

'Did the suspect and the victim ever meet in Afghanistan?'

'Yes. Sergeant Daniels was also Jones's doctor.'

DI Fields nodded. 'Okay … then let's go and talk to this son-of-a-bitch and see what we've got.'

Chapter Nineteen
Then

Aimee's Mother's House, August 2009

It's strange being back in my childhood bedroom. Everything is exactly the way I'd left it, right down to the faded posters on the walls and the dark Blu Tack stains. My mum has clearly kept up her rota of dusting and vacuuming once a week, but otherwise has left it alone, a shrine to her oldest child, a secret hope that one day I'd return.

Since leaving home I've never had a place of my own. I'd moved from here to Pirbright, where I'd completed my basic training, then I'd been posted to Aldershot where I'd lived in a military accommodation block; a single room with an en suite. All of these moves had been within a twenty-mile bubble of home, which had pleased my mum at first, thinking that I'd be back every weekend for Sunday lunch. However, I'd rarely returned, even though I'd been close by, preferring to focus on my job, my new friends, my new life. Now, I'm back where I started, with no idea of the direction I'm supposed to be heading in next.

I sit down on my bed, wincing as I sink into the soft mattress. A week ago I'd had a part of my female anatomy removed and I still feel hollow inside. The pain is gradually dulling, but there's an ache that's constantly growing and I don't know what it is. Everything is an effort; walking, talking, even breathing. I don't want to admit it to anyone, but there's a part of me that is beginning to agree with what Jones had said. Maybe it would have been easier if I'd never made it back from Afghanistan. My mind drifts to Jones briefly and how he might be getting on. I assume he'll have been medically evacuated back to the UK by now, recovering either at a civilian hospital as I'd done, or been transported directly to the rehabilitation facility.

I look up at the sound of my bedroom door opening. 'Hi Daffy, come in.'

My grandfather smiles as he steps forwards with his cane. 'Hasn't changed a bit, has it?'

'Has Mum even changed the bedding?'

Daffy laughs. 'She changes it every week.'

I shake my head at my mum's ridiculousness. 'I guess I never realised how much my leaving would affect everyone. I just signed up and left and didn't think about any of you.'

Daffy smiles warmly as he sits next to me, grunting softly at the effort. 'Do you remember what I told you after you'd signed up?'

'Always keep your feet dry.'

'Well, yes, and I still stand by that, but I meant the other thing I told you. I said that joining the Army would mean you would have to sacrifice a great deal, and you wouldn't know what you were sacrificing until it was too late. I also said that it would be one of the most incredible adventures of your life, that it would change you as a person, not just physically, but mentally as well, and you would need to prepare yourself for what that would entail.'

I nod, staring down at the ugly carpet; massive pink swirls and red spots. What had I been thinking when I'd chosen it at eleven years of age? 'I remember. I just didn't understand what you meant at the time.'

'Of course you didn't. You were too excited to start a new chapter of your life. Even if I'd have told you not to go through with it you still wouldn't have listened, would you?'

'I wanted to make you proud. I wanted to be like you. Also ... I have a ... confession to make.' Daffy looks at me, his head titled to the side. My mouth turns dry as I begin speaking. 'I lost the set of dog tags you gave me. I think I lost them during the explosion. I emptied all my pockets looking for something and they must have fallen out. I'm so sorry, Daffy, I know how important they were to you.'

Daffy pulls me into a hug and plants a soft kiss on the side of my head. 'My dear girl, those tags aren't important. The main thing is that you're alive and they did their job. They kept you safe.'

'But am I jinxed now?'

Daffy chuckles. 'I'm afraid that was merely an old man's whimsical story.'

I nod, but there's still a small part of me that believes it's my fault I'm in this situation.

A long silence follows, but it isn't awkward; it feels right, but I need to break it with a loaded question. 'What happened to you in the Army, Daffy?'

'You've never asked me that before.'

'I know, and it was wrong of me not to, but I'm asking now and I want to know everything. I can handle it, whatever it is. I think I need to hear it.'

Daffy reaches down and takes my trembling hands in his, squeezing them, allowing his warmth to seep into my skin. 'I know you can. You know, I never even told your mum the whole truth.'

'What about Granny?'

'Not even Granny.'

'Why?'

'You see, back then, things were different than they are today. No one talked about their feelings or told people what was troubling them. We never discussed the horrors of war, not even with each other. We all just … kept it inside and, believe me, that's the worst thing you can ever do. It will eat you up and poison the rest of your life, if you let it.'

'But you seem happy, Daffy. I've never known you to be anything but happy.'

'That's because I am, love. I'm very happy. After the war I had a wonderful life with your Granny. We had your mum and Auntie Rachel not long after. I got a job and we made a good life for ourselves, but … there's always been a dark place inside, deep down inside, that I've never shown to anyone. I saw a lot of awful things no human being should ever have to see. I saw friends and comrades torn apart by explosions right in front of my eyes. I dragged my commander for nearly two miles before I realised the bottom half of his body was gone. I attempted to hold together a man's torso as his innards fell out onto the floor and watched him die slowly. The terror in his eyes is something I see every time I close mine. And now I think to myself … why did *I* survive? What makes me so goddamn special that I survived and they didn't? I ask myself that when I look in the mirror every morning, but you know what else I tell myself?'

I shake my head slowly, biting my lip to stop from crying.

'I tell myself that I *survived* … and I must honour their sacrifice and continue to survive no matter what. Even if it's gets really, really dark. Even if things seem so bad, so hopeless, that you don't know how you can make it through another minute … just remember that you survived for a reason.'

My emotions overwhelm me; tears erupt from my eyes and great big sobs rattle my body as I struggle to form words. 'B-but I can't h-have children a-anymore. Y-you had Granny and M-Mum and Auntie Rachel. I-I have no one.'

Daffy envelopes his arms around me again, being careful not to squeeze too tight. 'My dear girl. You have me, your mum and Zoe. You will always have us.'

'I'm not sure I c-can do this, D-Daffy.'

'You can. You will. You must. Because … you *survived* for a reason.'

Later that evening I join my family downstairs for dinner, the first family dinner I've had in over a year. I watch Zoe scoop the majority of the mashed potato onto her plate from the serving bowl, barely leaving enough for anyone else. I witness my mum filling her own wine glass up to the brim, accidentally slopping a bit over the side. It would have made me laugh, before …

Daffy pours thick gravy over my plate so that the chicken and vegetables are swimming in it. Everyone is acting so … normal, as if nothing has happened and this is just an ordinary family dinner where no one has just been blown up or had their ability to have children ripped from them. Here they all are, drinking wine and eating a roast dinner, chatting and laughing, but I'm not laughing. I sit quietly and eat slowly, one tiny mouthful at a time. I'm not even hungry, but I'll only get moaned at by my mum if I don't finish my plate. She always says I'm too thin and she's right, I have lost a lot of weight since the incident. I catch Daffy looking at me every now and then and he offers me a quick, reassuring smile.

'So … apparently Aimee met a man while she was away,' says my mum out of the blue, taking a slurp of wine. The way she says *while she was away* makes it sounds as if I was merely on holiday and it grates on my already fragile nerves.

Zoe looks up from shovelling chicken into her open mouth and rolls her eyes. 'I'm pretty sure that's not news to everyone, Mum. There are loads of men in the Army. I heard that they outnumber women ten-to-one.'

'No, silly. I mean she met a man who actually likes her. Apparently they're an item.'

I snap my head up. 'We're not an item, Mum … and no one even says *item* anymore.'

'Is that who those flowers were from?' asks Zoe.

'Yes and he wants to visit her soon.' My mum is positively beaming with happiness and cheer, and it makes my stomach roll.

'What's his name?'

'James Daniels.'

'Actually,' I correct, 'it's *Sergeant* Daniels.'

'Is he hot?'

'Apparently so,' says my mum, 'and he's black,' she adds, winking at me.

I can't help but roll my eyes as I eat a tiny piece of roast potato.

'Oooh … Does he look more like Will Smith or Idris Elba?'

'Neither.'

'Interesting.'

I look sideways at Daffy for backup, but he merely shrugs and chugs his beer. It seems that I'm on my own with this one. 'Can we not talk about him, please?'

'Okay, fine. Can I bring some friends round tomorrow to meet you? I want them to meet my sister, the hero.'

I open my mouth to speak, but Mum gets there first, as usual. 'I don't think that's a good idea, Zoe. Let Aimee settle in for a few days, okay?'

Zoe's face falls, but she reluctantly nods.

I close my eyes, relieved that I don't have to be paraded around like a prized bull. It's the last thing I want to do. I have a lot to think about and it's going to be a very long road to recovery, and the dark feeling inside me, whatever it is, is most likely going to make it even more difficult. I'm not sure I'm strong enough to battle the darkness.

Chapter Twenty
Now

Aimee struggled to focus as she followed DI Fields through the corridors of the station to the interview rooms in the back. The station had two of them, both fairly small and simple in design. There were no pictures hanging on the walls, no bright colours to lighten the dull rooms, not even a window to allow in natural light. Her vision blurred, her legs wobbled and her stomach was performing somersaults again. She prayed she wouldn't have another panic attack. Cindy wasn't anywhere around to save her this time and she had to keep up appearances and stay strong. She had no idea how Jones was going to react to seeing her after all this time. She'd seen him briefly at the rehabilitation facility during her recovery, but he'd barely acknowledged her. Back then he'd been an empty shell and now ... now she hadn't a clue what he'd be like, but he was suspected of murder; she knew that much. Could it really be true? Why would Jones have murdered James? They'd barely known each other ...

DI Fields led her into a room situated next to Interview Room 1. It was small and dimly lit with a huge mirror on one wall. Numerous recording and computer equipment were set up on a desk underneath the mirror; a young officer sat on a swivel chair. He stood up and shook Aimee's hand. If he noticed it felt clammy and shaky he didn't mention it, which she was grateful for.

'This is DC Forman. He usually conducts these interviews, but, as I said, I'll be taking the lead on this one. He'll be monitoring the interview and taking notes of anything I may miss. I'll be going in alone to start with to get things going. I'll give DC Forman a signal if I need you to come in, okay?'

Aimee nodded and took a seat at the desk next to DC Forman. At the moment the mirror showed her own reflection; puffy eyes, dry lips, her shoulders hunched forwards.

God, she thought, *I look a mess.*

'Here we go,' said DC Forman.

With a flick of a switch the mirror changed from a reflective surface to a window and Aimee's eyes landed on the man she'd pulled from the burning vehicle all those years ago. She gasped at the drastic change in his appearance. Not only was he obviously older, more lines around his eyes, but his hair was long, so long in fact that it was tied back in a rough ponytail, a few wispy bits escaping at the sides. He sported a long, unkempt beard that looked in dire need of a wash. Aimee didn't like to be prejudiced against people, but he looked as if he lived on the streets and hadn't eaten a decent meal in years. His once muscular physique was all but gone, at least from what she could see, replaced by a much slimmer figure, and his eyes were hollow shells, his once charming and arrogant spark completely gone. Due to the way he was sitting she couldn't see his legs under the table, so she didn't know if he had a prosthetic leg fitted or not.

'Oh my god,' said Aimee, covering her mouth with her hand. She watched as DI Fields wordlessly took a seat in front of Jones, who wasn't paying him any attention whatsoever.

DI Fields slurped some liquid from his plastic cup and placed it lightly on the table, pausing for a few extra seconds before finally speaking. 'For the record, this is DI Tony Fields interviewing Mr Thomas Jones on the 15th of July 2021. The time is 12:04.' He cleared his throat, leaning back in his chair, ignoring his notebook and pen for the time being. 'Do you know why you're here, Mr Jones? Or can I call you Thomas?'

Jones made no sound or movement.

'If you have no objection then I'll call you Thomas. Do you know why you're here, Thomas?'

No answer.

DI Fields allowed the silence to fill the room for several long seconds, clearly at ease, having done this countless times before. 'I understand you were in the Army. How long were you a soldier?'

Jones made the tiniest of movements with his head but continued to stare blankly at the table in front of him.

'Thomas ... you may think that saying nothing is going to help you in the long run but, honestly, if you continue to say nothing then we'll end up keeping you here longer. I just need some answers to a few simple questions, that's all.'

No answer.

'Okay ... let's try something else ... How did you lose your leg?'

Jones shifted an inch in his chair.

'I bet that was difficult for you ... losing your leg and then being medically discharged from the Army, but you must have had a hefty compensation lump sum awarded to you.' DI Fields let the words hang in the air.

Aimee didn't take her eyes off Jones. He wasn't going to talk; that much was obvious. She knew it was only a matter of time before DI Fields gave DC Forman the signal, whatever it was, but she didn't feel ready. Would she ever feel ready to come face to face with the man who blamed her for ruining his life? An uneasy, cold tingling sensation crept up her spine and her heart hammered in her chest, preparing her for flight or fight.

'Would you like something to drink?' asked DI Fields.

'That's the signal,' said DC Forman. 'Out the door, turn immediately left, first door on the right. Knock three times.'

Aimee took a deep breath as she rose to her feet, her mouth so dry she thought she might suffocate as she followed the officer's directions. She stood at the door and knocked three times.

'Come in,' came the immediate response.

Aimee pushed the door open and stood in the doorway, unsure how to proceed. Jones still stared at the table. He'd obviously heard the door open, but had no intention of turning to see who had entered. She cleared her throat, but he didn't respond. It was time to be brave, so she walked a few short paces and stood by the second chair that was next to DI Fields.

'Hello, Jones,' she said as calmly as her quivering body would allow.

At the sound of her voice Jones lifted his head and locked eyes with her, his mouth twitching.

Chapter Twenty-One
Now - Jones

Last night was a blast. In fact, I don't remember a lot of it and that may have had something to do with the amount of beers I drank. The blonde was fit though, although she turned her nose up when she got too close to me. Most women do these days; can't say I blame them.

My body's shaking as I'm bundled into a tiny interview room at the local station. I've got a vague idea of why I'm here, but I have no intention of saying a word. They can't hold me or charge me with anything because I've done nothing wrong. It was all a matter of being in the wrong place at the wrong time. My mouth is dry; I could really do with a drink, and not an alcoholic one either. I've been sitting here for over an hour. What the hell are they waiting for? Just fucking question me already so I can get the hell out of here.

Some dimwit detective left me here. He looked like a twat, all dressed up in his shirt and waistcoat. Who does he think he is … Chris Hemsworth? I'd have punched him for the look he gave me, had he not been a detective. When I was brought in here everyone stared at my leg, like they'd never seen a guy with a prosthetic limb before.

The door creaks loudly behind me and Detective Dimwit enters and takes a seat without a sound. I don't even look up. He doesn't deserve my attention. He asks me a few stupid, random questions, attempting to act like he's friendly and approachable and I can just spill my guts to him and everything will be okay. Then he asks if I want a drink, and, even though I'm parched, I still don't answer him. Why the hell should I? We sit in silence for a minute or so and then the door opens again.

Great, another fucking detective.

I can tell it's a woman by the way she's just cleared her throat. Her footsteps echo around the room as she walks to the chair next to Detective Dimwit.

'Hello, Jones.'

That voice. I know that voice.

I slowly lift my head and clamp eyes on the woman who both saved and ruined my life. My mouth twitches into a small smile as I take in her appearance. She looks ... like shit. But then, I expect I don't look any better right now. She could do with a decent night's sleep and there's a sheen of sweat on her forehead. She's nervous; I don't blame her. I'm fucking nervous too. I haven't seen her in what? ... Eleven years ... Has it been that long?

'I believe you know Aimee Price,' says Detective Dimwit in a condescending tone.

Ah, so that's her first name.

Honest to god, I've only ever known her as *Price*.

I'm glued to the spot, unable to believe what I'm seeing, but I fight to save face and keep up my silent attitude. I don't want to talk to her with Detective Dimwit breathing down my neck. I lock eyes with her, wincing as a jolt of electricity shoots through my heart. Jesus Christ ... those eyes of hers are full of pain and unanswered questions. I narrow mine slightly, hoping that she remembers my silent signal that I'd perfected back in Afghanistan whenever I needed to get her attention while we were working, but didn't want Sergeant Miller to notice. She frowns at me and then asks Detective Dimwit for some water.

There's my girl. I knew she'd remember.

Chapter Twenty-Two
Then

Military Rehabilitation Facility, September 2009

A month later and I've apparently recovered enough from surgery so I can start my recovery programme at the Military Rehabilitation Facility, located in Surrey. It's less than a thirty-minute drive from Woking, which Mum is obviously thrilled about, meaning my family is nearby and can regularly visit me. Mum, Daffy and Zoe all come with me on my first day and attend the walking tour of the facilities and the grounds. Mum asks about a million questions while I stay relatively silent, soaking it all in like a sponge.

It's a spectacular mansion that houses approximately two hundred staff from all three services' medical and nursing branches, comprising physiotherapists, occupational therapists, speech and language therapists, social workers and cognitive therapists. Not only does the facility deal with patients who have physical disabilities, but also those who suffer, or who are likely to suffer, from post-traumatic stress disorder. The grounds are vast, the lawns and gardens a welcoming and relaxing haven to injured military personnel.

Upon arrival I sit down with a group of medics – physiotherapists, consultants – and look at everything that I want to accomplish (or am told I should accomplish) in the next few months. Together, we set goals and I'm given a strict timetable to stick to, ensuring I'm given the best chance of making a full recovery as quickly as possible. After speaking with the medical professionals I feel somewhat optimistic for the first time about my future. The physiotherapists agree I should be able to make a decent recovery physically, however the psychiatrists want me to start one-to-one therapy sessions as soon as possible, which I'm not exactly thrilled about. My first appointment is in a week's time.

Once I say goodbye to my family I'm left alone to explore the grounds and the facility. I have two hours before dinner is due to be served in the mess hall. So, now I'm able to walk around with very little pain, I decide to go for a walk to see the famous tunnel of trees and the long expanse of lawn, which is often, apparently, considered a rite of passage for lower-limb amputees to conquer using their new prosthetic legs.

One thing I notice while strolling around is that everyone has a smile on their face and they all say hello as they pass me, or at least nod a greeting. I've always felt a strong comradeship within the Army, something I've never experienced in civilian life. Yes, I've experienced pretty severe bullying and sexual harassment, but I'm almost certain it was never targeted at me directly. Almost every female soldier I speak to or have made friends with has been on the receiving end of some form of bullying, but, despite that, the Army has always felt like a safe place, especially here among the injured soldiers who are all fighting a different type of fight now; the fight to recover and survive.

The first night I spend in my new bed I hardly sleep. Whenever I close my eyes I see orange flames and bright red blood, often mingling together, forming a strange pattern. It makes my head spin and I wish I could turn off my brain just as easily as turning off a light.

Chapter Twenty-Three
Now

Jones's eyes were like sharp daggers piercing her soul, but she didn't dare look away. She couldn't. She held his stare with the same intensity before DI Fields broke it, clearing his throat loudly and obviously.

'I believe you know Aimee Price,' he said, gesturing to her.

Jones flared his nostrils and then narrowed his eyes at her. She titled her head slightly, recognising the gesture almost immediately.

Aimee slowly sat down, attempting to hide the quiver in her voice as she asked, 'Please may I have a cup of water, Detective?' She realised she was possibly pushing the boundaries of their professional relationship by asking a superior to fetch her some water, but she hoped he'd take the hint to give her and Jones a few moments alone. They hadn't discussed this, so she wasn't sure how DI Fields would take it. She knew they'd be continually watched and recorded from behind the glass, so it wasn't like she had something sinister to hide, and she wouldn't be able to ask Jones something without being overheard. She simply wanted five minutes alone with him.

DI Fields stood up, shoving his chair backwards with slightly too much force that it toppled over. He left it lying on the floor. Aimee assumed the display of dominance was his way of saying that he was the bad cop and she was the good cop, for all intents and purposes.

Aimee waited and listened to the sound of his footsteps getting quieter and quieter. Then she focussed her attention on Jones, studying his introverted body language.

'I expect you're a little surprised to see me ... or maybe you're not. I'm not quite sure. I only found out you were here about two hours ago.'

Jones lifted his head and stared at her. She tried to see past the long hair and beard to the man he'd been before, but she couldn't see him. He wasn't the same. Something in him had changed; broken, even.

'You look so different, I barely recognised you,' said Aimee softly.

Jones inhaled deeply and then exhaled in one big breath. 'Price.' The sound of his voice saying her name sent warm shivers up her spine, which tickled the back of her neck. It wasn't an altogether unpleasant feeling, she realised. 'What's a girl like you doing in a place like this?'

Aimee smiled at his line; the same line he'd used to chat her up all those years ago, albeit drunkenly. He remembered. He was still there ... somewhere.

'A girl's got to work,' she replied.

'You a cop?'

'No. I'm a civilian here, but when Tony' – Jones snorted at his name – 'realised we had a history he brought me in to help.'

Jones raised his eyebrows. 'A history? Is *that* what we have?'

Aimee shrugged her shoulders. 'I'm not really sure what else I'm supposed to call it.'

'How much does Detective Dimwit know exactly?'

'Everything.'

'Everything?'

'For the most part.'

Jones folded his arms across his chest and made another grunting sound. 'Nothing gets by Detective Dimwit, huh?'

'I'd probably not call him that to his face if I were you.'

Jones grinned. Aimee was surprised to see that he'd retained his beaming smile, the one that had once made her stomach flip in hatred and passion. 'You shagging him? You seem to be on a first name basis.'

'No. I only call him Tony when he isn't around, otherwise our relationship is strictly professional.' Aimee prayed that her face wouldn't let her down and redden at the embarrassment. Jones had always been good at embarrassing her.

'Hmmm.'

'How are you, Jones?' Aimee tried a different approach.

Jones raised his eyebrows again. 'Is that a serious question?'

'Of course it is. Why wouldn't it be?'

'Let's see ... How am I? Well, I'm doing peachy ... How about you, Price?'

Aimee narrowed her eyes. He hadn't changed, not really. He was still an annoying, arrogant dickhead who took pleasure in messing her about and giving her a hard time. Aimee was looking forward to DI Fields returning and putting him in his place.

As if on cue the door opened and DI Fields walked in carrying a plastic cup.

'Hope I'm not disturbing anything.' He set the water down on the table with a thud, spilling a few drops. 'All caught up are we?' Jones sniffed loudly and grunted yet again. 'What was that, Thomas?' snapped DI Fields as he picked up his chair and set it straight, taking a seat. The two men glared across the table at each other, neither one breaking eye contact.

'I think he prefers to be called Jones,' said Aimee shyly.

'Does he now? Not Tom? Maybe I should call him Tom Jones.'

Aimee winced as she watched Jones's upper lip curl. He'd always hated it when people called him that, attempting a joke at his expense.

'It's *Jones*,' he growled.

'I prefer Tom Jones.'

'And I prefer Detective Dimwit.'

Aimee leaned forwards and picked up the cup, taking a sip, wishing she could sink into the floor and escape the testosterone-filled room. The air practically stank of it.

'So ... are you ready to answer some questions now?' asked DI Fields, ignoring his obvious attempt at belittling him.

Jones shrugged. 'Depends if they're stupid questions or not.'

'How about I be the judge of that? Let's start with a fairly simple one. Do you know why you're here?'

'No,' came the abrupt reply.

'You sure about that?'

'Stupid question. Next.'

'How well do you know James Daniels?'

Jones screwed up his face. 'Who?'

Aimee leaned forwards in her chair. 'Sergeant Daniels,' she clarified. 'He was the doctor who treated us in Afghan.'

DI Fields held up his hand to Aimee. 'Thank you, Aimee, but I'll ask the questions ... Well?'

'Stupid question. Price already answered it.'

'I want to hear it from you. How well do you know him?'

Jones sighed loudly. 'He was the doctor who treated me in Afghan when I got my fucking leg blown off.'

'And you haven't seen or spoken to him since?'

'Stupid question. Next.'

This time it was DI Fields's turn to sigh loudly. 'Fine. Let me make it perfectly clear for you. You're here because you were found at the scene of a crime — a murder, actually — James Daniels's murder. So, I'll ask you again ... When was the last time you saw or spoke to him?'

Jones raised his eyebrows at Aimee, who did her best not to react. She took another sip of water to moisten her exceptionally dry mouth. Her skin felt sticky with sweat even though the air conditioning was on full blast.

'The last time I saw Daniels was at the rehab facility where Price and I spent time recovering in 2009.'

Aimee's breath caught in her throat and she choked on the last drop of water on her tongue. She glared at Jones, managing to get her coughing under control, and gave him the slightest of head shakes.

Don't say it, she thought.

'What was he doing at the rehab facility?' asked DI Fields. 'I thought he only treated you in Afghanistan?'

Jones's eyes darted sideways at Aimee for the briefest of moments before he shrugged. 'I dunno. He was a doctor. I assume he was treating other patients there.'

Aimee closed her eyes and allowed her shoulders to relax. Jones had lied for her without knowing the reason. Why had he done that? Because she'd wordlessly asked him to or for his own hidden agenda?

DI Fields glanced down at his notebook. 'What were you doing at Maynard's Place at one o'clock in the morning?'

'Stupid question.'

'I beg to differ.'

'It's a bar … *Clearly* I was drinking.' Was that an eye twitch Aimee had just seen as he'd said that?

'You didn't see the body of your former doctor with his throat sliced open and stab wounds all over his body?'

Jones laughed. 'That's got to be the stupidest question so far.'

'Yes or no?'

'No.'

'Were you with anyone at the bar who can corroborate your story, that you were just *drinking*?'

'Sure.'

'I'm going to need a name.'

Jones chewed on his bottom lip for several seconds. 'Just some skank for a hook-up. I think she worked there. I don't do names, but she was tall, blonde, had the most perfect pair of double D's I've ever seen and an ass just perfect for—'

'Thank you, that's quite enough of a description. I think I know who you're talking about.'

Jones grinned. 'Of course you do, *Detective*.' He winked at him.

DI Fields glanced at Aimee for a few seconds, appearing to gather his thoughts, and then continued his verbal assault. 'What was your relationship with Aimee back when you worked together in Afghanistan?'

Aimee saw Jones tense his jaw. 'You just answered your own stupid question. I'm beginning to think you're not a very good detective.'

'So you worked together?'

'Yep.'

'And before that? Before Afghanistan ...'

'We met while we were in deployment training several months before Afghan.'

'Aimee tells me you were a bit of a dickhead.'

Jones tipped his head back and laughed loudly. 'She would say that. It's cos she had a thing for me. All the ladies did.'

'In your dreams,' muttered Aimee.

'No, Price ... in *yours*.' Jones kissed the air in her direction.

Aimee stopped herself from physically shuddering. The nausea was building up again, broiling underneath the surface. The walls were closing in, inch by inch, minute by minute. She needed to get out of here ...

'Okay,' said DI Fields loudly, 'let's move on. Why are you in Woking? According to your most recent address you live in Milton Keynes.'

'Fancied a change of scenery.'

'Did you know that Aimee lived here?'

'A happy coincidence.'

'In a murder investigation we don't believe in coincidences.'

Jones shrugged. 'Don't know what else to tell you, *mate*.'

DI Fields clenched his teeth in clear frustration and then blew out a long sigh as he leaned back in his chair, tipping it and balancing on its two back legs. 'Well, unfortunately, I don't have enough to hold you, but I'm sure I'll have more questions for you, so make sure you stay in town. I need to talk to the owner of the bar and your ... blonde woman.'

Jones nodded curtly. 'Right-o.'

'I need to be able to get a hold of you. Please write down your phone number and where you're staying.' DI Fields pushed a piece of paper across the table at him.

'I don't have a phone and the place I'm staying doesn't have an address.'

DI Fields frowned as he asked, 'What do you mean?'

Jones rolled his eyes. 'I'm staying at this great little bus stop that's out of the way. Keeps the rain off, you know. It's just by the small Tesco Express in town. You can find me there if you have any further questions.'

A silence followed, one that Aimee spent quickly thinking up a plan. Before she could change her mind she sighed and stood up abruptly, her chair scraping loudly across the floor.

'That's ridiculous, Jones.' She turned to DI Fields. 'If you need to speak to him then call my number. He'll be staying with me, Detective.' By the smug grin that appeared on Jones's face she knew she'd probably regret her decision within the hour.

Chapter Twenty-Four
Then - James

Military Rehabilitation Facility, September 2009

James was happy to be back on home soil. His third tour in Afghanistan had left him tired and questioning his sanity, wondering why he'd become an Army doctor in the first place. He'd seen so many brutal injuries, so many lives lost or ruined; it was enough to make anyone crazy. Yet, despite the horrific brutality of the war, two months ago he'd met Aimee Price and somehow she seemed to make his days a little brighter, a little less mundane. He only had to think of her and a smile would appear on his face from out of nowhere.

It had probably been slightly forward and inappropriate to send flowers and chocolates to her hospital bed, but he wanted her to know how much he was thinking about her, that he hadn't given up on her. He had only been back in the UK for four days, hadn't even travelled to see his mum and dad and brother yet; he had a stop to make first.

The rehabilitation facility where Aimee was being treated was familiar territory to James. He'd been posted here once before, a few years ago, and knew several of the military staff as close friends. He popped his head round the door to the staffroom and caught sight of Simon Kilner, a fellow medic who'd gone through basic training with many years before. Simon was a tall, lean man with thick, brown hair that looked like it was overdue for a cut.

'Daniels?'

'Yeah, Kilner, how's it going?'

Simon leapt to his feet and embraced his old friend, slapping him on the back. 'It's great to see you. How was Afghan? When did you get back?'

'Ah, you know, Afghan never changes. Got back a few days ago. What's with the boy band hairstyle? I'm pretty sure that's not regulation.'

Simon laughed. 'Yeah, well, not been bollocked yet. What the hell are you doing here, Daniels? You can't have missed me that much.'

'Actually, I'm here to see someone, a patient.'

'Ah yeah, she cute?'

'Yes, as a matter of fact, she is. Aimee Price ... you know where she might be?'

Kilner cocked one eyebrow. 'Ah yeah, Price. I've seen her around. If you ask me she seems a bit ... unstable.'

'Unstable? In what way?'

Kilner shrugged. 'In the way anyone would be after being blown up.'

James nodded slowly. 'Right. You know where she is?'

'I think she's probably just about finishing her therapy session. She likes the gardens, so try there first.'

'Thanks, I will. Hey, it's good to see you, Kilner.' The men shook hands.

'You too, Daniels. And listen ... be careful with her, yeah?'

Five minutes later James stepped outside and breathed in the fresh air, expanding his lungs to full capacity before exhaling hard. The cool air was a welcome relief compared to the stifling heat of Afghanistan, which often burned his nostrils whenever he breathed in. The gardens still looked breathtaking and full of colour and life.

He scanned the immediate area, hoping for a glimpse of brown hair, but there didn't seem to be anyone around. He took a step forwards, about to trot down the stone steps, but was halted by a loud scream ...

Chapter Twenty-Five
Then

Military Rehabilitation Facility, September 2009

I open the door to the brightly lit office and peer inside. It's a week later and time for my first therapy session with Doctor Watson and, to be perfectly honest, I've been dreading it the entire week. I've attempted therapy once before, back when I'd thought I was depressed at university, but after one session I quickly realised that I hadn't actually needed therapy because it appeared that talking about my issues made things worse, not better. So I skipped my next session and the next, until I was told that I'd be taken off their books because I'd missed too many appointments, but by that time my dark mood had started to improve, thanks to me deciding to quit university and move back home. But now I have no choice but to focus and talk about my issues. I can't run away from them anymore. It's going to be difficult, probably even more difficult than the physiotherapy sessions I endure daily. Despite them being painful, they are enjoyable because I'm slowly starting to see small improvements, even after only a week. It won't be long until I'll be able to walk down a flight of stairs without wincing.

'Aimee, come on in,' says Doctor Watson, beckoning me forwards with her hand. I still find it strange to be called by my first name, rather than my last, even though I'm in a military establishment. Back in basic training I'd spent the first ten weeks of my training completely unaware of the first names of the other recruits. It wasn't until day release that we shared our first names with each other.

'Hello,' I mutter, taking a seat in the overly soft armchair. I sink into the red leather and fold my hands awkwardly on my lap.

'Nice to meet you, Aimee. I'm sure you're a bundle of nerves right now, but honestly there's no reason to be. I know that probably won't make you feel any better, but I promise you whatever you say in here is dealt with in the strictest of confidences. What's said within these walls will be kept between us. The only time I would need to intervene and speak to someone else would be if I thought you were a danger to yourself or to others. I hope you understand that.'

I nod, recognising the almost exact same speech I'd heard in my first therapy session at university. 'Yes.'

'Great, thank you. Now ... I've read your file, so I know why you're here and what you went through, but I'd like to hear it from you, if that's okay. Why are you here, Aimee?'

And there it is ... the dreaded first, and extremely loaded, question.

Why am I here?

Of course, there's a very obvious and simple answer, but I assume the doctor doesn't want the simple answer, or maybe she does ...

'I'm here because I was injured while on tour in Afghanistan.'

The doctor smiles, as if she knew that was going to be my answer. 'Yes, of course. That's why you're here at this establishment, but why are you here in this room with me today?'

I stare down at my fingernails, noticing that they are still a bit dirty from taking part in the earlier gardening activity. I had, along with several of the other patients, planted a rose bush in the garden, and I'd pricked my finger on a thorn. 'To be honest, I don't really know why. I've been told I'm at risk of developing PTSD, so maybe that's why.'

'That's interesting the way you just said that … you were *told* you're at risk of developing PTSD. Can I assume that means that you don't *think* you have it?'

I shrug my shoulders. 'I don't know.'

'What *is* PTSD, Aimee?'

It's a stupid question coming from a military doctor, but I oblige her anyway. 'Post-Traumatic Stress Disorder.'

The doctor nods and smiles. 'Yes … and do *you* think you went through something traumatic and stressful in Afghanistan?'

I close my eyes. I'm engulfed in fire and blood. The smell of burning flesh curdles my stomach. I'm dragging Jones across the hot sand, his leg torn to shreds. I shudder and gulp back the nausea.

'Aimee?'

'Yes, I do.'

'Great, so now we know *why* you're here … let's make a start, shall we?' Her tone sets me on edge and I can already tell that the next hour is going to be excruciating.

An hour later I leave the room with knots in my stomach and a pounding headache. I've even been given bloody homework to do. I have to write everything I'm feeling down in a diary. Apparently, I don't have to show her what I write, I merely need to put words down on a page. I can't think of anything worse to be honest because it's hard enough expressing my feelings out loud, let alone on paper.

I softly close the door behind me, despite wanting to slam it with such force that it falls off its hinges, and lean against it with my eyes closed for a few seconds.

I seriously want to scream ... like, properly scream until my voice cracks.

No ... I *need* to scream.

But not here, not in these quiet corridors where I'm bound to be heard and cause a scene.

I retreat outside as fast as I can, jogging down the stone steps to the garden and walking past the flower garden I'd attended to earlier. During my gardening hour I'd been in such a good mood, but now I want to cry and shout in frustration and anger, like an overly tired and hungry toddler. Apparently, so Doctor Watson had said, it's perfectly normal to feel these sorts of emotions, especially during the first therapy session. I'd wanted to throw something at her there and then, but, luckily for her, there'd been nothing within arm's reach.

Upon arriving at a secluded area I lift my face to the blue sky and scream. The sound that comes out of my mouth is more of a garbled cry, but I let it out anyway as tears stream out of my eyes, my vision blurring.

After thirty seconds of screaming I sit on the grass and begin counting each individual strand. It's the perfect distraction technique.

'Price?'

Confused, I lift my head, feeling as if it weighs a tonne, immediately losing count of the blades of grass, and look over my shoulder.

There he is ... walking towards me with a smile on his face, dressed in a normal outfit of a black t-shirt and jeans.

Sergeant Daniels.

Jinx

Chapter Twenty-Six
Now

It took several hours before Jones was free to leave the station. The officer who logged him into the system seemed surprised at the fact he didn't have an address or a phone number, so Aimee went back to work and assured him she'd come back at five to collect him.

DI Fields had not been happy about Aimee's suggestion of Jones staying with her. In fact, he'd attempted to talk her out of it in the interview room, eventually agreeing when she'd refused to change her mind. He even suggested sending a police escort home with her; Jones was a possible suspect after all, but Aimee had dismissed that idea. She was convinced that Jones wasn't dangerous.

In the end, DI Fields agreed to let Jones stay with her, thanked her for her cooperation and told her she also needed to stay close by in case she was needed further on this case. Aimee asked if they had any other suspects, to which he replied that they didn't, but his team were looking into Jones's background in more detail, as well as James's.

At ten minutes past five Aimee collected Jones from the holding room and ten minutes later she opened the door to her flat and ushered him inside, all too aware that prying eyes and ears were nearby, hoping for the next piece of juicy gossip. She breathed a sigh of relief when she finally slammed her door shut, having managed to avoid Mrs Leamington.

Jones whistled as he walked in a circle, inspecting her kitchen diner. 'Well, it certainly beats a bus shelter.'

Aimee placed her bag on the kitchen countertop with a loud thud. 'Have you seriously been living under a bus shelter since you've been here?'

Jones shrugged. 'It depends on the weather.'

Aimee sighed as she opened the washing machine and pulled out the wet bedding. 'I don't understand ... what about your compensation money? Why haven't you—'

'Hello! Who do we have here?' Jones spied Darth's cage and stuck a finger through the bars, allowing the hamster to scurry over and sniff it.

'That's Darth Vader.' Aimee hung the damp bedding across the backs of the chairs in the dining area.

'Cool name, dude,' he told the hamster.

'Actually,' corrected Aimee, 'Darth's a girl.'

'Of course she is. Is she evil? She's not going to bite me, is she?' Jones was already opening the cage and beckoning the animal to crawl into his open palm.

Aimee smiled. 'No, she doesn't bite. Here ... this will help.' She placed the last pillowcase across the back of a chair, opened the hamster food bag and dropped a few pellets into Jones's hand. They watched silently as Darth took a few tentative steps and eventually made herself comfortable in his palm as she nibbled the food. He stroked her gently with one finger as he continued to walk around Aimee's home, looking at her hanging pictures and random ornaments.

'Where's all your pictures of you in uniform? Where's your medal?'

'You know about that?'

Jones paused for several seconds before replying, 'Yeah, I heard that you'd been given one.'

'I don't keep it here on display. My mum has all my Army photos, including my medal.'

'Why?'

Aimee chose to ignore his question. Instead, she filled up the kettle and flicked it on. She heard Jones behind her take a seat on the sofa. It was a large corner sofa, too big in reality for one person, but she loved nothing more than lying across it, legs outstretched. When she turned around his dirty feet were propped up on the glass coffee table.

'Get them off my table,' she said with a sigh. 'If you're going to stay here then I expect you to at least be civil.'

'Hey, you're the one who invited me here. I was perfectly happy under my bus shelter.'

'You can't honestly expect me to believe that you're actually homeless ... You must have been awarded even more compensation than I was.'

Jones said nothing as he continued to stroke Darth who had now taken up residence on his shoulder and was burying herself in his greasy hair.

At that moment the front door burst open and Dot entered, carrying several shopping bags and a suitcase. She looked slightly flustered with her rosy cheeks and her thin blue jacket falling off one shoulder. Her bleached blonde hair was shaved on one side of her head and longer on the other, her fringe falling across her eyes stylishly.

'Hey! Hope you don't mind that I let myself in, but that's why I have a spare key, right? Anyway, I'm here now so let's get cracking on and ... Hey, Aimee ... why's there a homeless man sitting on your sofa?' Dot stopped mid-stride and dropped everything she was carrying on the floor.

130

Aimee spun round. 'Shit, Dot, sorry … I forgot you were coming over.'

Dot backed up a few paces, took out her phone and held it up. 'Do you need me to call the police?'

'No, no … he's fine. I invited him here.'

Jones grinned and waved, acting far too comfortable for Aimee's liking.

Dot sidled up to Aimee and leaned in close to her ear, lowering her voice. 'No offence … but you can do a *lot* better.'

Aimee held back a laugh. 'Don't worry, it's nothing like that. This is Thomas Jones. He's … staying with me for a while.'

Dot narrowed her eyes at Jones, taking in his attire. 'Tom Jones, huh?' Then her eyes widened as she gasped. 'Wait … Jones? As in … the guy you saved while you were in the Army?'

'Uh … yeah.' Aimee poured hot water over a teabag and stirred.

'Why does he look homeless?'

'No idea. I'm still trying to work that one out.'

Dot straightened her top as she took a few tentative steps towards him. 'I'm Dot.'

'Hey Dot, I'm Jones … You a dyke?'

Aimee gasped in horror and threw him a dirty look.

Dot laughed. 'I like him!'

Jones shrugged his shoulders. 'You look like a dyke.'

'Actually, yes I am, Mr Homeless. Are you disappointed?' Dot folded her arms and batted her long eyelashes at him.

'Yeah … I am. You're fit.'

Aimee rolled her eyes at his typical Jones response. 'Well, even if she were straight you'd have no chance with her looking the way you do,' she snapped. 'Plus, you smell like something has crawled under your clothes and died.'

Dot screamed and clapped her hands together, jumping up and down on the spot like an excited child. 'Oh my god! I've just had a fantastic idea. Let me do a makeover on you!'

Jones frowned. 'Hell, no.'

Dot looked at Aimee for backup. 'No,' said Aimee sternly.

'Oh please! Look, I can run home and grab my hair clippers, a blow torch and some disinfectant, and I'll be back in ten minutes – fifteen tops.'

Aimee added milk to both of the cups. 'Don't you have a date tonight?'

'I can skip it.'

'No, you can't. You told me yourself you're excited about this date, so you're going. I'll help you choose an outfit and get ready like we planned.'

'Fine, but tomorrow's your day off, right?'

'Yeah.'

'Then I'm coming over first thing tomorrow to give this guy a makeover.'

Aimee glanced at Jones and raised her eyebrows. There was no way she'd be able to get Dot to change her mind. The woman was like a rabid wolf. Once she got her claws into something she wouldn't let go.

'On one condition,' he said.

'Name it,' answered Dot.

'I want you to get me two six-pack of beers and a packet of fags.'

'Done!'

Chapter Twenty-Seven
Then

Military Rehabilitation Facility, September 2009

I blink against the sunlight, raising my hand to shield my eyes. I can't quite believe who I'm seeing. Are my eyes seeing things that aren't really there, the way they do whenever I close them? Now I'm seeing things when they're open too? What's he doing here? My mind races with endless questions and possibilities and I'm still so stunned by his appearance that my mouth is hanging open as he jogs the last few paces and stops beside me.

'Hey, I thought that was you. May I?' He gestures to the ground beside me.

'Of course ... sorry ... I'm just a bit surprised to see you, Sergeant.' Understatement of the century. When he'd said that he'd visit me I hadn't actually believed him. I'd just assumed he was being nice.

'I did say I'd visit you and please, call me James. I'm off duty.'

'Only if you call me Aimee.'

'Deal.'

We share a smile, and a tiny spark of ... *something* ... jolts my heart. 'You didn't happen to see me just now ...'

'Screaming at the top of your lungs? Nah ... but I certainly heard you. At first I thought someone might be hurt, but then I saw you.'

My face catches alight. 'Sorry,' I whisper.

'Rough day?'

'Something like that.'

James nods. 'Want to tell me about it?'

'Not really.'

'Brutal honesty, I like it. That's okay. I suck at listening anyway. Did you get the flowers?'

'Oh yeah, thank you. My mum practically had a heart attack on the spot.'

James laughs. 'That wasn't my intention, I can assure you.'

I look away from him and out across the gardens, taking in the vivid green of the grass and trees. The gardens are so well maintained here, yet I never see any groundskeepers. It's so surreal sitting here with the man who saved my life.

'It's beautiful here, isn't it?' he asks.

'Yeah. Have you been here before then?'

'I was posted here a few years ago. Got some good mates here now. How long do they reckon you'll be here?'

'How long's a piece of string?'

'Right.'

'I guess I'll be here as long as it takes to recover.'

'How are you doing with that by the way? You look good.'

I smile weakly, still avoiding his gaze. 'Thanks. I'm doing okay, I think. I'm not in pain all the time now. My physio is going well and my scars are healing and I'm recovering from my surgery.'

'You had surgery?'

I mentally kick myself, knowing that revealing to the man I have a crush on that I've had a hysterectomy isn't the best topic of conversation. 'Just some internal wounds that needed stitching, but nothing major.'

'Glad to hear it. I know you were still in bad shape when you left my care and needed further treatment. I'm glad you pulled through. You're a fighter, that's for sure.'

'I'm not so sure about that.' I allow a few beats of silence to pass. 'How was Jones when you left?'

'He got sent back to the UK about two weeks after you. He … was still having a hard time. We had him on suicide watch.'

'Oh god.' Another jolt inside physically turns my stomach and not in a good way like before. As much as I detest the man for the way he treated me I can't help but feel responsible for his suffering.

James reaches out and covers my hands with one of his own. 'I know what you're doing. You're blaming yourself. Please don't. You can't worry about him. You have to think about yourself and get through this. Don't let him drag you down with him.'

I allow the warmth from his touch to seep into my skin. The tiny hairs on the backs of my arms are standing to attention and for the first time I feel an electric buzz of exhilaration. I want him to touch me. Since the incident I've barely allowed anyone near me, apart from a hug or two from my family, but with James it feels different. I feel safe when I'm with him. It was the same feeling I had in Afghanistan and now he's here I want to continue to have that feeling.

'Now,' says James before he quickly clears his throat, as if he's shaking off nerves, 'I need to ask you what I came here to ask you and I'd better do it quickly before I chicken out.' I finally turn and look at him, giving him my full attention, tilting my head as I wait for him to continue. 'Would you like to go on a picnic with me?' he asks.

I fight back a laugh, which I quickly turn into a cough. I don't want him to think I'm rude, but the idea of having a picnic sounds so strange coming from his mouth. 'A picnic?'

'Yeah. Wait ... let me make it a little clearer ... What I probably should have said was *a date*. Would you like to go on a date with me? The picnic is the date ... Shit, I'm really bad at this, aren't I? You'd think I'd never asked a woman out before.' James runs a hand over his head and down the back of his neck, stretching it.

This time I do laugh. 'Has it been a while?'

'A little while, yeah. I'd bring the picnic supplies, obviously. These gardens are perfect for it. I know how strict the schedules can be here so you just tell me a time you're free and I'm yours ... That is ... if you want me to be yours ... Fuck ... Should I just start again?'

'I think that might be best.'

'Okay ... Aimee ... would you like to go out on a date with me?'

'Yes, I would like that very much ... James.'

Chapter Twenty-Eight
Now

Dot had left to buy the beer and cigarettes five minutes ago. Aimee handed Jones one of the cups of tea she'd just made.

'You still take it NATO, right?'

Aimee was pleasantly surprised that, even after so many years, she could still remember the Army terminology for a cup of tea with milk and two sugars. It was what the Army referred to as NATO Standard, a dark-brown colour with full-fat milk and two heaped spoonfuls of sugar. Anything less than that was not considered to be a real cup of tea. She'd laughed when she'd learned that a black cup of tea with no sugar was called a "Whoopi Goldberg" (a black nun) and a tea with milk and no sugar was called a "Julie Andrews" (a white nun). The first time she'd said it out loud when she'd started working at the police station Cindy had burst into hysterical laughter and then told her that HR would probably have words if she continued to use those phrases, so she'd had to quickly adjust back to the civilian way of speaking.

Jones took the cup and stared into its contents. 'You remember?'

'Don't look so surprised. I used to make you a lot of cups of tea. I remember how you like it.'

'Oh, do you, huh? I bet I can remember how you like it too.' He winked as he took a sip, a playful yet annoyingly arrogant smirk across his face.

Aimee glared at him. 'Do you always have to be so crass?'

'No, I don't always have to be, but I like to pick my moments.'

'How about no moments? If you're going to stay with me then I expect you to treat me like a human being and not some piece of shit you just scraped off your shoe, or one of your goddamn whores you used to shag every weekend.'

Jones raised his eyebrows. 'There she is … I was wondering when the old Price would make an appearance.'

'The *old* Price?'

'Yeah, you know, the one who used to stand up for herself and not take any shit from anybody. You used to love all that witty banter.'

Aimee leaned against her kitchen counter. 'I'm going to let you in on a little secret, Jones … All that *witty* banter, all those sexual jokes, those derogatory terms you used to call me … I didn't *love* them, not even a little bit. They slowly killed a little bit of my soul every day and I hated and resented you with every inch of my body.'

Jones took a deep breath, held it for five seconds and then let it out. 'If you say so, Price.'

Aimee gritted her teeth, took a step forwards to begin another verbal assault, but Dot striding into the room carrying a shopping bag put an end to it.

'Ta-da! Beer and fags.' Dot chucked the bag at Jones who caught it and immediately tore into the beer, setting the cup of tea aside.

'Cheers!' he said as he took a big slurp.

Aimee grimaced and turned to Dot. 'He's bad enough when he's sober. Now I'm going to have to deal with him when he's drunk.'

'Well, you know how to rectify that, don't you?' answered Dot as she handed another bag to her. Aimee peered inside and brought out a bottle of white wine. Dot cheered. 'If you can't beat them … join them! Now, come and help me decide what to wear on my date.' Dot grabbed Aimee's hand and dragged her towards the bedroom.

Aimee glanced over her shoulder at Jones and called out as she walked away, 'No feet on the coffee table!'

'You got Sky Sports channels?'

'No!'

'Lame.'

Aimee slammed her bedroom door and rounded on Dot, needing to vent her frustration. 'Oh my god, why did I think it was a good idea to let that man into my house? He's been here less than ten minutes and I already want to throw him out of a window.'

'Why the fuck is he even here?' asked Dot as she began laying out the clothes from the suitcase that she'd brought in earlier.

'He's a suspect in a murder investigation.'

Dot froze. 'You let a *murderer* into your flat? Are you crazy?'

'No … I mean … he's a suspect, but I don't think he did it.' Even though she had no evidence to prove it, she had a feeling that he wasn't the murderer. It seemed so ridiculous, but there was definitely something that didn't add up, something he was potentially hiding.

Dot looked towards the closed door and lowered her voice. 'You sure about that?'

'Pretty sure.'

'Pretty sure as in ninety-nine percent sure, or pretty sure as in ninety-five percent sure? Because there's a big difference.'

'More like ninety percent sure.'

Dot ran her tongue over her teeth. 'Still ... I'd maybe keep a knife under your pillow tonight, just in case.'

'Gee, thanks.'

'Just trying to look out for you! Now ... green or blue?' Dot held up two pairs of leggings, both as shockingly bright as each other.

'Blue. You think I should ask him to leave?'

'After inviting him in? Would be a bit rude, don't you think? The silver or the red?' Dot held up two tops, both pretty, but not too revealing. Dot wasn't like Cindy in that department.

'The silver. Why do you think he's here in Woking?'

'How the hell should I know? A black or a pink jacket?' Dot lifted up the two examples.

'Black. Oh god, what if he did it ... What if he really did kill James? But why would he do it? He barely knew him ... unless he did. What if he knew about me and James?'

'Wait ... who the hell is James? Hoops or studs?' She placed one of each style of earring by her ears.

'Hoops. James ... the guy I nearly married eleven years ago. I told you about him, right?'

'Briefly ... what's he got to do with anything? Black heels or silver flats?'

'Flats. James is the guy who was murdered.'

'What!' Dot dropped everything she was holding onto the floor. 'Why the fuck didn't you tell me that to begin with! Holy fuck, your ex-fiancé was murdered? Are you okay?' Dot ran up to her friend and wrapped her arms around her. Aimee hugged her back, resting her head on Dot's shoulder.

'I'm fine, really.'

'Do you know why? Like … what the hell happened?'

'I don't really know. I've been so busy today I've barely had time to think, let alone sit down and watch a news broadcast. I don't know anything about the murder, only that Jones is a possible suspect and it happened at Maynard's Place, just down the road, but Tony let me in on the interview when he found out I knew both the victim and Jones.'

Dot let go of Aimee and began to sort her clothes out. Aimee sat on the edge of her bed and fiddled with the hoop earrings, twirling them round and round her fingers.

'I have an idea,' said Dot as she got undressed. 'We should totally call Cindy and let her know and then tomorrow, after I've turned Jones into a beautiful man, we should have a snoop around and see what we can find.' Dot wiggled her hips from side to side as she slid the leggings up.

'What do you mean by *snoop around*? Snoop around where?'

'You know, check out the crime scene. You work at a police station, don't you?'

'I'm an Evidential Property Officer, as I've told you many times. I'm not a detective, not even close.'

'But you're part of the investigation, right?'

Aimee shrugged. 'Sort of. Tony said he needed my help with it.'

'Great! Then we'll go and see what we can find.'

'I don't think it's a good idea. What if I get in trouble?'

Dot rolled her eyes as she pulled the top over her ample breasts and straightened it out. 'Why do you always have to do as you're told all the time?'

'I was a solider … it's kind of drilled into you from the start. If I disobeyed an order or disappointed anyone in any way then I'd be made to do push ups or hill sprints until I puked.'

'Uh, sounds vile, but you're not a soldier anymore.'

'I could still get in trouble.'

Dot grabbed the earrings from Aimee and put them on. She slipped into her flats and pulled on her jacket, striking a pose. 'What do you think?'

'You look great.'

'Thanks. Now … about tomorrow. You in?'

Aimee let out a long sigh. 'Fine … I'm in. That is, if I survive the night with a homeless guy sleeping on my sofa, who may or may not be a murderer.'

Dot clapped her hands together. 'Yes! Oh, and you'll be fine. Just grab the biggest knife you can find from the kitchen and wedge a chair behind your door.'

Chapter Twenty-Nine
Then

Military Rehabilitation Facility, September 2009

Despite my hectic schedule and regular physiotherapy sessions I find myself excited and looking forward to having my first date with James. It's still weird to call him by his first name, especially since he's a senior rank, but he doesn't care, so neither do I.

I have a free afternoon on a Wednesday, as most soldiers do in the Army. It's collectively known as a "sports afternoon", although playing sports is rarely involved. In fact, many a time, I've seen people skiving off to the pub or going home early. Today, I'm no different because I'm using my "sports afternoon" to go on a date.

James has sorted out everything and kept it a massive secret from me so I have no idea what to expect, just that I know we're having a picnic. I've only ever been on one other first date before and that was when I was thirteen and my mum chaperoned me and my date to the cinema. I can't remember what film we watched. It had been the most humiliating experience of my life because my mum is embarrassing and annoying at the best of times, let alone on a first date. I can't even remember the poor boy's name; he'd avoided me like the plague at school after that and, to be perfectly honest, I didn't blame him. I inwardly cringe at the memory.

James texted me earlier to say that I needed to make my way down to the end of the lawn, turn right and I'd be able to find my way from there. He said to arrive at 13:00 sharp, so at 12:50 I begin a slow walk down the steps and into the gardens. Once I reach the end of the lawn and turn right, I let out an audible gasp. There, laying neatly on the ground, is an array of colourful foliage and flowers spread out in the shape of an arrow, pointing in the direction of the water garden.

Somewhat dazzled and impressed, I follow the flower arrows down past the hedge maze, which I really need to visit soon because apparently there's a spectacular hedge shaped like a horse rearing up on its hind legs in the centre. When I turn the corner into the water garden, I stop and stare open-mouthed, not quite believing what I'm seeing. On the grass next to the large fountain, complete with water lilies and a stone statue, is a huge chequered blanket. On top of the blanket is enough food and drink to feed a small army; cakes, mini hotdogs, doughnuts and salad as well as a bottle of champagne in an ice bucket and a selection of non-alcoholic drinks.

'I wasn't sure if you were allowed any alcohol so I covered my bases,' says a voice from behind. I turn and see James walking towards me carrying a small tray of sandwiches. 'You're early,' he adds.

I smile as he comes to a stop beside me. 'I don't like to be late for anything.'

James nods as he sets the tray down on the blanket next to the rest of the food. 'Hope this is all okay. You wouldn't believe what I had to do to convince the staff to let me do this. Luckily, I'm good friends with the head chef.'

'Do you know everyone around here?'

James winks, not answering the question, and gestures for me to take a seat. 'Please, help yourself. Would you like some champagne? If not, there's also elderflower lemonade.'

'I'm sure one glass of champagne won't hurt.'

'Good choice.'

I sit down on the blanket, wincing as my muscles protest at the movement. Getting up and down from the ground is still quite difficult thanks to my injuries, but I'm slowly getting better at it. I watch as James expertly uncorks the bottle without spilling a drop and pours a small amount of the fizzy liquid into two plastic flutes. He hands one to me first.

'They drew the line at carting glass champagne flutes down here.'

I laugh as I take it from him. 'Can't say I'm surprised. Thank you.'

We raise our flutes. 'To … the future, whatever that may bring,' says James. We clink them together and each take a small sip. The cold bubbles fizz on my tongue and tickle my nose, sending chilly shivers down the back of my throat. I've never tasted proper champagne before.

'I still can't believe you did all this,' I say as I glance around at all the food.

'It was nothing. Maybe one day I can take you to a proper restaurant.'

'I'd like that.'

James grins and takes a large gulp of his drink. 'Can I offer you a tuna sandwich? There's also cucumber or cheese.'

'Wow, very posh. Tuna please, my favourite.'

I giggle like a silly schoolgirl as I take one. There are a few moments of silence while we eat as we admire our surroundings. I must admit that he's picked the perfect day for it. There's not a cloud in the sky and the sun's rays gently warm us. I can't help but dwell on the fact that winter will be on its way soon. Dark days and darker nights, cold weather and rain are just on the horizon, but, today at least, we're able to enjoy the last of the autumn sun.

'I hope you don't mind me asking,' I say, 'but are we going to get in trouble for this? For going on a date, I mean. I'm not really sure what the policy is on dating a higher rank because, obviously, I've never done it before.' I colour slightly.

'Well, as far as I'm aware there's no strict rules to say we can't. It's not like we actually work together. We're not even the same cap badge. I think we're safe.'

I nod, quite satisfied with his answer. 'You're right. Sorry I brought it up.'

'It was a valid point.' James shifts slightly so that he's a little closer to me, propping himself up on his elbow while munching on a sandwich. 'However, first dates are supposed to be all about getting to know each other, so how about we take it in turns to ask each other one question after another, sort of like a quick-fire round?'

I pop a mini hotdog into my mouth and nod. 'Okay.'

'Okay ... I'll go first. Where did you grow up?'

'Woking.'

'Ah, nice town. Love the Martian statue.'

'My turn,' I say. 'Do you have any brothers or sisters?'

'One twin brother.'

'Oh wow! You're a twin? What's his name?'

James frowns. 'I'm pretty sure it's my turn to ask the next question.'

I roll my eyes. 'Fine.'

'Do *you* have any brothers or sisters?' he asks.

'I have a half-sister called Zoe who's nine years younger than me.'

'Nice. Okay, now it's your turn.'

'What's your brother's name and are you identical?'

'Um, excuse me, but that was two questions. You're really bad at keeping to the rules.'

I laugh, finding myself completely at ease as I take another sip of champagne. 'Okay, fine … just his name then.'

'His name is Adam … and yes, we're identical, but there are some small differences. I'm much more handsome than he is for a start. By the way, since you asked two questions, I think it's only fair that I ask two now.'

I fake a laugh. 'Deal.'

'What's your favourite colour … and can I kiss you?'

I gulp down the mouthful of champagne I'd just taken before I start choking and smile. 'It's purple … and yes, you can.'

James sits up and leans in towards me. We're both smiling as our lips lightly touch. He tastes of champagne and cucumber and all my senses come alive at once as my head spins slightly, but not from the alcohol. It's the most romantic and the most perfect moment I've ever had.

James pulls away gently. 'Purple's a great colour.'

'I'm glad you agree.'

'How about a picture, to remember this moment, in case I fuck it up and when I'm old and grey and alone I can look back on this moment with you and know there was a time when I was perfectly and completely happy.'

I raise my eyebrows. 'Is that speech rehearsed?'

'One hundred percent made up on the spot, I swear.'

'I'm impressed.'

James grins at me again as he takes out his phone. I don't have mine on me. In fact, it's been spending a lot more time hidden away in my bedside drawer lately. Since being here, I've found that I've not needed it. It's been quite liberating.

James and I lean in close for a selfie, smiling like idiots. He takes the picture and we both check it out.

'Perfect,' he says.

'Will you send me a copy? You know, so that if I fuck this up I can look back on this moment and remember that I once went out on a date with a man who made me forget about all the bad things going on in my life right now, and how he made me feel so happy that I never wanted this moment to end.'

We lock eyes for several seconds and then he says, 'Okay, you totally stole my romantic speech.'

I laugh out loud and drink my champagne.

Chapter Thirty
Now

Jones was still on the sofa with Darth perched on his shoulder when Aimee and Dot emerged from her bedroom fifteen minutes later, after Dot had helped Aimee remake her bed with clean bedding. He'd already drank one beer and was halfway through his second. The television was blaring a random comedy show that Aimee had never seen before and he was laughing like an idiot, acting completely at ease, as if this were his own home. A spark of annoyance gurgled in the pit of her stomach as she glared at him.

Dot leaned over to Aimee and whispered in her ear. 'At least get him to take a shower ... your flat's starting to smell.'

'I'll try, but the thought of him being naked in my bathroom actually makes me feel a bit sick.'

'Well, maybe next time you should think twice before you invite a homeless person into your flat. Anyway ... I'm off! See you tomorrow, Mr Homeless.' Dot waved at Jones, who merely raised his can of beer in response, his eyes never leaving the screen. 'That hair and beard is coming off tomorrow by the way,' she added. Jones just snorted.

Aimee saw Dot out and then slowly turned around to face Jones, hands on her hips, her mind made up. 'I'm going to get you a fresh towel and then I suggest you have a shower. I'm surprised Darth hasn't passed out from the smell.' There wasn't going to be any discussion. He *was* taking a shower, whether she had to force him in it or not.

Jones poured the last of the beer down his throat and crushed the can with one hand. 'A shower would be great, Price. I need a leak anyway. Where's your bathroom?'

'Down the hall to the left.'

Jones nodded and stood up. He carefully scooped Darth up in his hands and placed her back inside her cage. 'She likes me.'

Aimee didn't reply as she watched him walk to the bathroom and slam the door. She rummaged around in her hallway cupboard, found a clean towel and knocked on the bathroom door a few minutes later.

'I'll leave the towel outside the door,' she called out.

Aimee barely had time to straighten up before the door flung open. Jones stood there, naked from the waist up. Scars slashed across his torso, small shrapnel wounds from the explosion. He had definitely lost a lot of muscle mass, compared to what she remembered, but his body was still strong and defined. Just different ... and scarred ... like hers.

'Didn't mean to scare you there, Price. You got any clean clothes?'

Aimee took a deep breath, finally able to drag her eyes off his scars. 'No, I don't, but I'll ask my neighbour if I can borrow some.'

'Cool.' Jones picked up the towel and slammed the door.

Aimee clenched her teeth together, squeezing her fists tight at the lack of a thank you. She felt an overwhelming urge to punch something. She slipped out of the flat and hurried across to Nathan's door, tapping it lightly. She was surprised when it opened within ten seconds.

'Aimee,' said Nathan with a smile, 'I wasn't expecting a visit so soon.'

She returned his smile. 'Um, yeah, actually it's not about a date or anything, sorry. I was wondering if I could ask you for a favour?'

'Of course.'

'Do you have any spare clothes I can borrow? I'll have them back to you clean and dry in a few days … Not for me, obviously. They're for … my brother. He's just popped into town for a surprise visit and uh … didn't bring a spare set of clothes with him … the idiot.'

Nathan raised his eyebrows. 'Your brother? Of course, yeah, hang on …' Nathan turned, leaving the front door to his flat open while he went into a nearby room. Aimee couldn't help herself and peered round the door, glancing at an immaculate hallway which was tastefully decorated in pastel grey tones. Nathan appeared a minute later. 'Is a t-shirt and trackie bottoms okay?'

'Perfect! Thanks Nathan.'

'How long's your brother staying for?'

'Hopefully not long.'

'You don't get on?'

'You could say that.'

Nathan smiled. 'Ah, you're lucky you have a sibling.'

'You don't have brothers or sisters?'

Nathan held her gaze for a few moments before replying, 'No.'

Aimee nodded. 'Well … thanks again … I owe you one.' Aimee took the items from him.

'How about taking me up on my offer of a date?'

'Yes, I promise I'll get back to you soon. It's just I've been so busy lately and … um …' Aimee's eyes darted to the side as she heard another door opening nearby; Mrs Leamington's door. 'Look, sorry … gotta go, talk soon!'

Aimee scurried back to her flat and slammed the door, peering through the peephole to check if Mrs Leamington had made an appearance. She could just about make out Nathan still standing in his doorway, watching her door with his brow furrowed. She watched as the pink outline of the old woman wandered across the hall and towards the stairs. Aimee breathed a sigh of relief, knowing she'd dodged a bullet.

Aimee laid the clothes outside the bathroom door. She listened as Jones sang "You're the one that I want" at the top of his lungs. She clamped a hand over her mouth to stop herself from laughing as he attempted the high notes and failed miserably. In the end she had to run away from the sound because her sides were aching from holding back her laughter. He certainly was a different person now. The last time she'd seen him he'd been in a wheelchair, staring out across the lawns at the rehabilitation facility, refusing to even make eye contact with her.

Jones emerged fifteen minutes later, by which time Aimee was halfway through a glass of wine. Dot, as always, had chosen a delicious one. She turned the volume down on the news as Jones entered the room. His hair and beard were still there, but they were freshly washed. Nathan's plain black t-shirt was slightly too big for him and the tracksuit bottoms sat low on his hips. As Aimee lowered her eyes to the floor she remembered, for the first time since seeing him today, that he only had one foot, which was bare. The other was prosthetic. She'd seen many different shapes and sizes of prosthetics, both arms and legs, while recovering at the facility. She couldn't see the whole thing due to the length of the trousers, but the foot part looked to be made of a strong, lightweight material, possibly carbon fibre or even plastic. It was badly scuffed and dirty.

Aimee didn't realise she was staring until Jones cleared his throat. She flinched, almost spilling her wine over her lap. 'Sorry,' she said quickly.

'It's fine. I'm used to it.'

'I didn't mean ... sorry, I just ... forgot. You walk really well with it.'

Jones grabbed another beer, which Aimee had put in the fridge, and took a long drink. 'I forget too, and then I trip over thin air, and it all comes rushing back to me.'

'Does it hurt?'

Jones started opening cupboard doors at random. 'You got any food? I'm starving.'

'I was going to order a pizza.'

'Perfect. I'll have a large spicy pepperoni.'

Aimee sighed. 'Would it kill you to say please or thank you?'

'It might. By the way ... you'll have to pay for mine, I've no money.'

Aimee rolled her eyes as she stood up. 'Of course you don't. It's not like you got awarded hundreds of thousands of pounds in compensation for having your leg blown off.'

Jones drank his beer in silence while Aimee ordered the pizzas. She poured herself another glass of wine and stood in the kitchen, watching Jones feeding Darth on his shoulder again.

'I need to know,' she said finally. 'Why are you homeless? It makes no sense. I put a deposit down on this flat with my money and paid off some of my debts. I made sure my mum and sister had some and I put the rest in a savings account, but you … you I don't get.'

Jones stroked Darth several times as he took a seat on the sofa, in her usual spot, which set that spark of annoyance alight again. 'It's blood money.'

Aimee frowned. 'It's not blood money. You didn't die. It's there to help you.'

'I don't want it.'

'You might not want it, but I'm pretty sure you *need* it.'

'I don't want it. I don't need it.'

'Where is it?'

'It's buried in a secret location that can only be found by finding three parts of a treasure map and linking them together … Where'd you think it is? It's in a fucking bank.'

Aimee took several large gulps of wine. 'You're ridiculous,' she muttered.

'Hey, what you choose to do with your blood money is your business and what I choose to do, or not do, with mine is my business.'

Aimee shook her head. 'But you're homeless! You actually would prefer to live on the streets and beg for food rather than use the money to buy somewhere to live. Why? Tony said your address is in Milton Keynes. Is that true?'

'Why do you even care, Price? You haven't seen me in over a decade and now, suddenly, you care about what's happened to me.'

'I've always cared, however, I remember you telling me, quite explicitly, that you never wanted to see me again. I wanted to help you and be there for you, Jones, I really did, but you pushed me away. You weren't the only one who lost a piece of yourself that day. I did too, yet you're so fucking selfish and up yourself that you don't give a shit about anyone other than yourself.' Aimee ended her speech by taking another large mouthful. Her heart thumped hard in her chest, her pulse so loud she could hear it. She'd never met anyone who could infuriate her as intensely as Thomas Jones.

Jones stared at her. 'What did you lose?'

Aimee closed her eyes, annoyed at herself for letting that small piece of information slip. Trust him to have picked up on it. 'Nothing. Forget it.'

'No, go on … since you started this conversation. I lost my leg. What did you lose?'

Aimee opened her eyes and shook her head. She couldn't believe she was even considering opening up to this man, but something inside her was being drawn to him. 'I lost … I lost the ability to have children.'

Jones stopped drinking, lowering the can away from his mouth. 'What do you mean?'

'Once I returned home the doctors discovered that my uterus was damaged, so they had to remove it. I have scars and some slight damage to my left hip and thigh, but it's the damage that was done on the inside … That's what I lost and I'm pretty sure you couldn't give a shit about what I've been through, but let's just say that this scar … this one I didn't get when that vehicle exploded.' Aimee held up her left arm, showing off a large puckered line of skin that ran from the middle of her forearm to her wrist. She lowered her arm and hid it behind her back, her cheeks flaming with regret.

Jones stood up and walked over to her. Every fibre in her body told her to run away, to hide, but she held her ground, trembling as he gently took her arm and traced a finger down her scar. Tiny bolts of electricity shot through her skin. Then, he showed her both of his forearms.

'Snap,' he said.

Aimee's eyes widened as she stared at the two jagged scars on his wrists. She blinked back the tears, feeling his warm skin under her fingers.

'I'm sorry I let you go through all that alone,' said Jones softly. 'I was an angry idiot back then, Price. I hated everyone, including myself.'

Aimee smiled. 'Me too. I should have tried harder to stay in contact with you even if you didn't want me to, but I have to ask … Why are you such a dickhead to me, even now?'

Jones laughed. 'Way to ruin that little moment we were just having, Price.'

Aimee laughed too. They had moved closer to one another, but now that he smelled and look slightly better she didn't mind. 'Sorry … I just meant … you can actually be a decent human being when you stop being such a dickhead. I'm sure you can even be charming and funny.'

'I *am* charming and funny.'

'No, you *think* you're charming and funny. There's a big difference.'

They shared another laugh just as the doorbell rang, which made Aimee jump. 'That'll be the pizza,' she said as she moved away, but Jones grabbed her wrist and held her back.

'We still have a lot to talk about, Price.'

Aimee nodded her agreement, trying to ignore the flutter of nerves and excitement growing inside her at the touch of his skin against hers.

Chapter Thirty-One
Then - Jones

Military Rehabilitation Facility, October 2009

I would literally rather be anywhere but here at this fucking camp for injured soldiers. Actually, scratch that, it's better than being at my parents' house being treated like a piece of scum. I was only there for two days and during that time my dad and I had argued at least a dozen times. I'd been so close to hitting him, but of course I couldn't, because I'm a fucking cripple and stuck in a wheelchair now. *She* did this to me. I swear to god if I ever see her fucking face again I'll—

'Hello, Thomas, my name's Simon Kilner. I'm one of the doctors here.' A bloke with a stupid haircut approaches me, his hand outstretched. I ignore it and stare straight ahead as he sits down on a chair next to me and continues to talk. 'I've got you booked in with a therapist first thing tomorrow. I realise you still have a lot of recovery to do, but I'd also like to get you booked in to be fitted for a prosthetic leg, if you're happy with that. It takes a while for them to be made.'

I stare across the gardens from my bedroom window. It's raining, the clouds thick and heavy, hovering over the grounds like a shadow.

'I realise that this must be difficult for you, but we're here to help—'

'What makes you think I want any help?' I spit.

'Thomas, I'll be honest with you ... without our help you'll possibly never walk again.'

I snort my response as I stare down at my fucking pathetic excuse for a body. The bandaged stump glares back at me, taunting me. 'I don't care.'

'You do care. We all care and we want to see you get better, but you have to be willing to help yourself first, which is why I feel it's necessary for you to talk to a therapist.'

'I don't need to see a fucking shrink.'

Simon sighs and stands up. 'I'll leave you for a while to sort your things out. There's a call button by your bed if you need assistance. Someone will come and get you for scoff later.'

'I'm not hungry.'

'Meals are a Scale A parade around here.'

I clench my jaw together and only release it when he leaves and the door closes. The rain is battering against the windowpane, which is quite soothing actually. It fills my head with white noise rather than the usual torrent of negative thoughts that swirl around inside.

There are two people outside walking in the rain, holding hands. Even through the murky window I can tell they are talking and smiling. My stomach clenches as I recognise the woman is Price. Who the fuck is she holding hands with? I lean forwards in my wheelchair, my body responding stiffly and painfully, to get a better look.

It's that fucking doctor from Afghan.

My fists clench at my sides. Why the hell do they get to be so fucking happy, and I'm stuck in this wheelchair like a pathetic cripple?

Chapter Thirty-Two
Then

Military Rehabilitation Facility, October 2009

The nights are growing darker, creeping ever closer to the start of winter. Despite this, October's my favourite time of year; the leaves are starting to turn all the different shades of brown and gold, the air is cool, but warm enough not to need to wrap up in layers every time you step outside. It's the nights that I fear the most. Not the darkness though; sometimes the darkness feels safer than the light.

It's sleep itself I fear.

My dreams are filled with vivid, blood-red images, decapitated limbs and screaming – so much screaming. Jones hunts me in my sleep, stalking me with a huge machete, threatening to chop my leg off, or worse, for what I did to him. I often wake up drenched in sweat, shivering uncontrollably, and scream until my voice goes hoarse or the night guard comes running to my aid. Then a nurse is called and they usually offer me a sedative, but I refuse because I don't want to stay asleep. It's too dangerous and horrifying in my mind. At least if I'm not sedated I can wake up on my own, but what if one day I don't wake up? Sometimes it feels as if I'll be trapped in a nightmare forever. Maybe I'm already in one, living it on a daily basis.

The only glimmer of hope, in any of this, is James. We've been casually dating for almost a month now and we've been on three official dates. So far, neither of us has fucked things up. He's still on pre-deployment leave so is able to visit me fairly often, but he also has his own family who obviously want to see him after being away for so long. I keep telling him that he should go and spend time with his family for a while, but he always says he'd much rather spend his free time with me. We go on walks together around the grounds, even if it's raining. However, I have had a few raised eyebrows from staff members when he's appeared from my room. We haven't had sex yet and that's mainly because I'm petrified to take that next step, which he says he understands and, luckily, he isn't pressuring me in any way. We're both enjoying each other's company and taking things slow and, for now, that's enough for me.

My physiotherapy sessions are progressing well. In fact, I'm ahead of where the doctors expected me to be at this stage of my recovery. My scars are healing nicely and my left leg is finally starting to regain full movement and coordination. If I don't walk with James then I walk with some of my fellow patients and listen while they swap stories about how they sustained their injuries and how their recovery is going. I'll sometimes join in, but I've never told anyone about the small scar across my abdomen, the one I hate most of all, the one that reminds me every damn day that I'll never be a mum.

There's one person I keep looking out for, but either he hasn't arrived yet or I keep missing him. He is always on my mind. There's so much I want to say to him. I can't help but wish he was here with me so we could get through this together. Despite there being dozens of people in the same situation as me, I don't feel a connection to any of them, but I do to Jones because he was there. I'm not sure how much he remembers, probably nothing as he was basically unconscious the entire time, but we still survived together. We share that strange bond and, without him, I feel completely alone in my dark thoughts.

Last Tuesday, it was a particularly sunny, crisp morning and I'd got up early and performed my rehab exercises that the physio had given me to do upon waking. They mainly helped to stretch my tight muscles and prepare my body for the upcoming day. I was going to get to breakfast early so I could go for a walk before one of my twice-weekly therapy sessions. Therapy is the one thing I hate about being here. I know I technically *need* it, but my mind is always fighting me and I'm struggling to control my emotions and anxiety. I'd had my first panic attack that day during that particularly brutal session. The horrific flashbacks overwhelmed me, forcing me back into a dark place, back into the burning vehicle and the only way my mind could see a way out was to break down. The panic consumed me, my whole body shaking with violent and uncontrollable convulsions. A nurse had been summoned and I'd been given a mild sedative to sleep off the side effects of the terrifying experience.

A week later and I'm doing slightly better. I've put that harrowing experience out of my mind and I'm determined to make today's session a better one. I'm the first in line for breakfast again. While I watch the chef plate up my eggs and beans I glance out of the nearest window and see a man roll past in a wheelchair, his head down, jaw clenched. I yelp as I realise … it's Jones.

'I'm sorry,' I quickly tell the chef, 'can you just leave it on the side. I'll be back for it in a second. Thanks.' Without waiting for his answer I swiftly leave the mess hall in search of the nearest exit that will take me outside onto the main patio.

'Jones!' I call out when I see him. He's parked on the edge of the patio looking out over the gardens. He doesn't even turn his head to acknowledge me as I stop beside him, slightly out of breath. 'When did you get here? It's good to see you. How are you?'

Jones continues to stare into the distance. Although I can only see the side profile of his face I can tell he's withdrawn and exhausted. His eyes have sunk into his sockets, his skin grey and dull, his hair longer now.

'Jones. Aren't you going to say anything?'

'There you are!' cries a voice from behind me. I spin around and see a male doctor jogging towards us, shaking his head. He grabs hold of Jones's wheelchair. 'Hey, Aimee. He always does this. Gets away from me when I'm not looking.'

'Hi, Simon.' James informed me a few weeks ago that Simon was one of his best friends from basic training, so he and I vaguely know each other now, although he's not my doctor. 'How long has Jones been here?'

'A couple of weeks.'

'Why didn't anyone tell me?'

'He asked us not to tell you he was here, but you were bound to run into each other eventually.'

I position myself so I'm standing in front of Jones, directly in his line of vision. He can't *not* be able to see me. 'Jones. Talk to me. Please.' My voice cracks as I fight back tears, but Jones ignores me, not even flickering his eyelids. It almost looks as if he's in a coma with his eyes open.

'He's not doing well, I'm afraid,' says Simon.

I slowly reach out my hand and place it on Jones's left shoulder. He flinches.

'I better get him to breakfast, see if I can convince him to eat anything today. See you later, Aimee.' Simon turns the chair around to push Jones away, but as he does Jones catches my eye. His eyes are black, soulless orbs. They send cold shivers down my spine.

If looks could kill.

Chapter Thirty-Three
Now

Aimee rolled over underneath the covers, pulling them further over her head as the curtains were ripped open and sunlight poured into her bedroom. She made a gargling, groaning sound, cursing herself for drinking the entire bottle of wine last night.

'Wakey, wakey, eggs and bacey!'

Aimee frowned at the male voice that appeared from somewhere above her. She peered out from under the duvet. Jones was standing next to her bed holding a breakfast tray with a smile across his face, looking far too fresh and enthusiastic for someone who had drunk six beers the night before. Why didn't he feel as if a mini steamroller was flattening his skull?

'Jones? What are you doing?' she croaked.

'I made breakfast. Thought you might need it. You know, I remember you used to handle your booze a lot better. What happened?'

'I turned thirty.'

Jones perched on the edge of the bed and lowered the tray so she could see what was on it. Her eyes widened as she saw a freshly brewed cup of coffee, eggs and bacon on toast and a glass of strange looking green liquid that looked suspiciously like slime.

'What's that?' she asked as she gestured at the glass, but, instead, picked up the coffee cup.

'Ah, that's my special hangover cure. I guarantee you, once you've drunk that, you'll feel amazing. Trust me.'

'I'll pass.' Aimee sipped the hot coffee, feeling it travel down her throat and warm her stomach.

'Suit yourself.' Jones picked up the glass and downed the contents in one go. Aimee resisted the urge to gag at the sight of him swallowing the lumpy concoction.

'Why did you make me breakfast?' Aimee sat up straighter as Jones handed her the tray.

'Just my way of saying thank you for letting me stay with you without actually saying thank you.'

Aimee smirked as she took a bite of toast. 'You're welcome.'

'By the way, your neighbour knocked on the door this morning asking for you.'

'Which neighbour?'

'The old lady in the pink dressing gown.'

'Oh fuck.'

'She dropped off some newspapers.'

Aimee mentally kicked herself for forgetting to do it after work yesterday. 'What else did she say?'

'Nothing much, although she did ask who I was and if I was your boyfriend.'

'And what did you say?'

'I said no—'

'Good.'

'—We're just fucking.'

'You said what!'

'She caught me off guard.'

Aimee groaned loudly into her coffee cup.

Aimee emerged from her bedroom half an hour later after she'd demolished her breakfast and had a long shower in her en-suite. She found Jones standing at the kitchen sink doing the washing up with Darth perched on his shoulder. Aimee smiled as she watched him chatting to the rodent as if they were having a serious conversation. Her eyes casually dropped from the top of his back to his hips and then to his surprisingly firm butt.

The doorbell interrupted her thoughts. Grateful for the distraction, she padded to the door and found Dot on the other side, a huge bag slung over one shoulder and dragging a small suitcase along with the other hand. She looked surprisingly fresh and radiant this morning and had a big smile across her face, which lit up her eyes.

'What's all this?' asked Aimee.

'Everything it's going to take to turn Mr Homeless into a prince.'

Aimee rolled her eyes. 'He had a shower last night, so he already smells a lot better.'

'Good to know … Just how close did you two get last night for you to be able to smell him?'

'Urrgg, don't make me gag again.'

'Too much wine?'

Aimee nodded as she closed the door behind Dot and followed her into the lounge area. 'How was your date?' Aimee asked as she flopped down on the sofa. Her head was spinning again and her legs were like jelly. It had been a long time since she'd drunk an entire bottle of wine. What had even happened last night after they'd eaten the pizza? After their serious moment Jones had retreated back to his annoying boyish ways so they'd not finished their conversation. Aimee racked her brains, but no solid memories would form.

Dot spun around in a circle, her arms wide open. 'I think I'm in love.'

Aimee cocked her head to the side. 'Really?'

'Yeah, really. She's so … cool … and sexy.'

'You wouldn't be talking about me now, would you?' asked Jones as he joined them in the lounge.

Dot stopped spinning. 'Afraid not, Mr Homeless. Have you looked in a mirror lately? Maybe when I'm finished you'll look cool and sexy, but right now? Uh-uh.' Dot shook her head. Jones shrugged as Dot approached him and tickled the top of the hamster's head. 'Hey, cutie.'

'Right, well, while you transform Jones I'm going to die slowly on this sofa. If I'm still alive when you finish then wake me up.'

'Got it.' Dot started carting all of her bags into the kitchen area.

'I told you, you should've drunk my special hangover cure. You'd have been feeling better by now.'

Aimee buried her head in the sofa cushion. 'You got any more?'

'Coming right up.'

Five minutes later Jones handed her a glass of the green liquid and a big bowl. Aimee frowned as she took them. 'What's the bowl for?'

'In case you hurl it all back up again.'

Aimee grimaced, held her breath for three seconds and then downed the whole glass. 'Ack! What the fuck is in that?' She coughed, swallowing the last dregs. Jones opened his mouth. 'Actually, don't tell me. I'd rather not know.'

Jones took the empty glass and bowl back to the kitchen, leaving Aimee to curl up on the sofa under a blanket.

She closed her eyes as she listened to the low murmurs coming from the other room and when she woke up an hour later she heard a hair dryer. She sat up and stretched, amazed at how good she felt; no nausea, no headache.

Damn ... what is in that hangover cure?

Aimee joined Dot and Jones in the kitchen and was startled when she saw Cindy there too, casually leaning against the side, drinking a cup of coffee.

'Hey, babe! How you feeling?'

'Better, thanks.'

'I told you that stuff works,' said Jones, but Aimee barely heard him because she was too distracted by his short, neatly trimmed hairstyle and a rugged, yet sophisticated spread of facial hair. He looked ... different. Not like the old Jones, who'd worn his hair at a grade 1 all over and always had a clean-shaven face, but a new and improved Jones.

'Look at her, she's speechless,' joked Cindy.

Aimee closed her mouth when she realised it had dropped open. 'Sorry ... I ... I wasn't expecting such a big change.'

'He scrubs up well,' said Dot as she fiddled with the last few strands of his hair. 'Aaaannnd ... done! Behold, my finest work yet.'

Cindy erupted into applause while Aimee continued to stare, not quite able to pull her eyes away in time for Jones to catch her. He grinned, but didn't say anything as he stood up, admiring his reflection in a hand mirror. He and Dot then high-fived and did a complicated handshake as if they were best friends.

'Right,' said Dot, putting the hair dryer back in her bag, 'you nearly ready, Aimee?'

'Ready for what?'

'For snooping around Maynard's Place. Cindy is on board with the whole plan.'

Jones stepped forward. 'Wait ... what are you three doing?'

'We're going to have a look around the crime scene and ask a few questions in the area,' answered Dot.

'What the hell for?'

'Um ... to solve the mystery of why Aimee's ex-fiancé was brutally murdered ... duh!'

Jones rolled his eyes over to Aimee who immediately wanted to shrink back under the blanket again. 'It wasn't my idea,' she said, holding her hands up in defence.

'Wait ... ex ... fiancé?'

Aimee's face drained of colour. 'I thought you knew.'

'I knew you used to go out. I saw you walking around the gardens a few times holding hands. I didn't know you were supposed to marry the guy ... What happened ... he get cold feet?' Jones chuckled to himself, but all three women glared at him.

'No ... I did,' replied Aimee sternly.

Jones raised his eyebrows. 'Okay ... that's definitely a story for another drunken night, but right now I have to say that snooping around a crime scene is a bad idea.'

'Why?' Aimee was on the offensive now.

'Why? You work in a police station. You really want me to spell it out for you?'

'Maybe you don't want me snooping around because you're afraid of what I might find.'

'Yeah, or maybe I don't want you snooping around because you'll get yourself in trouble.'

'Why do you even care?' she snapped back.

Cindy stepped in between them. 'Sorry to break up … whatever *this* is … but babe, we really should get going. I've got a pole dance lesson to teach at one and it's already nearly eleven.'

Jones's attention gravitated towards Cindy. 'You teach pole dance lessons? Cool.'

Aimee wasn't finished. She side-stepped past Cindy and squared up to Jones again. 'What *were* you doing at the crime scene, Jones? I find it hard to believe that both you and James were there on the same night and didn't run into each other.'

'I told you, I was meeting some skank for a date.'

'I don't believe you.'

'Well, gee, let me just pick up the broken pieces of my heart.'

Aimee stamped her foot and barged past him, grabbing her jacket from a nearby chair. Cindy and Dot stood rooted to the spot, glancing from Aimee to Jones in rapid succession.

'You girls coming or what?' Aimee snapped.

'Coming!'

'See you later, Mr Homeless,' said Dot as she high-fived Jones again.

'Later, Dyke.'

Aimee whirled round, eyes blazing. 'Don't call my friend that!'

'It was a term of endearment. Back the fuck off, Price.'

Dot nodded. 'It was … I call him Mr Homeless. He calls me Dyke.'

'What are you … best friends now?'

Dot shrugged her shoulders as she and Jones swapped glances. Aimee rolled her eyes and stopped herself from screaming by storming towards the front door. She needed some fresh air. She hoped to god she didn't run into Mrs Leamington in the hallway otherwise the old woman was going to get a mouthful.

Chapter Thirty-Four
Then

Military Rehabilitation Facility, October 2009

I see Jones from time to time over the next week. I can't believe he'd been here two weeks already and I hadn't seen him. He always has a nurse or a doctor with him, and he just stares down at the floor or straight out in front of him. I don't attempt to approach him again. I remember what James said about him being on suicide watch back in Afghanistan and what Simon said about him not doing well at the moment; it's enough to make my stomach turn. The fact that he's feeling *that* low is all my fault. I really want to help him, despite his previous attitude and treatment of me. All I need is someone to speak to who's been there with me, but Jones is clearly being his usual stubborn self and refusing help from anyone.

I'm in my room reading a book during one of my breaks. I was planning on going for a walk with James when he gets here, but the rain is beating against the window with torrential force so I don't think a walk will be happening today. Sometimes I don't mind walking in the rain, but I'm having a particularly low day today and can barely summon the enthusiasm to read.

A loud vibration interrupts my reading of a particularly intense scene. I quickly pick up my phone, expecting it to be James saying he's running late, but it's my mum. She hardly ever calls me because she's aware I don't use my phone very often and uses the phrase "I don't want to disrupt your recovery" as an excuse.

'Hi, Mum,' I answer in a cheery tone, determined not to allow her to worry about my downward spiral.

'Darling. I'm so sorry to call you. I know you have enough to deal with right now and I don't want to disrupt your recovery, but Daffy isn't well. He's in hospital.'

At this I chuck the book aside and sit up straighter on the bed, clutching the phone tighter. 'What's happened?'

'They think it was a heart attack. He's very weak. They say ... they say ...'

'Mum?'

'They say he may not have much time left.'

My heart constricts so tight in my chest I feel as if I might pass out. 'Oh god ...'

'Obviously if you're busy, darling, then don't worry, but—'

'Mum, stop it, of course I'll come. I'm leaving right now. I'll be there as soon as I can.'

'Okay, darling, thank you. Message Zoe when you're at the hospital and she'll come and meet you outside.'

'Bye, Mum.'

'Bye, darling.'

I leap off the bed and grab my bag and a light jacket. I move around the room at lightning speed, picking up everything I might need, wrench open the door and collide with James, slamming into his chest. My body responds badly to this visible barrier and I push him aside with considerable force, not even realising what I'm doing.

'Woah!' James grabs me before he topples over. 'Where are you off to in such a hurry?'

'I'm so sorry, but I have to go. Daffy's in the hospital and it isn't looking good.' I'm already halfway down the corridor.

James jogs to catch me up, immediately switching to a serious demeanour. 'I'll drive you.' I've told him all about my family so he knows how important Daffy is to me. He doesn't even stop to think about it and the kind gesture touches my heart.

I sigh with relief. 'Thank you. I just need to let the staff know I'm going.'

Chapter Thirty-Five
Now

Aimee, Cindy and Dot crammed themselves into the lift, all silent apart from Aimee's loud, erratic breathing. She refused to look either of her friends in the eye. She would have preferred to take the stairs, like she always did, but she knew how much Cindy and Dot detested them.

'Okay,' said Dot finally, 'are you pissed at me for becoming friends with him?'

Without missing a beat Aimee rounded on her friend. 'You don't know what he's really like. You've known him less than twenty-four hours, Dot. That man was so horrible to me. He called me names and I just had to stand there and take it because – as he put it – it was *only banter*. He then blamed me for ruining his life and said I should have left him to die. He's made me hate myself all these years.'

Dot placed a hand on her shoulder. 'I'm sorry, I didn't think, so I'll back off, but Aimee … maybe he's changed. He said you two had a good time last night catching up.'

'We did, but that's the thing with Jones. He lulls you into a false sense of security. He makes you think he's charming and funny and a good guy and then suddenly he does or says something awful that reminds you of what a shitty human being he really is. Trust me. I think he's hiding something and I'm going to find out what it is.'

'I thought you said you didn't suspect him of murdering your ex?'

'I don't, but I still think he might be hiding something else. There has to be a reason why James and Jones were both in Woking at the same time.'

Dot and Cindy shared a look as the doors pinged open, knowing better than to question their slightly unstable friend, especially when her mind was made up. They all walked out into the brilliant sunshine together.

'Okay,' said Cindy, 'I get it babe, I do, but I reckon you should give him the benefit of the doubt and try and keep him on your good side.'

'You're only saying that because you fancy him now that he doesn't look like a homeless person. And that's another thing … the man was no doubt awarded a large sum of money at some point, yet he chooses to live on the streets. I don't buy it.'

'Wait … he's loaded?' asked Cindy.

'You remember I told you about the compensation money I received? I was able to use it to put a deposit on my flat. Well, Jones would have got a lot more than I did, but apparently it's just sitting in a bank account doing nothing because he doesn't want to spend it because he thinks it's blood money.'

Cindy raised her eyebrows, but didn't say anything else on the subject.

'We need to come up with a plan,' said Dot as they rounded a street corner, all three of them in a line. 'The bar's still going to be crawling with police.'

They stopped at the end of the road where there was a police barricade blocking the way. Maynard's Place was up ahead and to the left, but Dot appeared to be wrong because there wasn't a huge police presence, not from the looks of the outside.

Maynard's Place was the local late-night singing bar where musicians could come and showcase their work. It was also a notorious place for local drug dealers and had been raided by the police on more than one occasion, but they'd never found anything stronger than weed within its walls. The bar held a lot of memories for Aimee because it had been where she'd first met Cindy and Dot, so they often recreated their first encounter by going on nights out there. The paint was peeling from the walls and the floor was usually sticky, but it was a welcoming bar … Except now it was a murder scene.

'Right, here's the plan. I'll distract the officer out the front while you two slip round the back and go in through the side door,' said Dot as she fluffed up her hair and straightened her bra.

'Babe … you're gay … No offence, but I think I'd be better at distracting the guard. Mine are bigger.'

'I may be gay, but he don't know that. Boobs are boobs to men.'

Cindy tilted her head and nodded. 'The woman's got a point. Fine. Go do your thing.'

Aimee and Cindy watched as Dot strutted towards the policeman at the front door, swaying her hips provocatively from side to side, her chest pushed out as far as possible. They couldn't hear what was being said, but from the huge, dopey smile on the policeman's face they assumed the plan was working and he was thoroughly distracted. Aimee and Cindy crept underneath the tape barrier and scurried over to the nearest wall, flattening themselves against it.

'Doesn't it feel like we're in some sort of murder mystery movie?' asked Cindy.

Aimee pressed a finger to her lips. 'Shhh!'

Cindy zipped her lips closed and threw away the key.

Aimee led the way along the wall and down the alley. She knew there was a side door because she, Dot and Cindy had been thrown out of it on several occasions after consuming too much alcohol and causing a scene by dancing on the bar, or by stealing the microphone from a singer who was just trying to get noticed. Aimee peered through the neighbouring window and, after determining that there was no one in the room, opened the door and ducked inside. The bar was silent, indicating it was almost certainly closed due to the murder. Usually, the bar would be open on a Friday at this time, gearing up for the start of the big weekend set list of singers. Aimee gestured for Cindy to keep quiet when Cindy accidentally knocked into a pile of stacked boxes.

'Sorry!' Cindy whispered.

Aimee heard faint male voices coming from somewhere in the building. She imagined they would be in the main bar area where all the tables and the stage was set up. As she crept through the narrow corridors towards the main room she kept trying to think of reasons as to why James would have been here in the first place. If he had been in Woking, then why hadn't he contacted her? Granted, they hadn't spoken since she'd broken off their engagement, not even once, but he must have been here for a reason. She couldn't get the idea out of her head.

'Yes, sir, we've logged all the evidence, including the photos of the scene.'

'Good. The victim's family have been informed and they'll be visiting the morgue later today to formally identify the body. I need to leave soon in order to meet them.'

Aimee signalled to Cindy to stop and listen as they crouched behind the bar. The floor was sticky with remnants of spilled alcohol and smelled distinctly like sweat and body odour.

DI Fields continued. 'Did you manage to get hold of the CCTV footage?'

'Yes, sir. It's been downloaded and sent to your email.'

'Perfect. Make sure that gets looked at today. And all the evidence has gone back to the station?'

'Yes, sir. Ready to be recorded and logged into the system.'

'Good. That'll be all.'

'Very good, sir.'

Aimee carefully peered over the top of the bar. She spied DI Fields at the far end of the room, his eyes glued to his phone. It was rare for DI Fields to be at a crime scene, since usually his team did all the leg work, but he seemed especially keen to work closely on this case. Aimee secretly wished that she was at work today so she would have access to the evidence that was being brought in, but she'd be able to look through it next week when she returned to work. Usually, she and Cindy worked Fridays, but they'd basically been forced to take today off because they had too many holiday days left which needed to be used up.

Aimee was aware she was breaking the rules by being here and she realised that if she were caught at the crime scene she'd be severely disciplined and most definitely removed from the application process to become a police officer. She was risking a lot by being here, but something inside her was telling her to keep pushing, keep prodding, because something didn't add up and DI Fields was clearly hiding information from her, and so was Jones.

Aimee kept her voice as a whisper as she spoke to Cindy. 'Go back out the way we came. I'm going to speak to Tony.'

'Are you crazy? You'll be fired.'

'No, I can make up some excuse and say I needed to see him and thought I'd find him at the crime scene. Trust me. I need to know what's on the CCTV footage. It can't wait.'

Cindy sighed. 'Fine, but be careful, babe.'

'Wait for me outside.'

'Will do.'

Aimee watched as Cindy crept back through the door the way they'd come. She peered over the bar again. It was time to act confident, even though inside she was falling to pieces.

Chapter Thirty-Six
Then

Woking Hospital, October 2009

James and I arrive at the hospital within the hour. During the drive the minutes seemed to tick by in slow motion. We hit every single red light and every traffic jam imaginable, almost as if some external force was trying to stop me from saying goodbye to Daffy. I can't catch my breath, convinced that a panic attack is imminent. The air is there, ready to be inhaled, but my lungs don't seem to want to work properly. My body's fighting against me.

I'm beyond grateful to James for driving me, otherwise I'd have had to rely on public transport to get me here, which no doubt would have resulted in a full-blown panic attack ages ago. He remains focussed and quiet on the drive, only glancing at me sporadically to check I'm okay, but I'm not okay, and I don't think I'll ever be okay again. My dark thoughts circle my mind like crows circling a rotting corpse and no matter how hard I try I can't make them leave. Why is life so hard for me? What have I done to deserve this torture? Daffy told me not long ago that I'd survived the *incident* for a reason, but at the moment all I can think of is how life would be easier if it just ended; like Daffy's is about to end.

Zoe is waiting for me at the entrance of the hospital. James drops me off and says he'll go and park and find me as soon as he can. Zoe runs into my arms and squeezes tight, burying her tear-stained face in my shoulder. She's only thirteen. She doesn't deserve to lose her granddad, the only male role model she's ever had.

We barely say two words to each other as she leads me through the maze of corridors that all look the same, through a busy ward and out the other side. Horrid memories of my own surgery and hospital stay come flooding back, whizzing around my brain, reminding me of what I lost when I was last here. Now I'm close to losing something else; *someone* else.

Zoe points to a room at the end of the corridor. 'I'll go and make sure James finds us,' she says as she turns to leave. Zoe hasn't even met James yet; neither has my mum. This isn't the type of first meeting I had in mind, but I can't worry about him now.

I grasp my sister's hand. 'T-Thank you,' I stutter. I want to say more, say something to comfort her because that's what big sisters are supposed to do, but the words are stuck somewhere inside me and I can't bring myself to say them, in case saying them out loud will jinx it.

Zoe nods and retreats back the way we came.

I approach the room one small step at a time, anxious to know what awaits me, yet also dreading the sight. I'm not ready to say goodbye to Daffy, the strongest man I've ever known or will probably ever know again. This is how it's all going to end for him; lying in a hospital bed, growing weaker by the second, his heart finally giving up on him. It isn't fair.

'Darling,' comes a shaky whisper as I step into the dimly lit room.

I force a smile onto my face. My mum is slouching in a chair beside the bed. It's been a few weeks since my mum visited me, but in that time it looks as if she's aged several years. Worry lines criss-cross her face, dark shadows stain the areas under her tearful eyes, but upon seeing me her eyes spark to life, if only for a second. She reaches out her hand, which I take, stepping closer to the bed.

Daffy has his eyes closed, his chest barely moving; wires and tubes enter his body at various sites and are connected to several machines which are quietly beeping. I watch the squiggly green line on the screen for a few moments, wondering when it'll eventually transform into one long one. Daffy looks like a shell of his former self and then a thought occurs to me. Maybe *this* is his true self, the way he feels and looks on the inside after what the horrors of war turned him into. I still remember the words he'd spoken to me on the day I'd come home from the hospital. It's something that will stay with me for the rest of my life. Is he at peace now that he knows the end is so close? Or will he continue to fight like he's been doing all his life? Is he relieved that his life will be over soon?

I place a hand gently over his, which is laying down by his side, outside of the thin green bed sheet. It's cold to the touch.

'He's quite heavily sedated, darling,' says my mum. 'I don't think he'll wake up again.'

'Is he in any pain?'

'I don't think so.'

'When did this happen?' My mum doesn't respond straight away, so I look away from Daffy towards her, my brows furrowed. 'Mum?'

'Three days ago.'

'Three days! And you didn't think to call me then?'

'I didn't want to worry you, darling. You have enough going on right now with your recovery and everything. After the first heart attack he seemed better and he told us not to tell you, but things started getting worse and then he had another one and now ... now it's only a matter of time.'

'If you'd called me sooner I could have had a chance to talk to him ... to say goodbye. Now, because of you, I'll never get the chance.' She flinches at my acidic words.

'I'm sorry, darling, please forgive me,' she whispers.

I wish I had the energy to argue my case, but I just shake my head slowly as I turn back to Daffy. 'Can he hear me?'

'I'm not sure, darling. Would you like a moment alone?'

I nod, blinking away the tears. I wait until my mum leaves the room to speak.

'Hi, Daffy. I'm here. I'm sorry I haven't been back home to see you lately. I've been trying to do what you told me and stay strong, but I'm really struggling to do that. I could really use some of your wise words right about now. Listen to me, going on about my own silly issues, when you're the one dying in a hospital bed.' I allow the tears to stream down my cheeks, unwilling to wipe them away. I squeeze his hand harder and lean down, resting my forehead against his cool skin. 'I'm glad you'll be at peace soon.' I kiss his hand.

Several minutes later I hear footsteps and look up to see James standing in the doorway, his head bowed, his shoulders hunched. Seeing him makes my heart split into two. I let go of Daffy's hand and run into James's arms, crying hard against his chest. He doesn't speak; he just lets me cry and holds me close as my legs threaten to buckle beneath me.

185

An hour later Daffy takes his last breath, finally free of his secret torment and dark demons, with his family by his side. I long to go with him, and yet hate myself for thinking that way.

Chapter Thirty-Seven
Now

Aimee steeled herself as butterflies fluttered in her stomach. She stood up behind the bar, hastily stepping over towards the side door to make it look as if she'd just walked in and not been crouched behind it. DI Fields's back was turned, his head still bowed low over his phone, which illuminated his face oddly in the fairly dim lights of the room.

'Hello, Detective.'

DI Fields snapped his head up. 'Aimee? What the hell are you doing here?' His voice had a sharp edge to it; for a split second he reminded her of Sergeant Miller when he would bark orders or shout at her for being too slow.

'I needed to speak to you and I was told you'd be here when I phoned the station, so I thought I'd pop down. I only live up the road.'

DI Fields narrowed his eyes as she stopped in front of him. 'You thought you'd *pop down* to a crime scene, a crime scene that clearly has barricades and yellow and black tape all around it? How did you even get *in* here?'

'Through the side door,' she answered as if it was no big deal.

'Uh-huh.' He didn't look convinced, nor did he look particularly happy, but Aimee quickly continued, hoping to distract his train of thought.

'I needed to ask you about something.'

'What?'

'It's about Jones. You said you have proof that he was seen here around the time the body was found, or close to it.

187

But who saw him and what was he doing? Did you manage to find the blonde woman he spoke about?'

'Has he said anything else to you?'

'No, nothing,' she lied.

'Yes, I've spoken to the blonde woman. Her name's Amanda Wilson. She's a works here as a waitress and sings twice a month, but on the night of the murder she wasn't singing. It was her night off. She was chatting with Tom Jones instead.'

'So she corroborated his story that he was just having a drink?'

'Yeah, a few too many drinks, but she said that she saw him leave by himself around midnight.'

Aimee sensed there was something on the tip of his tongue, so she pushed him a little further. 'Maybe we should check the CCTV footage in this place.'

'I have it already. I was just checking my emails on my phone when you walked in.'

'Can I see?' Aimee gave him what she hoped was an innocent smile, but DI Fields frowned at her.

'Aimee ... I know I said I needed your help, but—'

'I'll be able to look at it next week when I go back to work, along with all the other evidence you've gathered. It's kind of my job ... so you may as well show me now ... Detective.' She wasn't sure where her bravery was coming from, but it felt good to stand up for herself, for once. She bit her lip as DI Fields raised his chin ever so slightly.

'I'm probably going to regret this,' he muttered as he tapped his phone a few times. Aimee's heart lurched in her chest as she stepped forwards. 'I'm going to have to take a better look at it when I get back to the station,' continued DI

Fields, 'but from what I can see ... Jones spoke to the victim a few hours before he was killed.'

Aimee leaned forwards and watched the small screen, a burning annoyance building. If that was true then Jones had lied to her. She recognised him immediately; his shaggy hair and beard did little to disguise him, even on the small, grainy screen, but the second man in the frame was more difficult to make out. He was standing side on to the camera, but his facial features were very familiar.

'Can you confirm that that's James Daniels?' asked DI Fields.

Aimee squinted her eyes. 'I-I think so, but it's difficult to see properly.'

'Well, he's wearing the same jacket as the victim so I think we can safely say it's him.'

Aimee watched the video more closely. The two men were laughing, joking, and Jones even gave him a pat on the shoulder. 'They look friendly.'

'Hmm,' said DI Fields, 'which means Jones lied earlier when he said he didn't know him well and that the last time he saw him was back in Afghanistan.'

'But why would he lie?'

'You tell me.'

'How am I supposed to know?'

'I think you know a hell of a lot more than you're letting on.'

Aimee stood up straighter. 'Are you accusing me of something, Detective?'

'No, but I'd appreciate your complete and total honesty when answering this next question.'

Aimee's mouth turned dry as he reached over to a nearby table and picked up a clear sealed plastic bag, which held a torn photograph. 'Why would the victim have a photo of you in his pocket when he died?'

Aimee swallowed hard, taking the bag and studying the contents. There was a photo torn into two pieces, but the picture was easily recognisable. In fact, she had a copy of the same picture hidden away in a drawer at home. It showed her and James's faces squeezed close together, with a water fountain behind them. They'd taken it on their first date. Aimee opened her mouth to answer, but DI Fields cut her off.

'You two look pretty friendly too, wouldn't you say? ... James Daniels was more than just your doctor, wasn't he?'

Aimee nodded slowly. She'd been caught in another lie and now she'd have to deal with the consequences.

'Turn the photo over.'

Aimee did as he said, gasping loudly when she saw what was written on the back of the photo.

A single word.

Chapter Thirty-Eight
Then

Aimee's Mother's House, October 2009

The following few days pass by in a foggy blur as my mum hastily schedules the funeral and attempts to keep her emotions from drowning her. She puts on a brave face, as she always does, and soaks up the attention she receives from well-wishing neighbours and friends. Auntie Rachel flies over from Canada for the funeral, leaving her husband and children behind for a few days, and her and Mum flutter about the house, never resting, and drink more wine than usual.

Zoe spends a lot of time with her friends, only returning to the house for family dinners and to sleep. We're inundated with home-made freezer meals from the neighbourhood, each with a card attached or with flowers, so Mum's house looks like a flower shop and her freezer soon becomes full to capacity, enough meals to last us for months.

I, however, am not as strong as the rest of my family and retreat to my childhood bedroom because it's the only place I feel safe. I can't face friendly chit-chat with Auntie Rachel or nosey neighbours and I'm pretty sure Mum doesn't want me around anyway. I'll only get in her way or annoy her or do something wrong. I'm still quietly angry with her for not telling me that Daffy had a heart attack immediately after the first one happened, when he was still capable of talking.

James has been back and forth visiting me. He and Zoe appear to get on well and my mum can't get enough of him, even inviting him to dinner, which I find to be an odd thing to do considering she's just lost her dad. Maybe it's her way of dealing with grief, to have lots of people around her so she's distracted.

The rehabilitation facility has granted me two weeks of compassionate leave, but I already know I won't need the full amount as I'll be returning there as soon as the funeral is over. I don't want to be at home because home is where Daffy usually is, pottering about in the garden or snoozing in his worn out leather armchair or reading the newspaper with a cup of tea and a plate of biscuits nearby. Now he's gone it feels wrong to be here. I can't control my bad mood; it comes in waves, threatening to destroy me completely. I can't see a way through the darkness and, to be honest, I don't want to fight it any longer because I'm tired of everything and everyone.

The mattress is soft against my back as I stare at the ceiling. There's a dark spot up there, probably a damp patch, which is glaring back at me. I can't look away, almost as if it's drawing me in like a black hole, sucking me into its depths to be lost forever. I've been staring at the same spot for three hours when a loud bang interrupts me. Sitting bolt upright, I clench my pillow close to my body like a shield.

'Aimee?'

I hear my name somewhere in the distance, but the bang is ringing in my ears, getting louder and louder. It vibrates my whole body; then I see it – the blood, the fire, encircling me, covering me completely in its scorching embrace. An ear-piercing scream escapes my lips.

'Aimee!' Hands are grabbing me, shaking me as I scream. I kick out my arms and legs to try and protect myself, but they are forcefully holding me down and pinning me against the bed. 'Aimee, stop! It's me. It's James. Stop!'

I fling my eyes open, not even realising they were closed. 'Don't touch me!'

James immediately withdraws his hands, but the damage has already been done. I retreat further up the bed, away from him, squeezing myself into the corner, attempting to make myself as small as possible.

'I'm sorry,' he pleads. 'I'm sorry. I just didn't want you to hurt yourself.'

I bury my face into the pillow and weep. 'I can't do this anymore, James. I can't. I'm not strong enough.'

'What do you mean? I'm here. Let me help you.'

'I just want to be left alone. I want you to leave.'

'I can't leave you like this. I can't—'

My mum bursts through the door. 'What on earth was all that screaming? Darling, are you okay?'

'Mum, tell James to go away,' I shout like a petulant teenager.

James stands up and backs away from the bed. 'Aimee, you don't mean that. You're upset, just let me—'

'Don't tell me how I'm feeling! I'm sick to fucking death of people telling me how I should be feeling!'

'Language, young lady!' scolds Mum.

'Oh, Mum, get a fucking grip.'

James glances at my mum and sighs. 'I'm sorry, Mrs Price, but I think I'd better go. I don't want to make things worse.'

'Oh, James, love, I'm sorry she's behaving like this, but obviously we've all had a bit of a shock.'

I lift my head, my eyes wild with fury. 'Stop talking as if I'm not here. A bit of a shock, Mum? Really? Your dad dies and

I've barely even seen you shed a single tear. What the fuck is wrong with you?'

'Now, darling … I know you were close with Daffy, but I'm just—'

'Just go away, both of you.'

My mum sighs angrily. 'Fine, if that's the way you feel. You always were an attention seeker. Everything always has to be about you, doesn't it?'

My eyes fill with angry tears as I grasp the pillow and hurl it at my mum, screaming as loud as I can, 'Get out!'

Chapter Thirty-Nine
Then - James

James's Car, October 2009

James slammed his car door harder than he intended after making a swift exit from Aimee's mother's house. His body trembled from the argument he'd just had with Aimee; if you could call that an argument. It had mostly been Aimee shouting at him for trying to help her. He knew she was struggling, and he'd wanted to help her, but why was she pushing him away? Before her grandfather's death they'd been having fun together, never a sharp word between them, but there were times when she was distant with him. Sometimes her eyes glazed over, as if she were miles away and she'd forget he was even there.

James started his car, a black Audi estate, and pulled out of the driveway, taking one last look in the rear-view mirror at the house, at the window of Aimee's bedroom. He needed to help her, to get through to her somehow that his feelings towards her were genuine. He'd never felt like this about anyone before, never truly cared about someone else's well-being and it scared him, made him feel vulnerable.

The sound system switched on as a call came through on his mobile. James pressed the answer button on the steering wheel when he saw it was his brother calling.

'Hey, Adam, what's up?'

'Hey, just wondered if you want to come out for a drink tonight?'

James slowed the car to a stop at a junction. 'Uh, yeah, I guess I can now.'

'Why, did you have other plans with Aimee?'

'She's a bit messed up since her grandfather died.'

'Ah yeah, poor girl.'

James sighed. 'We had our first argument and she told me to get out.'

'James, sometimes you can't save everyone, you know that, right? She clearly has issues after what happened to her. I don't want her sucking you in to her madness.'

'It's not like that. And she's not mad. I really care about her … I … I think I love her, Adam.'

'Jesus … Right, that settles it. You're coming out for a drink or two or three with me tonight, no exceptions. We need to talk about this.'

A smile appeared on James's face as he signalled to turn left. 'Okay, I'll meet you at Mum's house in two hours.'

'Cool. Later.'

James disconnected the call and settled into his seat for the fifty-mile drive to his family home near Oxford. He'd been up and down the M40 and the M25 more times than he could count lately, visiting Aimee and spending time with his parents and brother. He didn't have his own place yet, but he'd religiously put money in a savings account every month towards a house deposit, so while he was on his post-deployment leave he'd been staying with his parents. It wasn't ideal because Adam was there too. He still lived at home, which James always gave him a hard time over. In terms of personality traits they couldn't have been more different. James was sensible with money, whereas Adam blew through whatever he earned within days, working as an estate agent.

James only usually entered into serious relationships, never having random one-night stands, but Adam seemed to be dating a different girl every other week. James could barely keep up with all of their names. Adam was a big drinker and often went on lads' trips away with his friends to various locations around the country, never remembering what had happened most of the time; James, however, liked the odd drunken night out, but rarely drank to excess, unless he was having a particularly hard day … like today.

Maybe it was time he let loose, to shake off these feelings and the tension in his shoulders. Maybe a night out with his brother was exactly what he needed.

Chapter Forty
Now

Aimee turned the photo slightly and aligned the letters like a jigsaw in her mind. The word was there, scrawled in untidy handwriting, in black ink.

Murderer.

Aimee knew DI Fields was staring at her, waiting for an explanation, but her heart hammered in her chest so erratically that she could barely draw breath to speak. There was nothing she could say to even attempt to explain what she was seeing. Her mind flashed back to that perfect day when she and James had laughed, flirted and kissed for the first time. She licked her lips, practically tasting the champagne and cucumber on her tongue as she had when she'd tasted his mouth.

'Care to offer an explanation, Aimee?' DI Fields had adopted his detective voice; stern, low and direct.

Aimee couldn't avoid the inevitable any longer, finally raising her eyes to look at him. 'I have no idea what this means.'

'But that *is* you and James Daniels in the picture, right?'

'Yes.'

'Smiling and looking very happy it seems.'

'We took it on our first date.'

'And you failed to mention that you'd had a romantic relationship with the victim ... why?'

'I ... I didn't think it was important.'

DI Fields folded his arms and sighed heavily, and Aimee was briefly reminded of the same actions her mum used to take when she was about to tell her off as a child. 'Anything else you want to tell me while you're at it?'

'Okay, yes … we were involved. A few months after this picture was taken I agreed to marry him, but two days before we were due to elope to Gretna Green I called it off and that was the last time I saw him.'

DI Fields cocked one eyebrow. 'You broke up with him two days before your wedding? Fuck.' Aimee imagined the cogs turning in his head; the judgemental thoughts whizzing around. 'Can I ask why?' And there it was, the inevitable question that she'd been dreading.

'It's personal,' said Aimee, her face turning pink.

'Personal? I'm afraid when it comes to a murder investigation, the word *personal* doesn't matter.'

Aimee gulped, staring down at the torn photo just to have something to do. She couldn't tell him. Not here, not now, not like this.

'Okay …' said DI Fields, changing tactics, 'so why do you think the victim wrote the word *murderer* on the back of a photo of the two of you?'

Aimee frowned. 'How do you know it's his handwriting?'

'Isn't it?'

'No, it's not. James didn't have handwriting like that.'

'Okay, so why would someone else, possibly the person who killed him, write it?'

'I have no idea. Honestly.'

'I think it's time my team and I dug a little deeper into the victim's past, don't you?'

Aimee held her tongue and nerve as she said, 'Detective, I knew James ... he never would have hurt anyone. He was a decent man.'

'Being decent has nothing to do with it. People change. You said yourself you haven't seen him since you dumped him ... Eleven years is a long time.'

Aimee had to admit that the detective was right. She didn't know James, not really, not anymore. 'I'd better go,' she said, handing the photo back to DI Fields.

'Do me a favour and bring Jones down to the station after five, will you? I need to have another little chat with him once I've spoken to the family of the victim, unless ... do you want to see them? His family, I mean. I can only assume that since you were due to marry their son they know who you are.'

'Actually ... I never met his family. I never even met his twin brother.'

This received another eyebrow raise. 'He has a twin brother?'

'Yeah. His name's Adam.'

'Good to know. I'll see you at the station after five with Jones then.'

'Is he still a suspect?'

'No, but I've found something out about him that warrants another chat.'

'What have you found?'

'Just bring him to the station. I'll explain then, and Aimee ... you may need to be interviewed as well.'

Aimee nodded, but she could barely draw breath as her mind searched for an answer she knew she didn't have. Was she now a possible suspect? What had DI Fields found out about Jones?

'Thank you, Detective. See you later,' she said as she backed away, wanting to put as much distance between her and DI Fields as possible.

'Oh, and Aimee ... don't let me catch you snooping around a crime scene again, yeah?'

Aimee smiled coyly before she walked out the door, her head held as high as she could muster, despite the agonising urge to bury it under the sand and hide away from the world. She met Dot and Cindy outside, both of whom were hiding behind the corner of the building and whispering. Their eyes widened in excitement when she joined them.

'So? You find anything?' asked Dot.

Aimee tucked a stray strand of hair behind her ear. 'I'm not sure. I need to speak to Jones ... alone,' she added, shooting Dot an obvious look. 'Tony is very suspicious of me. He caught me in another lie.'

'Which one?' asked Cindy.

'The one about me being in a relationship with James.'

'Ah ... shit.'

'Also ... it definitely looks as if the murder was pre-meditated.'

'Who'd want to kill a hot, ex-Army doctor?' asked Cindy.

'You still think you're connected somehow?' added Dot.

Aimee shrugged her shoulders. 'I don't know. I think I must be ... somehow.'

Dot rubbed her hands together. 'This is some proper serious Detective Poirot shit.'

'Tony knows more than he's letting on,' said Aimee, rubbing the back of her neck. The sun was beating down, the temperature rising by the minute. She didn't like the heat, not anymore, not after suffering through the hell of Afghanistan. Although, the British summer was like a mild spring day compared to that country.

'Well, he is the detective,' said Cindy matter-of-factly. 'It's his job to know.'

Aimee shot her a look. 'I need to talk to Jones and then take him down to the station for more questions. I'll see you both later.'

'Okay, but remember it's our girls' night tonight.'

'Uh … yeah … I might have to bail on that, but I'll let you know.'

Aimee hugged each of them in turn and then casually jogged back to her flat, her mind foggy with questions. She decided to take the stairs instead of the lift, her footsteps echoing in the empty hallways. Her heart rate quickened as she neared the top, not from the physical activity, but due to the fact she was going to have to confront Jones again.

Aimee stepped inside her flat and slammed the door, only releasing her breath when she'd bolted it.

'Jones?' she called out, leaning against the door. She walked towards the lounge, checking around for him, but he wasn't there. 'Damn it.'

Aimee kicked off her shoes and fed Darth a nugget. She watched the hamster's nose twitching in excitement as she scoffed the whole thing into her mouth pouch.

Aimee's mind flashed back to the photo that had been found on James's body. She closed her eyes, the moment he'd taken it clear in her head. Aimee smiled at the memory, but there was a niggle of doubt, of … *something* in the back of her mind that kept itching. She needed to know for sure …

Aimee headed to the nearby side cabinet and pulled out the middle drawer. Lifting up several pieces of paper and old notebooks, she finally found her old diary, the one she'd kept when she was at the rehabilitation facility. Her therapist had recommended that she keep one, which had been the bane of her life at the time.

Aimee flicked through the pages, not bothering to read any of it because she knew how dark and sinister the words were; words she never wanted to read ever again. She was looking for something in particular, something she'd stored between the pages long ago.

It wasn't there.

The picture of her and James that she'd tucked neatly away was gone.

'Looking for something?' Jones's voice made her jump, the notebook clattering to the floor.

Chapter Forty-One
Then

Military Rehabilitation Facility, October 2009

The funeral is held two days later, but I can barely force myself to put one foot in front of the other. It's like all of my life-force, my energy, my reason to keep breathing, has been sucked from my body and I'm now an empty shell.

It isn't just Daffy's death that's caused this; I know that, but it's certainly the situation that's finally pushed me over the cliff and into the icy waters below. My mum is like a whirlwind at the funeral, overseeing everything along with Auntie Rachel, even Zoe helps out, but not me. I sit in the corner in my black dress and jacket, contemplating. I don't care that people are talking about me in hushed whispers, giving me side glances as they eat their finger food and drink their cups of tea. I overhear one person, a middle-aged woman with dyed red hair, saying that I'm being selfish and lazy for not being there for my mum and helping out. I don't even have the energy or the motivation to stand up for myself. I've come to realise that nothing matters anymore; nothing at all.

I returned to the rehabilitation facility the day after the funeral, unwilling to spend the whole two weeks at home. I couldn't bear to spend another second with my mum and Zoe. They didn't deserve to see me like this and they both agreed that I was better off here anyway. They promised that they'd visit me soon, but by then it will be too late and they won't have to worry about me anymore.

I haven't heard from James either, not even a text, but something inside me tells me to leave him alone. I've got enough to deal with without trying to make him feel better by apologising.

I shuffle my feet, moving up in line for dinner. I don't have an appetite, but if I don't attend dinner then I'll have people questioning me about it and I seriously don't need the hassle. Jones is sitting in his wheelchair over by the window again, staring blankly. He never seems to eat anything and has lost a drastic amount of weight recently.

Fuck him.

Fuck everyone.

I reach the box of cutlery, the silver coating of the knives glinting in the florescent lights. They aren't particularly sharp, but it's the best I'm going to find around here. I grab one and slip it into my pocket, taking the dinner plate with a fake smile. It's a light-bulb moment, a sudden realisation that there is a way out of all of this … pain.

Soon the pain will be gone and I'll have nothing left to worry about. Zoe and Mum will be fine; I'm not worried about them. They have each other. No longer will I have to feel this overwhelming surge of panic whenever someone attempts to talk to me about what happened. It's too much to deal with and talking about it isn't helping. It's just making everything a lot worse. There's no other way out. I'm trapped like a caged animal, but now there's a glimmer of light ahead; the end.

I sit on the floor of my room a few hours later, the knife laid out ceremoniously on the floor in front of me, still gleaming in the light from above. I'm not going to leave a note. The reasons why will be abundantly clear. It's late, past midnight. No one will come and find me to ensure I'm up for breakfast for hours. I've got plenty of time. The pain that I'm about to endure doesn't scare me because I've been through much worse, and as for the blood ... I see the crimson liquid every time I shut my eyes anyway. It may as well be mine now.

A calming presence washes over me as I pick up the knife, the cool surface brushing my skin as it dances ... dances ...

Large angry yellow and orange flames lick at my feet. At first, it tickles, a small, uncomfortable sensation, but I scream as that sensation transforms into one of sheer terror and unimaginable pain. The heat envelops me, but I can't climb any higher to escape it.

The fire is growing and slowly climbing up my body, eating away at my flesh, turning my clothes to cinders. I keep attempting to climb up and out, but up and out of where? Where am I? I can't focus on anything because all I can feel is heat and the pain and see the bright colour of the flames, growing ever higher ...

I scream again ...

My eyelids flicker open, but they're so heavy I can't keep them open for longer than a second. It saps every ounce of energy not to fall back under again, under the flames ... under ...

'She's coming around. Aimee ... Aimee ... can you hear me? Aimee, stay with us. You're going to be okay.'

No.

No, that's not what I want.

I don't want to be okay.

The pain needs to go away, but it's following me, hunting me, torturing me.

Leave me alone!

I thrash my arms and legs in a blind panic as I remember the last time I was in this situation, waking up after the explosion.

'Hold her down!'

A sharp pain stings my arm, which feels as if it's on fire.

My arm is on fire.

The flesh is burning away and all I see is crispy, blackened muscle, tissue and bone.

'No,' I plead. 'Make it stop, please make it stop.'

'It's going to be okay, Aimee.'

'No!' But whatever's been injected into me is floating around my blood vessels, pulling me under, back towards the flames.

Maybe this is the end after all.

Blood ... so much blood.

I'm wading through it, chest deep, and it's slowly getting deeper, so deep, in fact, that I'm forced to start swimming, but the blood is thick and congealed, making my progress slow. It's trying to suck me under. I need to get to the edge, but where is it? The edge of what?

All I can see is a red ocean ... that reaches far into the distance.

'Aimee, can you hear me? Aimee ...'

That voice; it's one that's vaguely familiar, but I have to follow it. There is no other choice. Maybe it will lead me out of the red ocean. The waves are lapping over my head, drowning me. I cough up blood, whether it's my own I don't know …

'That's it … follow the sound of my voice.'

I open my eyes, squinting at the bright lights.

'She's awake. Just talk to her, try and keep her calm.'

'Aimee … it's Doctor Watson. I'm here to help you.'

I blink several times, attempting to connect my brain to my eyes. I see the outline of a woman standing next to me, but she's fading in and out of focus.

'Can you hear me?'

I slowly nod as my line of vision is drawn to the white bandage around my left forearm. What is this? What happened? I'm not in Afghanistan … I'm not where I'm supposed to be.

'Do you know where you are?'

I shake my head because it's the truth.

'Do you remember what happened?'

My mouth opens, but no words come out, so I shake my head again.

'Aimee … this is very serious. I know that you're healing well physically, but mentally is another matter. I'm going to help you through this. Things will get better for you, but you have to trust me. We have to work together on this, okay?'

'H-How?' I manage, before my voice is swallowed by an overwhelming surge of pain. I close my eyes against it, blocking it out.

'I can help you manage—'

'No … h-how did you find me in time?'

'It seems that one of the other patients saw you take the knife from the cafeteria. It took them a few hours, but they eventually told someone.'

'Who?'

'I don't know, I'm afraid.'

Chapter Forty-Two
Then - Jones

Military Rehabilitation Facility, October 2009

There she is, waiting in line for her scoff. My pathetic excuse for a meal is in front of me on the flimsy table, growing colder by the second. I've been told I need to start eating more, but it's such an overwhelming effort these days. My once strong, bulky physique is melting away before my eyes, my hard-earned muscle succumbing to atrophy due to lack of use. I can barely lift my arms above my head during my physiotherapy sessions, which are horrible to endure.

She has her back to me so I glare at the back of her head, wishing I had the power to make it explode all over the mashed potato. Why is she hovering by the cutlery? I watch as she picks up a knife and studies it, gently stroking the blade with her fingers. She glances around and then slips it into her pocket before taking her plate of food and walking away. At first I'm confused by her actions, but then I realise what she's doing and a smile creeps over my face.

The bitch wants to kill herself. Good riddance. She doesn't deserve to live after what she's done to me. My only regret is that I can't join her in the afterlife because I'm basically on twenty-four watch at the moment. My eyes flick over to the nurse sitting nearby; my guard. I can't believe I hate Price even more because she gets to fucking kill herself and I don't. Why does she get to end it and not me? I'm suffering more than she is.

I reluctantly pick up my knife and fork and begin to eat the cold mashed potato, one tiny mouthful at a time. I watch Price do the same. She's sitting over in the far corner now, eyes darting from left to right as if she's about to be caught out doing something naughty. Lucky bitch. I wonder when she'll do it? I bet she doesn't even have the guts to go through with it anyway. Maybe she'll attempt it tonight and slowly bleed out on her bedroom floor, lost and alone. Good …

I can't sleep; my mind is alive with visions of blood and screaming … of *her* screaming. She keeps shouting my name over and over, trying to get me to wake up. It's just gone midnight and my eyes are so heavy that I finally allow them to close, but whenever I do I keep seeing her fucking face. Why won't she leave me alone? She's probably dead by now. Even in death she's determined to ruin me.

There's an ache inside me that I can't seem to ignore. My heart is telling me to do something … something to save her, the way she saved me, but my brain is saying the opposite. What am I supposed to do? She needs my help, but I'm refusing to help her.

I adjust my body on the bed. I don't think I'll ever get used to only having one leg. It throws me off balance even when I'm lying down.

My eyes focus on the call button dangling on a wire beside my head …

And I finally make my decision.

Chapter Forty-Three
Now

'Fucking hell, you scared me.' Aimee bent down and picked the diary off the floor. 'Where've you been?'

'For a walk.'

'Right, cos that doesn't sound suspicious at all.'

Jones snorted. 'Not as suspicious as you snooping around a crime scene. Find anything then, Miss Detective?'

'Yes, as a matter of fact, I did. I found out that you're lying.'

'Oh yeah? About what?'

'About the fact that you haven't seen or spoken to James since Afghan.'

Jones narrowed his eyes. 'So?'

'So? The police want me to bring you back to the station later for further questioning. Are you going to answer with *so* when they ask you the same question?'

'I might.'

'I'm afraid you're going to need a better answer than that, especially if you want to keep yourself out from behind bars.'

'Too late for that.'

Aimee squared up to Jones. 'What's that supposed to mean?'

Jones sighed loudly. 'Nothing ... Fine, I saw him, I spoke to him. You happy?'

'No, I'm not happy. Far from it. I have an idiot homeless man living in my flat who refuses to act like a decent human being and answer a damn question properly. What's more, I'm pretty sure Tony thinks I'm somehow involved. It wouldn't surprise me if *I'm* brought in for questioning soon, or arrested.'

Jones shrugged his shoulders. 'Maybe you are involved.'

'Are you saying you think *I* murdered my ex-fiancé?'

'No, but I reckon you have something to do with it, whether it be directly or indirectly, I don't know.'

'Gee, thanks.'

'Just relax. I'm sure Detective Dimwit doesn't suspect a thing.'

'How would you know?'

'Cos he'd be stupid to suspect you of actually killing someone in cold blood, although granted he does ask a lot of stupid questions. If he knows you at all he'll know that you're incapable of hurting someone. You could have left me to die, but you didn't.'

Aimee bit her lip. It was the first time she'd heard Jones properly mention the incident and the fact that she'd saved his life. She rolled her head from side to side, feeling the crack of her tense muscles. She definitely needed to hit the gym soon and release her pent-up emotions on a punch bag, or maybe she needed a night out to let off some steam. An idea formed in her head, something she'd ask Cindy and Dot about later. It was girls' night after all.

'You seem tense,' said Jones. Aimee laughed sarcastically in response. 'What's that?'

Aimee glanced at the diary in her hand. 'It's a diary I kept back when I was recovering at the rehab facility. My therapist wanted me to keep one.'

'Ah yeah, I was forced to do one of those. What a load of shit. I burned mine as soon as I got discharged.'

'Shocking.'

'Why'd you have it now?'

Aimee frowned as she flicked through it again, hoping she'd just missed the photo she knew should be there. 'A photo was found on James's body. A photo of me and him. We both had a copy. I kept mine in this diary, but it's gone.'

'Okay, so maybe you did kill him.'

Aimee huffed. 'Not helpful, Jones!'

'Okay, fine ... let's think about this. Who's been in your flat recently who could have taken it?'

'But why would anyone take it? No one even knew about it except me and James.'

'Just answer the damn question.'

Aimee bit her lip again. 'Only Dot and Cindy ... and you, obviously, but you came into the flat after the murder had already happened. Neither Dot nor Cindy would take it. They knew about James, but not the details. They wouldn't have known the picture was in this diary.'

Jones folded his arms over his chest. 'No one else has been in here?'

'Zoe and Mum, but not for a while, months actually, and they didn't even know about the diary and the picture.'

'No booty call, no random bloke you picked up, no boyfriend?'

'No.'

'Jesus, you need to get a life.'

'Thanks a lot.' Aimee pushed past him into the kitchen, chucking the diary on the side where it skidded across the smooth surface and clattered to the floor. She ignored it, flicking on the kettle instead as she continued speaking. 'My family and friends would not have killed James. They barely knew him. Plus, Dot and Cindy never met him.'

'Okay, so that just leaves two options.' Jones followed her and stood against the kitchen counter.

Aimee stopped just as she was about to put sugar in one of the cups. 'Which are?'

'Oh, come on, you want to be a detective, don't you? It's no fun if you let me do all the work.'

Aimee rolled her eyes. 'Fine … let me think.' She turned her back on him as she grabbed the green-topped milk from the fridge. 'Either James somehow found me and broke into my flat and took it or … someone else did.'

'Bingo.'

'But who?'

'Well then, isn't that the million-pound question?'

Chapter Forty-Four
Then

Military Rehabilitation Facility, November 2009

The days seem to roll into each other like waves and the nights blur into one endless void of nothingness; nothing seems like it's getting better. I lie awake during the night in my hospital bed staring at the ceiling. My wrist throbs from the damage I've caused with the knife. The doctor says I was lucky I didn't hit a nerve, but I had almost severed the main vein. It hadn't been sharp enough to get the job done properly. Instead, it had just caused a huge mess.

A thought keeps buzzing around my head and, try as I might, I can't stop thinking it. Had I truly wanted to end it all? If I'd been serious about going through with it then why hadn't I ensured that the knife was sharp enough or found another way? I'd contemplated stepping out in front of a car, but that hadn't been a guarantee either. I could have ended up with a load of broken bones. Doctor Watson pointed out to me that it could have been a cry for help, and when she'd said that the first time I'd wanted to strangle her and watch her eyes pop from her head. Everyone always says that; they always say a failed suicide attempt is just because the person wanted some attention. I can't make up my mind what the truth really is. What I do know is that I'd reached the lowest point possible and hadn't seen any other way out. I'd tried to save myself, but now, it seems, I've been given a second chance.

Doctor Watson has prescribed me a course of strong anti-depressants, which I started two days ago. It's too soon to know if they're making a difference, as I'm told it can take up to two weeks or more for them to take effect. I've also been put on suicide watch, so I constantly have a nurse sitting by my hospital bed and the night guard comes to check on me every hour throughout the night.

I still want to be by myself and refuse to have Mum and Zoe visit me. Apparently, my mum has been told about my suicide attempt and I can only imagine what her reaction had been. She'd probably assumed, like everyone else, that I just wanted attention.

A niggle of regret and shame begins to eat away at me over the following days. Daffy has just died and here I am having attempted to kill myself merely days later. Aching feelings of remorse and guilt flood my body. I feel so inadequate and lonely; so lonely, yet I don't want to be around people. Hell, it's a strange sensation and, if anyone ever asks me to explain what being depressed feels like, it will be almost impossible to cover everything.

A week passes and I'm finally allowed to return to my room. The blood stains have been cleaned up, no trace of the *incident*, as Doctor Watson likes to call it, is left.

Now it appears I've had two catastrophic incidents in my life that will affect me for the rest of it. To be honest, I'm beginning to warm to Doctor Watson, despite her persistence at getting me to open up and talk. Sometimes we'll spend the entire hour of the therapy session in complete silence, but I quite like it, just sitting with someone. Yes, the doctor's overall goal is to coax me to start talking, but she's not being pushy about it, knowing I'll talk in my own time.

Doctor Watson watches me as I sit down on the bed, glancing around nervously. 'I have arranged for someone to come and visit you,' she says. 'I think it will do you good.'

'Who? I told you I'm not strong enough to see my mum yet, or Zoe.'

'No, it's not your family. James Daniels has asked after you. I've kept him at bay for a few days, but I think you're ready to see him.'

'I was awful to him. Why does he want to see me?'

Doctor Watson smiles kindly. 'Aimee, one thing you'll do well to remember is that, despite what you may think … there are people around you who care about you. Including me.'

I don't respond, avoiding the doctor's gaze. There's that guilty feeling again, rising up from within, making my insides writhe and itch.

An hour later a quiet knock disturbs me from a light sleep. After the doctor had left I'd curled up on my bed, pulled the blanket over me and attempted to sleep, which, surprisingly, I'd managed to do, albeit briefly.

'Come in,' I call out, sitting up and leaning back against the cool wall.

The door creaks open and James pops his head around it, a solemn expression across his face. He looks as if he hasn't slept in a week. 'Hey.'

'Hi … come in.'

'Thank you.' He closes the door and stands awkwardly in the middle of the room. 'Aimee … I … I wanted to come sooner, but they wouldn't let me.'

'It's okay. Thank you for coming now.'

'How are you?' I squeeze my lips together. 'Shit …
that's a stupid question, right? I'm sorry, I don't really know
what to say. I knew things were bad, but I thought you were
getting better. You never said anything.'

I shrug. 'I didn't want to burden anyone.'

'You're not a burden, Aimee.'

'I certainly feel like one now.'

James walks slowly across the room and sits on the
edge of the bed. I can see the pain in his eyes. I hate myself for
doing this to him. I should have known better than to get
involved with someone while I'm recovering and feeling
unstable. Maybe it's been a mistake, but, then again, James is
the only person I really want around. When I'm with him it
hurts a little less.

'I just want you to get better, Aimee. I know how bad
it was for you. I saw you when you were brought into Bastion
Hospital. I knew there and then that you'd have to fight to get
better, that it wouldn't happen overnight. I can help you, and I
will help you, in any way I can, but you have to let me.'

I slowly nod. 'Have you seen Jones?'

James's whole body stiffens. 'Yes, I've seen him
around. I've tried to talk to him, but he's in a bad place.'

'I wish I could help him.'

'I think you need to help yourself first. Jones is in the
right place for him, as are you. You just need to focus on
getting yourself better and let other people worry about
Jones.'

'But we're going through the same thing. We could
help each other.'

'Jones doesn't want any help.'

James doesn't understand and I know there's no point in trying to argue my case with him. Jones *does* need help; he does *want* help, but, like me, he doesn't know how to ask for it. I just know that if I can get through to him we can help each other, but everyone seems to want to keep us apart, James included. Why?

'You're right,' I say finally, 'it's time I focus on getting better.'

Maybe Jones will get better on his own one day … I can only hope he does.

Chapter Forty-Five
Now

Later, Aimee messaged the girly group chat to ask if Cindy and Dot wanted to join her tonight to go and see Nathan, her burly next-door neighbour, perform in a show. They usually scheduled a few drinks at a bar for their girls' night, or a movie marathon, but Aimee felt like pushing the boat out a little.

Cindy: I dunno … like, a theatre show or something?

Dot: Are you doing this as a favour to him?

Aimee: No, he just said that I should come and watch him sometime and I really need a night out away from Jones and all this stress.

Dot: Can't we just go drinking? He sounds like a creep.

Cindy: Yeah, babe … stay away. Let's do cocktails instead.

Aimee: He's a stripper.

Cindy: …

Dot: …

Cindy: I'm there! What time?

Dot: Meh … as long as he doesn't wiggle his dick in my face, I'm good.

Aimee allowed the front door to her flat slam shut, instantly regretting it, knowing Mrs Leamington was bound to have heard with her super hearing on high alert. While she'd waited for five o'clock to arrive she chucked Jones's clothes into the washing machine and added double the amount of powder that was recommended to ensure it erased the smell and grime, although she highly expected that his homeless clothes were beyond help. He was still wearing Nathan's borrowed items, but at least he looked more presentable than when he'd entered the police station yesterday.

Aimee glanced at Nathan's closed door as she passed it, praying that he didn't make an appearance, but clearly the gods weren't listening to her prayers today because the door opened and Nathan almost collided with Jones as he walked past.

'Oh, sorry,' said Nathan, as his brain caught up with who he was seeing. 'Ah, glad to see the clothes fit.'

Aimee cringed, knowing that this was about to go horribly wrong, so she attempted to play it cool. 'Hi Nathan. This is … Thomas. Thomas … Nathan.' It sounded so strange saying his first name; she'd only ever known him as Jones. She would bet money on the fact that he didn't know her first name.

Jones eyed Nathan up and down and snorted.

'Nice to meet you,' said Nathan, stretching his hand out. Jones took it begrudgingly and squeezed it hard. Nathan winced. 'You know,' he added with a laugh, 'you two don't look much alike.'

'And why the hell would we?' snapped Jones.

Aimee's breath caught in her throat. She stepped forwards. 'Ah, yeah, everyone says that. No one believes us when we say we're brother and sister.'

Jones shot her a sideways glance and then grinned sheepishly.

Nathan nodded. 'Going somewhere fun?'

'Not really. Just out for an early dinner to catch up.'

'Lovely. I'm off to work.'

'Ah,' said Aimee, 'actually … me and my girlfriends are going to come and see you perform tonight.'

Nathan's eyes lit up as he grinned. 'You are? That's great! I'll reserve a table for you at the front. How many of you are coming?'

'Three altogether. Thank you.'

'Great! It starts at nine. I'll leave the tickets at the front desk. I guess I'll see you then.'

Aimee nodded enthusiastically, avoiding eye contact with Jones. They watched in silence as Nathan walked down the stairs, rounding the corner until he was out of sight.

'I'm glad to see you took my advice.'

'What advice?'

'To get a life.' Aimee rolled her eyes. 'If you keep rolling your eyes at me they'll get stuck the wrong way round.'

'Shut up.'

'So what play is Loverboy in then?'

'He's not in a play. He's a stripper, if you must know.' Jones held his hand up for Aimee to high-five him. 'I'm not high-fiving you. What are you … twelve?'

Jones burst out laughing as Aimee ran away from him down the stairs, her face burning red hot.

Chapter Forty-Six
Then - James

Military Rehabilitation Facility, November 2009

It had been good for James to go out with his brother the other night. He'd had a few pints, not over done it and had a good time, even if Adam had done his best to convince him that he wasn't actually in love with Aimee.

'It's ridiculous,' he'd said, 'you've only known the girl a few months. You've not even shagged her yet!' It was a typical Adam response and James knew his brother meant well, but he didn't understand how he felt. Whenever he wasn't with Aimee he thought about her. He longed for a time when she was over her depression and injuries. It had devastated him when he'd found out she'd tried to kill herself. He should have been there for her. He couldn't imagine how lonely she must have felt, which was why he'd fought with the doctors there to let him see her, but they wouldn't allow him access, not until a week after it had happened. He didn't want to text or call her either because, not only did she rarely have her phone on, but it wasn't the type of conversation to have over the phone. He wanted to see her face, hold her hand and make sure she understood that he would always be there for her.

Thankfully, Aimee had seemed in good spirits when he was finally allowed to see her and they were able to salvage their relationship. But what was her fascination with Jones? He could sort of understand why she wanted to reach out to someone to try and help them because that's the type of person she was – she always wanted to help people. But why

Jones? He'd been nothing but horrible to her. Jones didn't deserve Aimee's friendship or attention and James was relieved when Aimee finally agreed to leave Jones alone and focus on herself. It seemed that she was finally turning a corner and putting the past behind her, where it should always be.

By the time he'd left her a few hours later he knew what he wanted to do. He knew the next step forward and it was enough to make his stomach bubble with excitement and nerves. He'd wait though, to ask her the question. She wasn't ready to hear it yet and he didn't want to scare or confuse her.

Next year ... next year he'd ask her.

Chapter Forty-Seven
Then

Military Rehabilitation Facility, January 2010

Time, apparently, can heal all wounds, but, to me, time is merely masking them, both physically and mentally. Two months pass and, while I'm doing better in therapy and often have good days where I feel somewhat normal, I'm constantly plagued by the viciousness of guilt and mind-numbing fear of losing everything. Some days I refuse to get out of bed or eat a single scrap of food, while other days I leap up at the crack of dawn and go for a walk or a jog with a smile on my face. Yes, my physical injuries are healing well and I can now jog for short periods of time, something I used to take for granted before the incident happened. Now, when running, I cherish each and every step, savour the burning in my lungs, glad of the fact that it's air I'm breathing in and not smoke. Sometimes I wake up from a particularly bad nightmare and find the room around me is on fire, but then, like a light switch, it turns off, and I'm left gasping for precious oxygen.

The people around me who haven't experienced depression or PTSD (my family, mostly and, to a certain extent, James) can't understand it, but my therapist does and she's kind and understanding, never pushing me too far in our sessions and knowing when to hold back. My mum says she understands, but how can she really when she's never suffered from PTSD? I can finally see a dim light at the end of the dark tunnel, but there are still days when that light retreats further away from me. Those days, I find, are the hardest.

James visits me as often as he can. His post-tour leave is over and he's had to return to his unit to continue his everyday job as an Army medic, but he's always at the end of the phone when needed the most. I allowed Mum and Zoe to visit me about two weeks after the incident and, for Christmas, I'd been given two days at home with them too, but it's a struggle in the outside world now. I still feel safer being at the rehabilitation facility. The civilian world is scary and unpredictable. At least in the Army I know everything is taken care of, such as my bills, food, clothing and accommodation. I'm not sure how I'd adjust to civilian life now.

However, the news I'd been dreading since *it* happened finally arrived yesterday and I'm still attempting to recover from the shock, despite knowing it was coming eventually. Unfortunately, I've been told that, due to my injuries and ongoing PTSD, I'll be medically but honourably discharged from the Army. Even though my lower limb injuries are healing well, I have a small level of nerve damage that will prevent me from continuing my career as a soldier.

The moment I was told it felt as if my heart had been ripped from my chest. Being a soldier is all I've ever wanted to do. I've sacrificed so much, lost so much because of it and now I feel betrayed by the very service I've sworn to serve. My career has been cut short, having only served a little over four years. I'd barely begun and now I feel as if I no longer have a purpose in life. What's the point in continuing? I have to keep reminding myself that I've been down this road already and it has led to some very dark places, places I never want to visit again. I know I have to keep fighting. It's what Daffy would have told me to do, but it's so damn hard to see the positive side of things when all I can see or focus on is the negative.

I was also told by my chain of command to put in an application to receive compensation for my injuries, so now I'm waiting for those results. Not that I care about how much money I'm likely to be awarded. If I had to choose between having thousands of pounds and the ability to conceive and carry a child then obviously I'd choose the latter.

I'm sitting alone in the airy and spacious reading room, on a particularly rainy and cold day in January. My legs are tucked up underneath me on the comfy chair, a blanket around my shoulders. It's almost time to leave this place. The physiotherapist has signed me off from her care and Doctor Watson is adamant that I'm ready to return home. I've only got a few days left and my emotions are beginning to overwhelm me, sending me down a steep spiral, but I keep fighting them back. The medication holds my mind together, but on some days I feel fuzzy, out of touch with the world, as if my mind and body aren't connected properly. Today is one of those days, which is why I'm alone and reading.

'Hey,' says a voice from the doorway. I don't need to look up to know it's James.

'Hey, yourself,' I reply with a smile, setting down my book; a thriller about a missing woman. A small part of me is irritated that he's interrupted my quiet time.

'Sorry, I know I usually call first, but I wanted to surprise you.' James enters the room and produces a huge flower bouquet from behind his back. I'd spotted them already as I'd looked up, could smell the strong scent wafting across the room.

I take them. 'Wow, they're gorgeous. Thank you, but what's the occasion?'

'No occasion. Just I know how difficult it must be at the moment with being discharged from the Army. I mean … I don't *know* exactly, but … I can only imagine how …' James stops and sighs sadly. 'I'm so sorry, Aimee. I know it wasn't the outcome you hoped for.'

'Don't be. Let's face it … I'm in no condition to go back to work or go back out on tour or shoot a rifle. The other night, during a bad thunderstorm, I was so sick and couldn't stop shaking because of the loud bangs.'

'Why didn't you call me?'

'It was the middle of the night.'

'I told you, any time, day or night, if you need me then call me. Promise me, next time that happens, you'll call me?'

I nod slowly even though I know I won't. 'I promise, but I'm going home soon so I'll have Mum and Zoe around.'

'Are you looking forward to it?'

'Yes and no.'

James nods. 'What about later on? Any ideas for the future?'

I shrug. 'At the moment I'm just focussing on one day at a time. I'd still like to stay close to the service side of things, so maybe I can get a job with the police or the Civil Service. I haven't looked into it, but it's an idea that's been floating around in my head.' I'd mentioned it to Doctor Watson the other day and she'd thought it was a brilliant idea.

'That sounds good. I'm glad you have a plan of action to get back out there. I'm so proud of you, Aimee.' James takes my hands and squeezes them, kneeling down by the side of my chair. 'I want to ask you a question. It's been one I've wanted to ask for a long time, but I knew you weren't ready to hear it.

I'm not sure if you're ready now, but I can't hold it in any longer ...'

'Okay,' I say timidly.

James's eyes widen and he takes a deep breath, his hands visibly shaking. 'Aimee ... will you marry me?'

Chapter Forty-Eight
Now

The station was surprisingly busy when Aimee and Jones stepped through the doors, the air conditioning hitting them full in the face, a refreshing welcome from the vicious heat of the late afternoon sun. The officer on reception waved Aimee through without stopping the conversation he was having with a walk-in. As Aimee led Jones through the corridors towards the interview rooms, several heads swivelled in their direction.

'Must be the new hair style,' muttered Aimee.

'Can't complain,' answered Jones as he winked at a passing female officer, who returned his gesture with a coy smile. Aimee fought the urge to roll her eyes. She really did need to stop doing that. She'd once rolled her eyes at her instructor in basic training (for what reason she could no longer remember) and had then spent the next two hours scrubbing the stones that decorated the outside of the parade square with a toothbrush.

It was then that Aimee saw him.

But no, it couldn't be him.

He was walking towards her, his hair was longer and messier, his face slightly rounder, but it was him.

She stopped mid-stride, all of her breath disappearing from her lungs in a single moment. Aimee squeezed her eyes shut, hoping it was merely her mind playing tricks on her. Maybe when she opened them he wouldn't be walking towards her. She had hallucinated in the past, but this seemed very real, like she could stretch out her hand and touch him ...

'J-James?' Aimee stuttered. He stopped in front of her. She could barely breathe; her heart was racing, as saliva filled her mouth.

'You must be Aimee,' he said. His eyes flicked over to Jones for a moment, but he didn't acknowledge him in any other way.

Aimee covered her mouth with both hands. 'Oh my god ... you're his brother. You're Adam. I'm so sorry.' Aimee swore her heart stopped for several seconds as it plummeted in her chest, the reality of the situation hitting her with such force she felt as if she'd been slapped across the face. It wasn't James after all, so why did she feel relief and not joy?

Adam shrugged his broad shoulders. 'It used to happen all the time. Don't worry about it.'

'I just wasn't expecting to ... God, I just ... I'm sorry, I'm babbling.'

'It's fine. I'm sorry I startled you and I'm sorry we never got to meet you all those years ago, but maybe it was for the best, huh?'

'Yeah ... maybe. I'm so sorry about ... what's happened. It came as a complete shock to me too. I can't believe it—'

'How dare you!' A shrill female voice interrupted the calmness of the corridor.

Aimee jumped and glanced past Adam to see an elderly woman storming towards her, nostrils flaring, eyes piercing straight through her. The woman barged past Adam and squared up to Aimee who couldn't help but step back to avoid being too close to her.

'How dare you,' the woman spat again. 'What are *you* doing here?' She turned her head and addressed DI Fields who had jogged along the corridor to catch up with her. 'What is *she* doing here?'

DI Fields placed a hand on the woman's shoulder. 'I'm sorry, Mrs Daniels. I didn't mean for you to run into Aimee.'

Aimee's brain clicked into gear as she studied the woman who, despite her small size, made up for that fact by having a very sharp, severe look about her. Her pale blue trouser suit was pristine, fitting her perfectly. Aimee couldn't see the resemblance to James, who, like his brother, would have towered over her by at least a foot and a half. She had never met James's mother, but he had shown her pictures and, apparently, had shown his mother pictures of Aimee too.

'Mrs Daniels, I'm so sorry for your loss,' said Aimee solemnly.

'Oh, don't give me that bullshit, you conniving bitch. You did this to him!' She prodded Aimee's chest with her rigid finger.

'What? No, I … I haven't seen James since—'

'You dumped him and broke his heart. You used him and then cast him aside, didn't you? I bet you don't even care that he went to jail and his whole career and life was ruined because of you … because of what *you* did.'

'I … I don't understand.' Aimee's head span with a million questions as they jostled for first position inside her head. Words such as *jail*, *career* and *ruined* flashed at her, rendering her speechless. What was Mrs Daniels talking about?

Adam stepped forwards, his hands held up. 'Mum, come on. You can't blame Aimee for what he did.'

'Don't you start!'

'Okay, look, why don't we all just move along,' said DI Fields, attempting to get Mrs Daniels to start walking again by holding out his hand to show her the way.

'Hmmppfff!' She shrugged his hand off her shoulder then pointed another stiff finger at Aimee, poking her in the chest yet again. 'He was too good for you. If I find out you had anything to do with his death ...' But she didn't finish her sentence. Instead, Mrs Daniels stormed off down the corridor, leaving a waft of strong perfume behind as well as a frigid atmosphere.

Adam turned to Aimee. 'Sorry,' he muttered.

'I don't understand,' said Aimee in a hushed voice. 'What's she talking about? James went to jail ... Why and when?'

'After you ended things with him he went on a drinking binge, which was very unlike him. He got really drunk and ... hit a girl with his car. She died.' Aimee clamped her hand to her mouth. Adam continued. 'He went to jail for almost ten years, and when he came out he wasn't the same. Obviously, he was dishonourably discharged from the Army during that time, lost his pension, lost everything.'

Aimee shook her head slowly as she lowered her hands from her mouth. 'I'm so sorry, I had no idea.' Her heart was beating so hard and fast she thought she might pass out at any second. Every fibre inside her was shouting at her to run, to hide, to shield herself from the truth, but she couldn't. She had to absorb the information and deal with it.

'I know,' said Adam.

'If I did I would have reached out to him, you know that, right?'

Adam shrugged. 'We never got to meet you. It all happened so fast. I told him he was crazy for proposing to you so quickly, but he didn't listen. Why'd you say yes and then change your mind, anyway? I've always wondered.'

Aimee glanced at Jones who was still hovering behind her, pretending to fiddle with his fingernails. DI Fields had followed Mrs Daniels, so was out of ear shot.

'I … I was in a bad place mentally when I said yes, but I accepted because your brother was the only person in my life that made me feel happy.'

'So why'd you end it with him?'

'I realised that we wanted different things in life. We should have talked about it sooner, but we were so caught up in the moment.'

Adam frowned at her answer, but had the decency not to press her any further. 'Well, for what it's worth … I'm sorry about what my mum said. She's just angry. I don't think she means it.'

Aimee smiled. 'Thank you, but I understand her anger. It was nice to meet you, Adam.'

'Nice to meet you too, Aimee.' Adam smiled, nodding politely at Jones, before walking away, his head bowed slightly.

Aimee watched him until he was out of sight and then turned to Jones who was glaring at Adam as he walked away. 'Whatever you're going to say I'd rather you didn't right now.'

Jones held up his hands in defence. 'My lips are sealed, but I'm pretty sure I've worked out why you dumped him.'

'Can we talk about this later? I can't deal with this right now. I've just found out that I ruined someone's life and was quite possibly the cause of a woman's death.'

'Don't be stupid. You had nothing to do with it.'

Aimee frowned. 'Wait … did you know about the woman's death?'

'No … I'm as shocked as you are.'

Aimee sighed. 'I still don't understand how *you* fit into all of this and why you met up with him on the night he died.'

'Well, maybe if you're a good girl, I'll tell you.'

Aimee blew out the excess air in her mouth. 'You're impossible. You'd better not lie to Tony again or keep anything back. If you do then you'll be arrested and charged. Hell, at this rate I'll be the one who'll get arrested and charged.'

Jones folded his arms. 'Fine, I'll talk, but I want you in the room with me.'

'I'll talk to Tony.'

Chapter Forty-Nine
Then

Military Rehabilitation Facility, January 2010

I stare open-mouthed at James for several seconds, slightly unsure whether I believe my ears. I've had a few instances lately where people have been talking to me and I've either completely blanked out the entire conversation or missed snippets of it, or I've thought they've said something when, in fact, they haven't said anything at all. I can't trust myself. The other day I forgot how to tie my shoelaces and in the end I just tied a massive knot in them. Plus, I also hear things that aren't really there; like gunshots or crackling flames.

'Aimee ... did you hear me?'

I blink, bringing myself back to reality. 'Sorry, I ... yes, I heard you ... I think, but—'

'I know it's soon and you're going through all this stuff at the moment and you haven't met my family yet, but there's time for all that. As soon as I met you I knew I wanted to spend the rest of my life with you. I want to be there for you, through your recovery and beyond.'

There are words stuck in the back of my throat, aching to be free, but I can't quite let them go yet. It's too soon and I'm going through a lot. Hell, I've *been* through a lot and it isn't even close to being over. *What the hell is he thinking?* Granted, James does make me feel better. He's my safe space, my warm and happy haven, but we've only known each other less than six months.

'Are you s-sure?' I stutter. Maybe that's the wrong thing to say. Of course he must be sure otherwise he wouldn't have asked me. The look on his face tells me I've upset him. 'I'm sorry ... I just ... I'm not sure I ...' I stop, think and rephrase my sentence. 'I ... I ... yes, I'll marry you.' The words escape and I have no idea how or why I've said them. I was supposed to say them in my head, but they've come out of my mouth instead and now it's too late to reach out and grab them, stuff them back inside. Sometimes my words get jumbled up and I can never remember if I've spoken them aloud or not.

Before I know what's happening James grins, lean towards me and wraps his strong arms around my frail body. Yes, I do feel safe with him, like nothing will ever hurt me again. We have so much to talk about, but maybe James is right. There's time for all of that.

'I love you, Aimee.'

The words float from my mouth before I can even think. 'I love you too, James.'

My body floods with tingly joy and I smile properly for the first time since the incident. This is it; the start of my recovery. James has saved me, in more ways than one. I'm happy. I'm truly, truly ... happy ... There's something else I can't quite put my finger on, a niggle, an itch, but I'll deal with it another day, another time.

'James,' I say, turning to him, 'I don't want a big wedding. I'm not in the right frame of mind to deal with all the stress that comes with planning a wedding.'

'How about we elope to Gretna Green and do it in secret?'

I laugh out loud. 'Mum and Zoe would kill me!'

'Then we'll only tell them.'

'No,' I quickly say, 'no … my mum would stress me out even more. You're right. Doing it in secret is the best idea.'

'Are you sure about this? We can always wait until you're better and then have a big wedding?'

'No, a small ceremony with just the two of us sounds perfect.'

'Then I'll get the planning started.'

Chapter Fifty
Now

Aimee waited for DI Fields outside the interview room while Jones went in and sat down, after complaining that he was hungry and needed a beer. She was still in shock from what Mrs Daniels and Adam had just told her. The fact that James had been in prison for killing a girl seemed unbelievable, inconceivable. Surely there was some sort of mistake, some piece of information she was missing. How had she not heard about it or seen it on the news? Then again, she'd boycotted television and radio for a long time, determined that she wanted to focus on getting better and starting her new job. James had never tried to contact her though, not even a text to beg her to reconsider and now she knew why. He'd just upped and left when she'd broken off the engagement. It had been a heart-breaking yet clean breakup, but now she wasn't so sure. She couldn't help but wonder if his death had something to do with the crime he'd committed.

Aimee needed answers and she knew exactly what she'd be doing later when she got home – research. Maybe she should cancel the girls' night out ... It had been silly to think she could go out and have fun when her ex-fiancé was lying in a nearby morgue. Or was it? She didn't know him anymore. Did she really owe him anything?

First, before she could decide what to do about tonight, she needed to get herself and Jones through the next round of interview questions. DI Fields was, no doubt, going to ask some very difficult questions, possibly open up old wounds, which she wasn't ready for. She needed to be ready. It was necessary to get to the bottom of why James was dead, to ensure she wasn't the one who was partly responsible.

DI Fields rounded the corner and locked eyes with her. 'I was hoping to avoid you running into them. Mrs Daniels lost it a bit when she saw the body earlier.'

'It's okay, I understand. I didn't realise they'd be here.'

'I needed to ask her some questions about James's time in jail and his past. It was strange seeing his twin brother standing next to the body. Pretty surreal.'

'Can I ask a random question? It's going to sound a bit crazy.'

DI Fields inhaled deeply. 'You want to know if it's possible that the body in the morgue is actually Adam and not James?'

'It only crossed my mind when I saw Adam. They are so identical, it freaked me out.'

'I've already checked. James's fingerprints definitely match the ones on file from his arrest eleven years ago. Adam's don't match.'

Aimee nodded slowly in acceptance. 'Jones is in the interview room now. He says he'll talk, but he wants me in there with him.'

DI Fields narrowed his eyes. 'He's clearly got a soft spot for you, but I'll allow it if it makes him talk. He may not like the direction the questions are going to take. Also … I have a few questions for you too.'

Jones looked up as Aimee and DI Fields entered. She gave him a quick smile as she sat down next to him. It was strange being on the opposite side of the table from the detective, like she and Jones were a team, except that she had no idea about the game plan.

'I have to say I agree with your new look ... at least you don't offend my nostrils or eyes anymore,' said DI Fields as he sat down, scraping the chair closer to the table.

Jones scoffed. 'Shame I can't say the same about you.'

'I hear you're ready to answer my questions properly now?'

'Depends.'

'On what?'

'On how stupid they are.'

DI Fields turned to Aimee. 'I thought you said he was going to be cooperative?'

'He is.' Aimee shot Jones a stern look.

Jones chuckled. 'Calm down. I'll answer your damn questions.'

DI Fields leaned over and switched on the recording equipment and then proceeded to say his name, their names, the time and date and the reason why they were there. Finally, he took a deep breath.

'Right, let's get started. Now, my first question is this ...' He opened the folder he had placed on the table and brought out a printout of a black and white picture. Aimee recognised it as a snapshot of the CCTV footage she'd seen earlier on his phone. '... Can you tell me why you and the victim are in this photo together? That is you, isn't it? You know, before you had a makeover.'

Jones glanced at the photo, a mere flick of the eyes. 'Yep, that's me, but that's not Daniels.'

Aimee frowned. 'Yes, it is.'

'Actually, it isn't. You'd think you'd recognise your ex-fiancé, but no, that's Adam, the guy we've all just seen out in the hall.'

'Are you sure?' asked DI Fields. 'Because I've just finished talking with Mrs Daniels and Adam and he didn't mention anything about being in the same bar as his brother on the night he was murdered. Also, you two didn't acknowledge that you knew each other.'

'Funny that.'

'What's that supposed to mean?'

'It means, *Detective*, that Adam has lied to you.'

'Why would he do that?'

'I suggest you ask him that. I reckon you'll be shocked at what you find out.'

DI Fields puffed out his chest and ran his fingers through his hair. Aimee watched him for a few seconds, noting his flushed cheeks and flared nostrils. 'Okay, next question … What were you doing talking with Adam Daniels in the bar on the night his brother was murdered?'

'Catching up, having a few drinks.'

'How do you know each other?'

Jones narrowed his eyes. 'I'm a friend of the family.'

Aimee shifted in her seat, wanting to ask a dozen other questions, but she held her tongue and allowed DI Fields to continue.

'Did you see James there that night?' he asked.

'Yeah, I saw him.'

'Did you speak to him?'

'No.'

'So you were having a catch up with Adam, yet didn't speak to James. Why's that?'

'We arrived separately. Me and Adam were meeting him there.'

'Why?'

Jones chewed on his bottom lip for several seconds, never taking his eyes off DI Fields. 'He wanted my help.'

'Help with what?' Aimee asked, taking the words straight out of the detective's mouth. She hadn't been able to hold them back any longer.

Jones flicked his gaze onto her. 'The truth is that Daniels and I were friends. After I got discharged from the Army I also spent some time in jail for a minor crime—'

'I'd hardly call assault and battery a minor crime,' interrupted DI Fields.

'Do you want to hear my story or not?' Jones snapped. DI Fields grunted and leaned back in his chair as Jones continued. 'As I was saying … I spent some time in jail and that's where we met, for the second time. I hadn't seen him since I was at that rehab place. I was slightly shocked to find him behind bars for killing a girl by drink driving. He never seemed like the sort. Anyway, he kept saying that it was an accident and he couldn't remember what happened. He said that he'd been out drinking with his brother and he'd blacked out and then woken up after the accident with no memory of what had happened. He'd pleaded guilty because all the evidence had been stacked against him.

'Anyway, long story short, we became mates in there after he … well, the point is he looked out for me. I looked out for him, but I was only in there a year and then got released, which was a shame because jail beats the hell out of living on the streets.'

Aimee wanted desperately to interject and quiz him again on the fact that he had a large sum of money sitting in a bank account, but decided against it. Her heart pounded in her chest as Jones continued his story.

'When Daniels got out of jail a few months ago he looked me up, but he wasn't the same. Prison changed him, but one thing I'll tell you about ex-soldiers is that you can always depend on them to have your back, no matter what, and when Daniels said he needed my help, then I stepped up and came to Woking with him.

'That's when I met his brother, Adam. I didn't like the guy from the moment I met him. There was something about him that didn't feel right. He clearly had a drinking problem and that's when I started to put two and two together. Daniels wanted my help to try and make amends for what he'd done to the girl's family, but I told him that he needed to take a step back and think about what he was doing. It was Adam. I'm convinced of it.' Jones leaned back in his seat, looking as if the entire speech had exhausted him. It was the most amount of words Aimee had ever heard him say in one go.

DI Fields tapped his pen on the desk, seemingly unaware of doing so as he spoke. 'Are you saying that Adam killed his twin brother or that Adam killed the girl?'

Jones looked at DI Fields with a stern frown. 'Possibly both, but so far I haven't been able to prove it.'

'So this is all just conjecture so far?'

'Yeah, but you've met him, right? Adam? He's gives off a weird vibe.'

'I'm afraid I can't arrest the guy on the fact that he has a *weird vibe*,' answered DI Fields with a roll of his eyes.

'So you won't even look into the possibility that Adam might be involved?' snapped Jones, folding his arms across his chest.

'Of course I will. I need to look into every possibility, but you still haven't confirmed why you were talking to Adam at the bar that night.'

Jones sighed deeply. 'Like I said, I was drinking. We were just catching up, all three of us, that's all. I wanted to meet Adam properly to get a feel for him and try and talk Daniels out of doing something stupid.'

'Like what?'

'Like looking up this one.' Jones nodded at Aimee, who jumped slightly in her seat.

'Me? He came to see me?'

'I think so, yeah. Anyway, that night I got distracted by the hot blonde and lost sight of Daniels. Adam was taking a leak. When he came back we looked for Daniels, but he was gone.'

DI Fields folded his arms across his chest, staring at Jones directly in the eyes without blinking. 'When did you next see him?'

'I didn't. Me and Adam looked for him for ten minutes and then Adam got a text from him saying that he was calling it a night, so I went back to chat to the blonde and Adam went ... well, I don't actually know where he went, but he left.'

'What time did Adam receive the text?' asked DI Fields.

'Ten, maybe? Just after ten. I left the bar around midnight after chatting to the blonde for a while.'

DI Fields glanced at Aimee who'd been holding her breath during Jones's speech. She finally expelled the air in her mouth. 'What time was his body found?' she asked.

'Half one in the morning. He was found in one of the storerooms, but there's no footage of him talking with anyone, not even this guy' – he gestured at Jones – 'now that it turns out it's Adam in the footage. I need to get him back in here and ask him some more questions.'

'Can I go now?' asked Jones, leaning forwards in the chair, readying himself to stand up.

'Not quite. I'm still not sure what this has to do with Aimee other than the fact Daniels may have wanted to look her up.'

Aimee raised her eyebrows. 'I've got nothing to do with it. I didn't even know James and Jones were in Woking at the time. I had no idea he wanted to find me.'

'You sure about that?'

'Yes!'

'But you're still connected to them somehow. It can't be a coincidence that James came to Woking looking to make amends and then landed up dead.'

Aimee frowned. 'He had nothing to make amends for, if what Jones says is true and that Adam killed the girl. And if he was here to find me to make amends with me then there was no need because I was the one who broke up with him.'

DI Fields tented his fingers together. 'Yes, so you were the one who basically started all this. Maybe he was here to finish it. Leave it with me … I need to get my team to look into a few things.'

Aimee sat up straighter in her chair. 'So that's it? We can just leave?'

'Actually ... I have to ask ... Why'd you break up with James in the first place?'

'I'd rather not answer that.'

'Why not?'

'Is this a serious question? Am I being questioned about the case?'

'No, you're not—'

'Then I don't have to answer.'

DI Fields smiled. 'Fair enough. You can both go ... but stay close in case you're needed again.'

Jones stood up abruptly, knocking over his chair. 'Right ... time for some beers.'

Chapter Fifty-One
Then

Aimee's Mother's House, February 2010

It's all happening so fast, I can barely keep up. How am I engaged and a mere two days away from getting married when it feels as if it were only yesterday I was free and single? I've still been living at home and my mum has practically been spoon-feeding me, constantly doing everything, which isn't what I want, but I feel as if I owe it to her to let her look after me because that's what mums want to do; they want to help and look after their children when they're sick and always want what's best for them. I want everyone to be happy because if they're all happy then I'm happy ... except I'm not, not really. I'm struggling, but everyone is going about their daily lives without a care in the world, seemingly oblivious to me and my feelings. I'm old news now; my injuries have healed and, because no one can see the scars on the inside, they've forgotten that I attempted suicide only a couple of months ago. They've blocked out the fact that I'd reached such a low point in my life that I'd tried to end it. But I haven't. The memory keeps slapping me in the face every time I catch a glimpse of my wrist, another scar to add to the ones I already have scattered across my body.

Why does no one care? Even James barely mentions it anymore, too wrapped up in the wedding planning to worry about me. Not that there's much to plan. He's booked a slot for us to attend where we'll have two random people to act as witnesses. Am I doing the right thing? I feel like I should tell my mum and Zoe. It's extremely difficult to keep it a secret, but I'm just not in the right frame of mind to have *that* conversation with Mum. It's exhausting to get out of bed in the mornings and slap on a smile, covering up how dark my mood really is. The anti-depressant medication is still helping and it really does do a good job most days, putting up a mental shield against my sinister and disturbing thoughts. Maybe there's another reason I haven't told my mum about my impending wedding ...

Everything is just unravelling and gaining momentum and I can't stop it. The day after I said yes to marrying James I realised that we've never had a serious discussion about the future, about our plans; the big topic being children. The unanswered question is eating away at my insides like a virus. It's bubbling up to the surface, threatening to spill out whenever I see him. He still doesn't know about my operation. He knows I'd suffered some damage because he treated me in Afghanistan, but he doesn't know the full details and that's what's scaring me. I haven't been truthful with him.

I have to tell him. I have to be the one to bring up the dreaded topic that most couples should have discussed long before their wedding day, but here I am, days away from saying 'I do' and my fiancé has no idea that I can never bear his children.

We're sitting outside in the garden. I love this small patch of grass and the few random flower borders. Daffy used to keep it so neat and clean, but it's been neglected somewhat lately so the grass is a little too long, the borders a bit too overgrown and wild. Even though it's cold and the sky is heavy with dark cloud I want to be outside. The fresh air keeps my mind clear and prevents me from feeling claustrophobic.

I have to tell him ...

No, it's too scary. What if he gets angry or upset?

I have to tell him ...

'You okay, Aimee?' James's voice is smooth and gentle, the way it always is. I've never heard him raise his voice or even say a bad word. 'You look like there's something on your mind.'

I smile. It feels so forced. 'I love how well you know me.'

'Is it the wedding?' He keeps his voice low because he knows that my mum and Zoe are in the house behind us. 'Are you nervous? It's perfectly normal.'

'I know,' I say quickly. 'I'm not nervous. It's just ... it's all happening really fast and I know I said that's what I wanted, but my mind has been all over the place lately. I feel like there's so much we haven't spoken about yet.'

'Like what?'

I have to tell him ...

I gulp back the lump in my throat, forcing it down so I don't choke. 'Like ... where are we going to live once we're married? Am I going to stay here with my mum until I'm better or are we going to move in together?'

James stares out across the garden. 'Well, I don't mind. I mean, since we're keeping it a secret, it's probably best we keep up appearances for a while. I want to make sure you're happy and recovered first.'

I nod. 'Okay ...'

I have to tell him ...

'T-There's also ... um ... something else we haven't spoken about yet, because everything's happening so fast.'

'What's that?'

I fiddle with a strand of my hair as I wrestle with my tongue to form the word. 'Kids.'

'Ah ... you're talking about the whole *how many kids do you want to have* question?'

'Yeah.'

'Well, I'd like us to one day have as many as possible, but only when you're ready. There's plenty of time.'

My heart sinks like an anchor to the bottom of my chest, down into the icy depths, slamming with a thud when it reaches the bottom. This is exactly what I've been afraid of and what's been stopping me from bringing it up before today. Reality is a cold slap across the face and now I've realised how stupid and reckless I've been in saying yes to him so fast and ignoring the obvious elephant in the room.

'Aimee? What's wrong?'

'I ... I don't ... what if I said I didn't want to have kids?'

James raises his eyebrows slightly. 'Is that what you're saying?'

'No, but what if I couldn't have any?'

James furrows his brow. 'Wait ... Aimee, what are you saying exactly?'

This is it; the final nail in the coffin. There's no going back now.

'James ... I can't have children. When I returned from Afghanistan the doctors found that my uterus was damaged and it was too dangerous to keep it in, so they removed it. I can't have children. I'm so sorry I haven't told you before, but we've never discussed serious stuff like this. Normally, couples get to know each other over several years before getting married and talk about their future plans, but ...'

James puts his hand up. 'Aimee, it's okay. I know this has all been a bit of a whirlwind. You're right, we should have spoken about it sooner. I blame myself. I'm sorry, but I'm glad you've told me now. It doesn't change anything though.'

'What do you mean? You just told me you want as many kids as possible.'

James shrugs. 'Yes, but ... there are other ways of having kids now; adoption and surrogacy. We can still have kids together, just not in the usual way, that's all.'

'Are you sure? It doesn't bother you that our future kids won't be genetically yours?'

James is silent for several seconds, which I know means he's lying. He's clearly trying to spare my feelings. 'No, it doesn't bother me.'

A cold sensation spreads over my body. I can't do this to him, destroy his future. My mind's already made up. A switch has been flipped and now I need to get out before I have a panic attack. It's almost as if I've been waiting for an opportunity to back out and here's my chance. I know it's going to hurt him, but I can't do this ...

'I can't do that to you,' I whisper.

James turns to face me. 'What do you mean?'

'We got engaged too fast. We're doing all this too fast, James. You shouldn't have proposed to me while I was in such a bad state. I barely knew what I was saying.'

'What are you saying now? Are you changing your mind?'

'Yes.'

James sits up straighter. 'Aimee, I know you're probably freaking out about the whole not being able to have kids thing, but we can tackle that later on down the line. It's not a *now* problem.'

'Yes, it is.' I stand up, my head spinning. James stands too. 'It will always be a now problem. It's not something I can ever fix. It's not something we can just shove under a rug and pretend it won't affect us later in life.'

'But—'

'I was wrong to accept your proposal. I can't ruin your life. I won't … It's over.' I pull the ring out of my pocket, the one we picked out together only a few weeks ago, and hand it to James, who just stares at it.

'Aimee … you don't mean this. Think about what you're saying.'

'I have.'

'Let's talk about this properly.'

'There's nothing else to talk about. It's over.'

Chapter Fifty-Two
Then - James

Aimee's Mother's House, February 2010

James stared helplessly after Aimee as she ran into the house, slamming the door behind her. What the hell had just happened? One minute they'd been sitting in the garden, perfectly happy, and the next she'd plunged her hand into his chest and ripped out his heart while it was still beating. He couldn't breathe, couldn't think straight as he ran after her into the house and almost collided with her mother, who assured him that she'd talk to her and told him to give her some space, but he was fed up with constantly giving her space. He'd given her his soul and she'd just thrown it back in his face like it meant nothing.

He should have stayed, should have fought for her, but the pain in his chest was too much to bear and he didn't want to stick around any longer in the desperate hope that she'd change her mind. She wasn't going to change her mind; that much was obvious. It did hurt that she hadn't told him before now about her inability to carry children, but it wasn't a deal breaker for him. Clearly it was for her, or maybe she'd never wanted to accept his proposal in the first place and had only said yes to avoid hurting his feelings. Surely not? They'd been happy ... Granted she wasn't always completely lucid and herself, but ...

James slammed his foot down on the accelerator, causing the tyres to skid on the gravel. It was over. He'd had enough of trying to tiptoe around her, constantly worrying if he'd say something to set her off on one of her foul moods. Adam was right; he'd be better off without Aimee.

James used the dashboard buttons in his car to dial his brother's number, who picked up on the second ring.

'Hey, man, what's up?'

'Aimee's called it off.'

'I knew it. I told you that you proposed too fast. You okay?'

'Not really.' James could feel his voice starting to crack.

'Come and see me. I'll get off work early and we'll go for a drink.'

'I don't feel like it, sorry.'

'Come on! It will make you feel better, I promise.'

James sighed, quietly annoyed at his brother for always using alcohol as the answer to all his problems, but maybe he was right. They'd had a good time when they'd gone out drinking previously.

'Fine. Text me when and where to meet you.'

'See you later, bro.'

'Bye, Adam.'

James blinked back tears, barely able to focus on the motorway in front of him. His life was falling apart. All he'd been able to think about for the past few months was Aimee and now she was gone. He had nothing left anymore.

Chapter Fifty-Three
Now

Jones kicked his shoes off into a corner as soon as he walked through Aimee's front door. He cracked open a can of beer from the six-pack he'd bought on the way back and started chugging it as he made his way over to the sofa. He flopped down, perched his feet on the glass coffee table and switched the television on using the remote, turning the sound up high.

Aimee glared at him. 'Feet off the coffee table!' Jones sneered as he slowly pulled his feet off, placing them on the floor. 'You know, if you're going to continue to stay here the least you can do is help me cook dinner. I need to eat, shower, change, do some research and then meet the girls at nine.'

'Wait … you're going to leave me home alone?'

'I'm sure you'll be fine. I'll leave all the emergency numbers on the fridge.'

'Funny. Where are you going?'

'To see a strip show.'

'Can I come?'

'It's not your type of strip show.'

Jones was silent for a few beats, then he turned the volume down on the television. 'You're going to watch Loverboy strip, aren't you?'

Aimee sighed. 'His name's Nathan. You still want to come?'

'I'll pass.'

Aimee's heart sank a little when he didn't press her further about Nathan. She had been ready to defend herself, to argue with him that it was none of his business, but he didn't appear to care. Did she want him to care?

'What are we having for dinner?' asked Jones when an advert interrupted the game show he'd been watching.

'Whatever I can find in the fridge.' Aimee pulled the fridge door open and scanned the bare shelves. Today was her usual food shop day, but it was already nearly seven in the evening and she'd been unable to run any of her normal weekend errands. Jones appeared beside her, sending a pleasant breeze across her skin.

'You need to go food shopping.' Aimee made a low growling sound. 'Okay, look, chill out. I'll make us some scrambled eggs on toast, happy? Why don't you go and get showered and changed, ready for tonight?' Jones gently pushed her out of the way and reached in to grab the eggs, butter and bread. 'Why do you keep bread in the fridge?'

'That's where I always keep it.'

'It goes stale quicker.'

'Maybe I like stale bread.'

'Has anyone ever told you that you're a freak?'

'Has anyone ever told you that you're a dickhead?'

'Many times.'

Aimee bit her lip to stop herself from bickering further. Jones began to open every cupboard looking for a bowl.

'They're in the right-hand cupboard,' said Aimee.

Jones flung the cupboard door open, but there were no bowls. Aimee frowned as she scanned the worktops in case she'd left them out to dry.

'That's weird,' she said, opening other cupboards. She eventually found them in the cupboard beside the sink. She handed one to Jones. 'Did you move my bowls?' she asked.

'Why the hell would I do that?'

Aimee shrugged, deciding to forget it. She stepped out of his way, finding it quite humorous to watch him as he moved around the kitchen with ease. Humorous and … enjoyable.

'Are you going to go and have a shower or do you plan on watching me cook this entire meal?'

Aimee jumped slightly, blushing as she scurried to her bedroom.

Half an hour later Aimee emerged having decided against washing her hair. Instead, she'd used dry shampoo, but she had showered and changed into a pair of black high-waist jeans and a black long-sleeved sparkly top, complete with leopard print heels and a matching clutch bag. She'd overdone the eye makeup to hide her tired eyes and added a touch more highlighter to her face to emphasise her high cheek bones. Jones eyed her as she sat down with her laptop at the kitchen counter.

'What?' she asked when she felt his eyes burning a hole through her.

'Nothing.'

'There's clearly something you want to say.'

Jones placed a plate of scrambled eggs and toast in front of her. 'You scrub up well, Price.'

Aimee flicked her eyes up to him to check whether he was being sarcastic, but she couldn't detect his usual tone of witty banter. 'Thank you,' she said slowly.

'Of course, if you plan on getting laid tonight a short dress would enable easier access than tight jeans … if I remember correctly.'

'And there it is.'

'What?'

'You've just ruined a perfectly nice compliment.'

'Do you?'

'Do I what?'

'Plan on getting laid?'

'Why do you care?' Her heart began thumping inside her chest, so loud she thought Jones might be able to hear it.

'I *don't* care,' he said, taking a bite of toast.

'Then you don't *need* to know my answer.'

Jones took another bite and then glugged the remaining can of beer. 'What are you doing?' he asked.

Aimee took a deep breath, attempting to dislodge the strange fluttering in her chest. She'd been typing on her laptop while they'd been talking. 'I'm looking up James's drink and drive accident online.'

'Why?'

'I want to know the details of what happened. I never saw it mentioned in the news back then.'

'I warn you ... it's not pretty.'

'You really think James was innocent?'

Jones shrugged his shoulders. 'It just seems strange for a bloke who barely drank to suddenly go on a drinking binge and crash his car into an innocent girl, even if he was broken-hearted after you dumped him.'

Aimee didn't reply as she typed his name and a few search words into Google. The first link that appeared was a news article dated the 24th of February 2010. The picture showed a black Audi with a dent in the bonnet and a broken windscreen with blood splatters dotted across the metal and glass. Aimee gulped back the lump in her throat as she scrolled down the page and read.

Jennifer Lincoln, 19, was walking home from a night out when she was struck by a car. The driver, James Daniels, was ten times over the limit for alcohol consumption. She was pinned underneath the vehicle and dragged for twenty feet before Daniels crashed the car into a building. He was found passed out merely feet away from the wreckage after attempting to escape. Jennifer was declared dead at the scene. James Daniels is a sergeant in the British Army and has recently returned from serving in Afghanistan. He has been arrested and is now awaiting sentencing after pleading guilty to drink driving and causing death by dangerous driving.

Aimee shuddered as she looked up at Jones who was buttering another slice of toast. 'There's no mention of his brother being with him.'

'Funny that,' answered Jones with his mouth full.

'This was literally the day after I broke it off with him.'

Jones forked another mouthful of egg into his mouth and chewed. He continued to stand while he ate. 'I know why you broke it off with him ... because he wanted kids and you couldn't give them to him.' The words echoed around the kitchen as the walls started closing in on her.

Aimee sat up straighter on the stool, ignoring the room, which was moving in and out of focus, and sighed. 'Yes.' Her eyes threatened to flood with tears, but she managed to control them by continuing to speak. 'It broke my heart too. I should never have even agreed to marry him. It was a mistake. My head was so messed up with the amount of meds I was on and it was only two months after I attempted suicide ... I mean, what was he thinking proposing to me in the first place!' Her voice rose a couple of octaves at the end. She grabbed a knife and fork and began eating, cutting the toast with a little more force than was needed.

Jones watched her as she wrestled with her cutlery. 'You know, maybe you should go a little easier on yourself. Cut yourself some slack. Most people couldn't even imagine what you went through.'

Aimee swallowed her mouthful and pointed her fork at Jones. 'What about you? How'd you even become friends with him? Tell me the real story, not that shit you told Tony.'

'Who said it was shit?'

'I say it's shit. You're an expert at making shit up.'

Jones finished his plate of food and chucked the dirty utensils in the sink. Metal clashed against metal, leaving a loud ringing in the air. 'I really did meet him in prison. It wasn't shit.'

'Who'd you assault?'

'Does it matter?'

'Yes. I want to know.'

'And I want to know what you see in a pretty boy fuckwit like Loverboy.' Jones took a swig of beer, but before Aimee could respond to his comment, he'd started talking again. 'I beat up my dad, okay? When I got back from Afghanistan he was ashamed of me, said I was weak, that I was pathetic for letting a girl rescue me. He called me a useless cripple.'

Aimee stopped eating. 'I-I'm so sorry.'

'He was a dickhead before that anyway. Never treated my mum right, called her a slut, roughed her up a lot, used to hit me when I was a kid. I just ... sort of lost it one day. He wanted the money I'd received in compensation, said I owed him for having to look after a cripple. I had a lot of anger in me.

Prison was actually a nice break. It was a pretty big shock to find Daniels there. He looked like shit. He told me he'd killed a girl by drink driving, but he never said why he was drinking so much in the first place. I didn't know you guys were engaged. He changed in there, Price. We became friends when ...' Jones stopped and Aimee noticed his eyes flick to the scars on his wrists. She wanted to ask him more questions, but he continued on. 'Daniels found me ... thanks to his previous career as a medic he was able to save my life before I bled to death in my cell. We became friends after that.'

Aimee nodded, silently grateful that he'd shared a snippet of his past. 'Did he ... did he talk about me?'

Jones paused for several seconds. 'Not once.'

Aimee pushed her empty plate aside and pulled the laptop closer. 'I'm going to do some research on Jennifer Lincoln.'

'Maybe you should let it go.'

'And maybe you should put the kettle on.'

Jones grinned as he turned his back to perform said task. 'You know,' he said, turning around to face her again, 'you're actually pretty okay, Price.'

'Gee, thanks.'

'You know the only reason I gave you such a hard time back then was because I liked you, right?'

Aimee stopped typing and slowly lifted her head up. Had she heard him correctly? Her stomach performed an excited flip, but then she started seeing red, the same colour as her cheeks turned. '*That's* your excuse? You treated me like a piece of shit because you *liked* me? Bloody hell, we weren't in primary school, Jones.'

Jessica Huntley

'Yeah, well, when you have a dad like mine it's hard to know how to treat women properly when all you've seen is the bad stuff.'

'How about a little common sense? Have you ever heard the phrase *treat people how you'd like to be treated*? I'm sorry about your dad, but there's no excuse for what you put me through.'

Jones was silent as he stirred sugar into a mug of tea. 'You're right. I'm sorry.'

Aimee took the tea from him, eyeing him suspiciously. 'I don't believe your apology, nor do I accept it.'

'Well, fuck you.'

'Fuck you too.' Aimee sipped her tea. 'That's a good brew.' They smiled at each other sheepishly. 'Okay, Jones, so what's your excuse for being a dickhead to me now?'

'Can I just point out the irony here? You're being a dickhead to me too.'

'It's warranted.'

'Is it?'

'Yeah!'

Aimee and Jones glared at each other while they drank. Aimee finally broke eye contact and looked down at the laptop screen. Staring into his eyes made her stomach do flips again and she wasn't happy about it.

'You fancy a round of boxing tomorrow?' she finally asked.

'That's a bit random.'

'On Saturday mornings I go to my boxing gym and let off a load of steam. I think we both need it.'

'You realise I only have one leg, right?'

'You have two hands to punch.'

'Touché, Price. You sure you won't be too hungover from your night out seeing naked men prance about?'

'I'm not drinking tonight.'

'Sure, okay. Good luck with that.'

The loud pulse of the music rattled her insides as she chugged another shot of Sambuca, feeling the burning liquid reach the back of her throat. Was this her fifth or sixth? Aimee didn't care. She watched the naked stranger gyrate in front of her, his large, thick thighs straddled wide over her lap. She suppressed a giggle as he grabbed her hands and clamped them on his hips, rocking backwards and forwards.

Cindy and Dot whooped and cheered beside her, egging the man to turn around so they could see his tight bum. He was wearing a barely-there silver thong, both of his round cheeks jiggling in time to the rhythm of the music.

Nathan was up on stage with three other dancers. Aimee blushed every time she looked at him. It was an odd experience to see her next-door neighbour practically naked, covered in tan and baby oil. He seemed perfectly at ease, no longer the awkward, slightly shy man she barely knew, but a strong, confident and, she hated to admit it, sexy dancer. As the man in the thong moved back towards the stage, Cindy leaned in close to Aimee's left ear and shouted, 'Babe, it's so nice to see you relax and enjoy yourself for once.'

Aimee grinned at her. 'I thought it was about time.'

'This wouldn't have anything to do with making a certain homeless man jealous, would it?'

'I have no idea what you're talking about!' Aimee shouted over the music.

Ten minutes later the set ended and Nathan made his way over to the table. He'd dressed in a casual t-shirt and jeans. All three girls clapped and cheered.

'Thank you, ladies. I hope you're enjoying yourselves.'

'We're having a f-fantastic time! Thanks for the free drinks by the way,' said Cindy, picking up a shot. The table was littered with empty shot glasses and was swimming in spilled liquors of all descriptions.

'As many as you want,' said Nathan with a wink.

'Keep them coming!' shouted Dot as she and Cindy clinked glasses.

Aimee stood up on wobbly legs and leaned against Nathan's body. He smelled like baby oil and sweat. 'T-tomorrow night,' she said loudly in his ear. Nathan frowned at her. 'Tomorrow night. I'll g-go on a date with you.'

Nathan grinned from ear to ear. 'Yeah? I'll pick you up at seven.'

'It's a date!' Aimee slumped back down into her seat, her body feeling as if it were made of rubber. Her hands were numb and tingly, but it was a pleasant sensation.

'Ladies, it was great meeting you, but I'm afraid I'm still on the clock, so I'll see you later.' Nathan turned and walked away towards another table of women.

'Yes! Yes, go and do your stripper thing, you sexy beast of a man, although I will point out that I'm gay and therefore I don't want what you're offering, but it's ever so nice of you to offer it …' Dot trailed off, suddenly realising that he was no longer around. Cindy gave her friend a playful slap across the head.

'Sorry, ladies, but he's all mine,' said Aimee, reaching across the table for another shot.

'Come again?'

'I just asked him out.'

'You did what! You cheeky bitch,' laughed Cindy as she high-fived her.

Cindy grabbed Aimee's bag off her shoulders and rummaged around inside, but her alcohol-infused brain couldn't make her fingers grasp the keys so she dropped the bag and all three women burst into hysterical laughter. It was nearly two o'clock in the morning. Aimee pressed her fingers to her lips and shushed her friends loudly as she stumbled against the wall.

'If you w-wake up Mrs Leammint-ton then we'll all be in t-trouble.'

'T-That old hag don't scare me. Hey Mrs … whasshername?' Dot leaned against the door, but she fell straight through it as Jones opened it.

'Fuck me,' he muttered under his breath as he took in the three giggling women in the hallway. 'Get the fuck in here before someone calls the police and complains about the noise.'

'Hey, Mr Homeless, I know I like pussy, but you wanna try and change my m-mind?'

Cindy and Aimee bent over at the waists and laughed until tears ran down their cheeks. Jones grabbed Dot and Cindy and managed to drag them into the flat, leaving Aimee in the hallway. He returned minutes later to find her sitting on the floor, leaning against the wall with her knees up to her chest.

'Your turn, Miss-I'm-not-drinking-tonight.'

'Where did my friends go?'

'I've managed to convince them to pass out on your bed.'

'B-But where will I sleep?'

'The sofa.'

'B-But where will you sleep?'

'The floor is good enough for me.' Jones bent down to her level. 'Do you think you can stand?'

'Tough call. The floor is m-made of lava so I'm n-not sure.'

'Right. How about I carry you?'

'But w-won't you burn up in the lava?'

'No, I have a special shield that will protect me from the lava.'

Aimee laughed as she leaned her head back and stared up at the ceiling, watching it swaying back and forth and in and out. 'Jones?'

'Yeah, Price?'

'Can I tell you a secret?'

'Sure.'

'I can't have c-children.'

'You already told me that. Come on, let's get you tucked up on the sofa.' Jones pulled her to her feet and she stumbled forwards into his arms, grasping his shoulders.

'You smell funny,' she said.

'I'm pretty sure that's you. You smell like baby oil and Sambuca.' Jones bent down and lifted her into his arms, faltering slightly as he adjusted his footing to compensate for his prosthetic leg. He carried her through the front door and made his way slowly to the lounge.

'Jones?'

'Yeah, Price?'

'I have another secret.' He reached the sofa and placed her down gently, her hair spreading across her face.

'Oh yeah?'

'Yeah, but I c-can't tell you.'

'Why not?'

'Beeee cosssss … you'll hate me.'

Jones walked to the kitchen, filled a glass with water and returned. 'I won't hate you.'

'But you do, you did, you hate me.'

'Maybe I did once, but not anymore.'

'You sure you won't tell anyone?'

'Cross my heart and hope to die.'

Aimee laughed again and closed her eyes. She took a deep breath and as she breathed out, on the verge of unconsciousness, she said, 'I aborted your baby.'

Chapter Fifty-Four
Then

Aimee's Mother's House, February 2010

I turn and run as fast as possible across the garden, up the uneven stone steps and into the house. James is calling my name, panic in his usually calm voice, but I blank him out, retreating to my bedroom, slamming the door with such force that a picture wobbles against the wall. Muffled voices come from downstairs; the concerned voice of Mum probably asking James what's going on and the low, polite voice of James attempting to explain the situation. A door slams, there's the unmistakable screech of rubber skidding on gravel and then, finally, there's silence.

I've made the right decision, but it doesn't make me feel any better. In fact, that nagging, pinprick of self-hatred is creeping back in again. It's bad enough that I've fucked up my own life. I can't let James ruin his by being with me. I've seen a way out and taken it. No one else has to suffer; it's better this way.

Mum knocks softly on the door. 'Aimee … Darling … James has just left in an awful state. He said you ended things. What's going on?'

I don't want to speak to her. I don't want to speak to anyone because my mind is retreating to that dark place again; a place I don't want to go. 'We broke up, Mum,' I reply loudly.

The door opens and Mum walks in, her eyes wide. 'What on earth happened? You two have been so wonderful together. He's so lovely and makes you so happy.'

'I told him.'

It takes a mere second for my mum to understand. She slowly walks to the bed and sits down, stroking my back. 'I'm sorry, darling.'

'He said he didn't mind, but he also said he wanted as many kids as possible one day.'

'There are other ways of having children, Aimee.'

'I can't deal with this right now, Mum. I shouldn't be in a relationship while I'm still trying to get better. It's too much to deal with.'

'I understand, darling. You have to focus on yourself first. I'm sure James will understand eventually. You did the right thing.'

I nod, relieved that she isn't picking a fight, for once. 'I know I did, but it still hurts.' Although I don't tell her that the ache in my chest isn't from breaking up with James. 'Can I just be alone for a little while?'

'Yes, of course.' Mum stands up. 'Oh, by the way, you've had some mail from the Army. Two very important looking letters. I've left them on the kitchen table for you, whenever you're ready.'

'Thanks, Mum. I'll be down soon.'

Chapter Fifty-Five
Now

The next morning Aimee cracked her eyes open to find that she was lying haphazardly on her sofa, fully dressed, minus her heels, with a small dribble of drool seeping from her mouth. She sat up slowly and wiped her mouth, her whole body groaning in protest.

'Morning,' said a rough voice. Aimee looked up at Jones, squinting against the bright light. 'Do you feel as bad as you look?'

'Fuck off,' she muttered. 'How did I even get home? What time is it? Why am I on the sofa?'

'Fuck knows how you managed to get home, but you made it to your front door somehow. It's almost seven and to answer your third question, because your bed's taken up by Sleeping Beauty One and Sleeping Beauty Two.'

'Cindy and Dot crashed here? I don't remember getting home.'

'That doesn't surprise me a bit. Coffee?'

'Do you seriously even need to ask me that?'

Jones turned and walked into the kitchen and began preparing her beverage. Aimee managed to haul herself to her feet, stumbling slightly as her head swam, and pattered over to join him. She headed straight for the sink, turned on the tap and drank from it, slurping noisily. Her mouth was so dry it reminded her of the deserts of Afghanistan.

'Good night?' Jones asked.

'Um ... from what I can remember, yeah.'

'We still on for boxing this morning?'

Aimee groaned. 'Can I have coffee first and a shower?' The thought of any form of exercise before either of those things was inconceivable.

'Sure.' Jones handed her a large cup of coffee and folded his arms. 'You remember anything else about last night?'

'I remember nothing after my seventh shot of Sambuca. It may have been my sixth.'

'After I dumped Thing One and Thing Two on your bed I picked you up off the floor and you told me a secret. Actually, you told me two, but I already knew one of them.'

Aimee rubbed fresh water from the tap over her face, not caring that she was smudging her makeup further. She could already feel her mascara running down her cheeks. She turned to Jones, frowning. 'What secrets?'

Jones stared at her for several long seconds before saying, in a quiet, calm voice, 'Why didn't you tell me that you got pregnant and then had an abortion before tour?'

Aimee's breath caught in her throat as her vision swam in and out of focus. Had she heard him right? She frowned at him and he responded by raising his eyebrows. Yes, she'd definitely heard him correctly.

Aimee retched into the sink, but because her stomach was empty, nothing came up. She retched again before wiping her mouth with the back of her hand, her whole body trembling as she turned around and faced Jones, who merely sighed.

'Okay, look, before you go beating yourself up or get annoyed and start yelling at me ... I don't blame you, okay? I'm not angry. Well, maybe a little bit, but I understand why you did it. I was an immature dickhead back then. Hell, I still am. If you'd told me I'd knocked you up I probably would have told you to get rid of it anyway. It's just that … well, now that I know you can no longer have children … what you must have gone through … fuck …' Jones ran both hands through his hair. 'Aimee, I'm sorry you had to go through that alone and I'm sorry about everything that happened. I wish I could take it all back, but I can't. I can only apologise.'

Aimee breathed a sigh of relief as a crushing weight subsided from her chest, but then she tilted her head to the side, wondering if she'd heard him correctly. 'You just called me Aimee. I didn't even think you knew my first name.'

'Well, I do, as it happens … I found out a few days ago when Detective Dimwit introduced us.'

Aimee clamped her lips together as tight as she could, not due to the threat of vomit, but because she was trying hard not to laugh out loud.

Jones smirked also. 'Do you accept my apology?'

Aimee nodded slowly. 'Only if you accept mine. I made a rash, snap decision. I wanted to go on that tour to prove to myself and everyone else I was a good soldier. I didn't think about you at all in my decision and I'm sorry, even though you would have told me to … you know …'

'You have nothing to be sorry about, Price.'

'We're back to Price now then?'

'Yep, the moment's over.'

'Do we need to talk about this any further?'

Jones sighed deeply. 'No, I guess not … it happened over a decade ago. What's done is done.'

'I'm sorry you had to find out this way.'

'Would you have ever told me?'

'No … I don't think so.'

Jones opened his mouth to speak, but then closed it.

Aimee took the opportunity to change the subject. 'Great, well, now that unpleasantness is over, if you'll excuse me, I'm going to take my coffee and drink it while having a very cold shower. Then we'll go to the gym.'

'Are you sure you're up for a boxing workout?'

'Yes, believe me, I need it. Cindy and Dot won't be awake for hours yet.'

Aimee was surprised to find that she felt much better after a shower. She dressed in her neon yellow gym leggings, a black sports bra and matching tank top. The gym was the only place she allowed her scars to be on show. No one cared what she looked like there, no one took any notice of her body, only her boxing technique. It was the one place where she could truly be and look like her real self.

'You really need to get new clothes,' said Aimee as she eyed Jones up and down. He was still dressed in the clothes she'd borrowed from Nathan.

'The longest I've worn the same clothes is ten weeks.'

Aimee gagged. 'Please don't say stuff like that in front of me right now. I'm very delicate.'

'Why do you look like a glow stick?'

'You don't like neon yellow?'

'Not really. It hurts my eyes.'

'Too bad.'

They walked down the stairs side by side and stopped by the front door of the building. It was tipping down with rain, a vast difference to the warm sunshine of the previous few days. They looked at each other and spoke at exactly the same time.

'If it's not raining, it's not training—'

'Jinx!' they exclaimed as they pointed a finger at each other.

'Ah, you said it this time,' said Jones.

Aimee laughed as she pushed open the doors. 'I'm not a superstitious person.' Then she stopped and looked at him. 'Actually, I never used to be, but then I lost something that belonged to my grandfather and … you know what, it doesn't matter.' She stopped and titled her head. 'Wait … you don't think … me not saying *jinx* back in Afghan … it caused the explosion?'

Jones patted her on the shoulder. 'Price, it was just a joke.'

'I remember you saying that we were all doomed because I didn't say it back.'

'Yeah, and I also said that I came top of my squad in basic training and won best at drill.'

'You didn't?'

'No. I'd say anything back then to make myself look good.'

Aimee stepped out into the rain, attempting to ignore the niggle of doubt growing in her mind. Despite the wet weather it was lovely and warm.

'I would say that we should jog to the gym as a warm-up … but since you only have one leg I'd feel bad for beating you.'

Jones sniffed loudly. 'Hey, I can think of worse things than watching you running from behind, Price.' Aimee rolled her eyes. 'Stop rolling your eyes at me or they'll get stuck like that,' he warned again.

'How about we just walk? It's not that far.'

'Fine. Lead on, Price. I'll say one thing.'

'What's that?'

'You certainly are lighting up this dull, miserable day with your neon yellow leggings.'

The boxing gym was heaving with sweaty bodies already, clearly all determined to work off their frustrations of the working week, or their over-indulgence on a Friday night. The air was musty and thick with body odour, but neither Aimee nor Jones minded as they put their belongings in Aimee's personal locker. They'd both experienced worse smells in the past, having lived and slept in a hole in the ground for over a week during training on several occasions. The gym was open plan so Aimee could see straight across the room to the other side. The far left corner held five punching bags; the far right a boxing ring; the near left had a small set up of free weights and the last corner housed the lockers. The middle of the area was a clear space for people to work on their foot drills or perform floor exercises.

'Hey, Aimee!'

Aimee turned and spotted Joe, her boxing coach, jogging towards her. He was dressed in his usual uniform of tracksuit bottoms and a tight white vest, which showed off his impressive upper body, complete with tribal tattoos. Sweat glistened on his forehead.

'Hey, Joe. This is … Thomas Jones, a friend of mine from way back in my Army days.'

The men shook hands using a firm grip.

'Good to meet you. So you're … Tom Jones?' Joe laughed slightly.

Jones nodded, apparently not bothered this time by the name. 'Yep ... my parents found it funny at the time. Most people just call me Jones.'

'Jones it is. You here to box?'

'Hell yeah.'

'Great, I'll grab you a pair of gloves. You guys can take bag number three, over in the corner. I'll let you know when the ring's free for a sparring session.'

'Thanks, Joe.' Aimee took her gloves out of her locker and closed the door. Joe had provided her with her personal locker several years ago, as she was now classed as a regular here, training up to three times a week and often competing in small fights for charity when Joe needed an extra body. 'Why didn't you punch him in the face for calling you Tom Jones?' asked Aimee.

'Have you seen that guy? His biceps are bigger than my quads.'

Aimee sniggered.

'Nice guy though,' added Jones.

'Yeah, he is.'

'There must be loads of single blokes here you could shag ... Why'd you have your sights set on Loverboy?'

'Why do you have such an issue with Nathan?'

'No reason.'

'Besides, I don't come here to pick up blokes. I come here to box.'

'You should ask Joe out.'

'He's happily married with a kid on the way.'

'So?'

Aimee hit him with her boxing gloves. 'You have no morals, do you?' She walked away before he could respond.

'You ever boxed before?' she asked as they came to a stop beside their allocated punch bag.

'Not properly, no, but I've been in plenty of fights.'

'Shocking … Okay, well, I'll show you the basics.'

'Hey, Jones! Catch!' Jones turned and caught a pair of gloves that Joe hurled at him from across the gym.

'Thanks, man!'

Joe gave him a thumbs up.

Jones watched Aimee while he strapped the gloves around his wrists. She bounced up and down and side to side on the balls of her feet with ease and fluidity, ducking and jabbing every few seconds. The bag swung when her fist collided with it.

'I'm impressed, Price. How long have you been doing this?'

'Eleven years.' Aimee stopped and performed a few static stretches with her arms. 'I started soon after I ended things with James. It helped me recover both physically and mentally.'

'You ever thought about competing in the Invictus Games?'

'I'm not that good.'

'Don't know until you try.'

Aimee merely smiled. The truth was that she had thought about entering the games, an international sporting event for wounded, injured and sick service personnel, both serving and veterans, but her fear of failure had prevented her from taking the final leap.

Jones began to copy what she was doing. 'Don't worry about jumping around if it's awkward,' she said, noticing how stiff he was when he started to move. 'Just focus on keeping your guard up and take small side steps instead.'

'Got it.'

Jones lifted his gloved fists in front of his face and performed a few test jabs; two with his right and one with his left, then repeated. Aimee followed suit and punched the bag, causing it to swing towards Jones who managed to sidestep out of the way in time to avoid being hit. After a few minutes both of them were breathing heavily, small beads of sweat forming on their foreheads.

'Aimee! The ring's free now if you two fancy a sparring session.'

'Thanks, Joe!' Aimee called out across the gym. Joe gave her another thumbs up and went back to coaching a young man. 'Fancy a round in the ring with me … and I swear to God if you answer with something dirty I'll punch you.'

Jones grinned. 'Ah, Price, you're no fun.'

Aimee led the way. She crouched under the elastic bars of the boxing ring and held them up for Jones to follow her. He moved well, considering his left leg was amputated below the knee, but there was a slight stiffness to his movements.

'Okay,' said Aimee as she jumped up and down on the spot, warming up her lower body and keeping her heart rate elevated, 'no direct head shots, I have a date tomorrow night.'

'With who?'

'Nathan.' Jones rolled his eyes. 'If you keep rolling your eyes they'll get stuck like that,' said Aimee, followed by a cheeky smile.

'Smartass. Fine, but no low blows … I like to keep my tackle in top notch condition.'

'Yeah, cos I'm sure you get laid all the time being homeless and smelling like a sewer.'

'You'd be surprised.'

'You're not really homeless, are you?'

'Are we here to chat or box, Price?'

'Box.'

'Then shut the hell up and let's see what you've got.'

Aimee shrugged her shoulders. 'You asked for it.'

Jones chuckled as he dodged her first punch. He darted to the side and retaliated with a right hook, which she easily side-stepped. They circled each other slowly, testing out their reflexes and movements for twenty seconds or so, then Aimee moved in for her first combination attack. Jones blocked two of her punches, but wasn't quick enough to avoid the third; a direct hit to the ribs on his left side.

'Oofff,' he grunted as he backed away slightly.

Aimee smiled as they circled each other again, their eyes locked on one another. Jones performed a trio of punches, which Aimee easily blocked and dodged, and she retaliated by moving close to his body and jabbing him in the stomach. Jones attempted to block her by lifting his fists, but she countered by darting to the side and performing another blow, catching him off guard. Jones tried to step backwards, but lost his balance.

'Oh shit,' he said as he started falling.

It all happened so fast. He lashed out at mid-air in an attempt to steady himself and caught Aimee by accident, sweeping her feet out from underneath her.

'Ahhh!' Aimee lost her footing and collapsed on top of him, their bodies pressed against each other as they lay on the dusty, sweaty floor of the boxing ring. They locked eyes, breathing hard.

'If you wanted to climb on top of me, Price, all you had to do was ask,' said Jones with a laugh.

Aimee thumped him in the chest with her gloved fist before shuffling off him. 'I swear you did that on purpose.' Jones held up his arm. Aimee linked her elbow around his and pulled him to his feet. 'Dickhead,' she muttered.

'Hey, you'll pay for that.'

Aimee lifted her gloves in front of her face. 'Round two?'

'I thought you'd never ask.'

An hour later Aimee and Jones walked back to her flat, stopping for a Burger King breakfast on the way. She also bought food for Cindy and Dot, knowing that they'd be in need of a greasy breakfast. They were climbing the stairs to her floor when Mrs Leamington appeared at the stop of the steps, dressed in her usual pink ensemble.

'Ah, hello Aimee, dear … Good workout?'

Aimee inwardly groaned. 'Yeah … thanks. Um … this is Thomas, my … friend.'

Jones gave an over-exaggerated gasp and pretended that he'd been punched in the heart. 'Ouch, I'm reduced to the friend-zone already.'

Mrs Leamington raised her eyebrows. 'We've already met.'

'That we have,' said Jones with a smile.

'Right,' said Aimee awkwardly, 'well, have a lovely Saturday, Mrs Leamington.'

'Thank you, dear.'

They watched as the old woman descended the stairs slowly, too slowly, as if she were waiting for them to start talking again so she could overhear.

'She seems nice,' said Jones.

'She's the nosiest old woman ever.'

'So am I really just a friend?'

'I'd hardly even call you that.' Aimee slid the key into her door.

'Ex-lovers?'

'We never dated and most certainly *love* was not involved.'

'Ex-fuck buddies?'

Aimee sighed and turned to face him. 'We were colleagues once, so that makes us ex-colleagues.'

'I think we're more than that now.'

'Do you?'

Jones pressed his lips together as he leaned against the doorframe, blocking her way. 'Then what are we? You can't deny that we've started to become closer lately.'

Aimee took a deep breath. She didn't have the patience for Jones's antics now. She was in desperate need of another shower and she wanted to finish her egg muffin in peace. Plus, she really needed to check on Cindy and Dot.

'Fine ... I'll settle for being friends.'

Jones narrowed his eyes at her. 'Friends,' he said slowly and then added, 'but you have a major crush on me.'

Aimee burst out laughing. 'Ha! That's a good one. Like *you* don't have a crush on *me*.'

'I never said I didn't and I don't hear you denying it either.'

Aimee stopped and stared at him, taking note of his slightly damp hair. He smelled like rain and salty sweat. She could almost taste him on her tongue. She licked her lips.

'Don't do that,' he said in a low voice.

'Do what?'

'Lick your lips.'

'Why not?'

'Because it makes me want to shove you against this wall and fuck you in this hallway and make you come so hard that you wake up your neighbours.'

Aimee's throat and mouth turned dry and she was suddenly very aware of a tingling sensation between her legs. 'I … um …'

'Relax.' Jones moved aside, allowing her to pass. 'It was a test and you failed … miserably.'

She exhaled loudly. 'God, you're such a dickhead.'

'So you keep telling me.'

Chapter Fifty-Six
Now - Jones

My muscles ache already from that boxing workout Price had just put me through. Can't lie though, it had been fun. That woman does something to me and she can do it without even trying, just by licking her fucking lips. As I stroll down the pavement my mind keeps wandering back to twelve years ago when we did it at the back of the club; the lights were low and the beat of the music ricocheted through the wall, or maybe that had been us thumping up against it. She looks even better now and I knew I had to get out of the flat quick or risk losing control.

When I came to Woking to help Daniels I had hoped to avoid her, but then he went and got himself killed and fucked things up. I've got no proof that it was Adam who killed him, but I'd bet all the money that's left in my bank account that he did. I guess I have to leave it in the somewhat capable hands of Detective Dimwit and his cronies and hope that they solve the case. But then what? I'm not sure I have the strength or the willpower to walk out of her life again, not when we're becoming ... *friends*, as she called us. I can live with being friends if that's what she wants. I owe it to her after all, but I do like to tease her still, get under her skin. I'll openly admit I was a dickhead to her back then, maybe I still am one a little bit, but I'm determined to change ... She's the only woman I'd change for ...

I stop at the police barricade that's blocking the road to Maynard's Place; it seems Price's little trip to the crime scene has warranted stronger security measures. I have a brief flashback of the other night when I was last here and I can't help but feel partly responsible for Daniels's death. We'd had a plan to confront Adam, to try and figure out if he had killed that girl, but things had fallen apart. Daniels kept saying he wanted to find Price, Adam kept telling him it was a waste of time and I was trying my best not to punch Adam in the face. Now Daniels is dead and I don't know what the hell is going on, but while I'm here I may as well continue with my work. I step around the barrier and cross the road to the building ahead, pushing the doors open.

'Tommy! Great to see you again.'

'Hi, Mark. What needs doing today?'

'Ah, the van needs unloading out the back, if you don't mind.'

'Consider it done.'

Chapter Fifty-Seven
Then

Aimee's Mother's House, February 2010

The dark spot on my ceiling keeps getting bigger the longer I stare at it, like it's expanding in front of my eyes. Maybe I'm the one who's making it grow by transferring all of my bad thoughts and energy into it, feeding it, nurturing it. My therapist told me to do that sometimes; put all my negative thoughts and bad energy into a box or an object and lock it away. I wish I could do that for real, lock away all of my bad decisions and take back all the horrible things I've done or that have happened to me. I hate myself for hurting James, but I know it's for the best. He'll see that one day when he has children of his own who look exactly like him; the same dark eyes and hair.

I traipse downstairs to the kitchen, mildly curious at the mail my mum told me about earlier. I can smell dinner cooking on the hob, the steam fogging up every reflective surface; it smells like casserole. I pick up the two white envelopes and tear open the first one.

Dear Pte Aimee Price,

Following your recent application dated 02 January 2010 to the Armed Forces Compensation Scheme, we are pleased to inform you that you have been found eligible to receive compensation for the injuries you sustained during your recent operational deployment.

The claim assessment board has fully reviewed your application and you are awarded the sum of £125,152. This amount is a tax-free lump sum and will be paid direct to your personal bank account no later than 10 working days from the date of this letter. Should these funds not be received by this time, please contact this office as a matter of urgency.

Yours sincerely,

Armed Forces Compensation Scheme

My eyes flicker over the payment amount several times. The numbers are fuzzy and don't quite make any sense in my already groggy brain. I had barely been functioning properly when I'd applied for compensation and had scarcely given it any thought since.

I open the second letter, my mind still on the first, and scan the words quickly. There's an official-looking Army logo in the top right-hand corner and a stamp at the bottom.

Dear Pte Aimee Price,

I am pleased to inform you that following the most recent Armed Forces Awards and Honours Board, you have been selected to receive the Military Cross. This is awarded in recognition of your act of exemplary gallantry during Operation HERRICK 10. Subsequent to this letter, you will be invited by the Central Chancery of the Orders of Knighthood to attend an investiture within 3 months of the announcement of your award.

May I take the opportunity to offer my heartfelt congratulations for this award. You have represented yourself with honour and the entire unit is proud of your achievement.

Yours sincerely,

Lt Col Benjamin Smith
Commanding Officer

What the ... hell?

My legs start shaking so badly that I grab the nearest kitchen chair and stumble into it, grasping the two letters so tight that I turn them into balls of paper in my clenched fists. This has to be a mistake. I didn't want this. In order to receive an award of this type someone would have had to nominate me and speak to my chain of command. Who the fuck would have nominated me? Then it hits me like a bullet to the heart ... *James*.

'Fuck!' I shout.

'Darling, language!' scolds Mum as she enters the kitchen. 'Did you get your letters? They looked very important.'

Zoe waltzes into the kitchen and perches on the table next to me, her legs swinging. 'What did they say?'

I keep staring ahead at the wall as I reply, 'I'm being given over £125,000 in compensation and I've been selected to receive the Military Cross for bravery.'

Zoe squeals and grabs the papers out of my hand and my mum drops a cup, which explodes into dozens of tiny pieces across the kitchen floor.

'Fuck me!' says Zoe as she scans the pages, her eyes wide.

'Zoe, language!'

'Mum ... Aimee's rich ... although ... you can barely buy a house these days with that money, especially around here. It seems a bit ... low.'

I open and close my mouth several times.

'It doesn't say who nominated you,' adds Zoe.

'I- I think it was James.'

'And you just dumped him?'

'Yeah.'

'Fuck.'

Mum shoots Zoe another angry look, but she doesn't say anything. 'Well … you may not be in the Army anymore, or at least not for much longer, but at least they've looked after you financially.'

Zoe rolls her eyes. 'It's not exactly a lot of money, is it? For almost dying, losing your womb and having a mental disorder that could last years.' Zoe's words cut me to the bone. Hearing them said out loud so bluntly makes them feel worthless, like they mean nothing. I know she doesn't mean to upset me.

'It's fine, Zoe. It's enough to get me back on my feet.'

'What's the first thing you're going to buy?' she asks, her voice a high-pitched squeal.

I stare at her blankly, my brain still not able to comprehend everything. 'I don't know.'

'Can we go on holiday? You know, somewhere hot with a beach.'

'Yeah, sure.'

'And can we get a hot tub and a new car?'

'Sure.'

'And can I have a new phone?'

'Zoe! This money is for Aimee to do with as she wishes, for her to set up a new life and ensure she's stable and looked after, not to shower you with gifts.'

Zoe lowers her head and chews on her bottom lip, like she used to do when she was a little girl and had been grounded.

I keep my voice low as I lean over to her. 'You can have a new phone.'

'Yes!'

Chapter Fifty-Eight
Now

Cindy and Dot were barely awake when Aimee strolled into her bedroom carrying the paper bag of takeaway food, but once the delicious aromas wafted past their noses they soon regained consciousness and hungrily scoffed their breakfast baps like ravaged hyenas, barely pausing for breath until every morsel was gone.

'Okay, so … how did we get here again?' asked Dot, wiping the crumbs from her lips. She was still in her skin-tight dress and jacket.

'I remember getting back to yours,' said Cindy, taking a sip of coffee that Jones had made earlier, 'but I don't remember much else. I can't believe you've already been up for hours and gone to the gym. Babe, you're crazy.'

'I needed to let off some steam.'

'And did you?'

'Yeah, it was fun, actually.'

'And I can't believe you asked Nathan out. I'm not sure what got into you last night, but I love your new-found confidence. It suits you.'

Aimee shrugged her shoulders. 'We'll see what happens.'

Dot stood up and pulled her dress over her bottom. 'Right, well, cheers for the breakfast. I gotta get back home. I'm supposed to be meeting Jenna for lunch later.'

'And Jenna is?'

'That girl I went out with Thursday night.'

'A second date?'

'Yep. I told you, I think I'm in love.'

'The naked stripper last night who gyrated on your lap for ten minutes didn't turn you then?' joked Cindy.

Dot covered her mouth, taking a deep breath. 'Uh, don't make me gag. I can still taste baby oil. Next time we go to a strip club it's going to be one with hot, naked girls instead.'

'Deal,' said Cindy with a nod.

'I second that,' added Aimee.

Aimee spent the rest of the day scrolling online for further information regarding James and the hit and run, but she didn't find anything new. She needed a new angle and really wanted to speak to DI Fields, but she'd see him tomorrow so was inclined to wait until then. Sunday was usually her day off, but she promised she'd meet Cindy for lunch. They arranged to meet at the station first so Aimee could quiz DI Fields on any new updates involving the case.

Jennifer, the young girl James had supposedly killed, had been studying at university to become a doctor. Her parents and her older brother, who hadn't been named, had been devastated when she'd died and the family had been torn apart. It was true what was often said; a family tragedy could either bring a family closer than ever or divide them forever.

Jones had disappeared after he'd made everyone coffee. He had showered and got dressed into his clothes he'd worn on the streets and said he would be back later. Aimee quickly chucked the clothes he'd borrowed from Nathan in the wash, making a mental note to return them tomorrow night before their date. Aimee was mildly excited about her upcoming date. She wasn't sure how much she actually liked Nathan. All she knew was that he was very attractive and that had to count for something, but there was a small sliver of doubt creeping over her, which she was adamant had nothing to do with Jones and the electric tingles he'd given her earlier, despite never touching her.

By the time Saturday evening arrived, Jones hadn't returned. Maybe he'd decided he didn't want to stay with her anymore. They had never agreed a time frame anyway. He was no longer a suspect in James's murder so there was no real reason for him to stay in Woking. There was no way he was truly homeless. It made no sense to her. If she'd thought of it earlier she would have followed him to find out what he'd been up to today. She didn't hear her front door open until gone midnight and, by that time, she was too tired to confront him.

When Aimee got up the next morning she smelled coffee and toast. Last night was the first night she hadn't had a nightmare. In fact, she'd slept soundly and deeply and had woken up very disorientated.

'Morning,' grunted Jones as she entered the kitchen. Darth was perched on his shoulder, nibbling a piece of bread.

'You were gone almost all day yesterday,' she said as she picked up a slice of toast from the plate on the side.

'Miss me, did you?'

'No, I'm just curious.'

'I had a few errands to run.'

'Like what?'

Jones's lips creased into a smile behind his coffee cup. 'You really can't stand not knowing everything about me, can you?'

'I just want to make sure you aren't doing anything illegal or dangerous.'

'Jesus, you sound like my mum. Anyway … what did *you* do for the rest of the day?'

'I did some more research on Jennifer Lincoln.'

'And?'

'And I'm going into the station today to meet Cindy for lunch. Hopefully I'll be able to talk to Tony quickly, see if he has any new leads.'

'It's not your job to pry. You're not a cop. Let Detective Dimwit do his job.'

'But that's just it … I feel like he's missing something or I'm missing something really obvious. It can't be a coincidence that James was murdered only a few streets over from where I live, can it?'

'Stranger things have happened.'

'But he came here to make amends for something. He must have been here either for me or for Jennifer.'

Jones shrugged his shoulders and took a long slurp of coffee. 'I don't know what to tell you.'

Aimee huffed as she shrugged her jacket over her shoulders. She needed to pop to the shops to get groceries as her cupboards and the fridge were dangerously empty. 'Well, you're a great help as always. When are you moving out?'

'I didn't know I lived here.'

'You know what I mean.'

'Do you want me to leave?'

Aimee opened her mouth, but quickly closed it. She bit her bottom lip and then licked her lips. The truth was that she didn't want him to leave, but if she told him that she'd never hear the end of it. Jones had a tendency to be stubborn and big-headed.

'You need to stop licking those lips of yours when you're around me.'

'They were dry.'

'Get some lip salve. Besides, you don't have to worry, I'll be out of your hair soon. As soon as I get the all-clear from Detective Dimwit that he no longer needs me to stick around then I'll leave.'

Aimee nodded. 'Fine. Good. Great. I'm going to the shops for food. Would you like to come?'

'Can't. I need to run some errands.'

Aimee twiddled her keys around her fingers. 'More errands?'

'Hey, I'm a busy guy.'

'How busy can you be when you're homeless?'

Jones tickled the hamster's belly. 'Don't you have to get to the shops?'

'Why do you constantly dodge my questions?'

Jones grinned. 'Have a great day, sweetie.'

'Don't call me that.'

'Baby?'

'What happened to Price?'

'Just trying something new.'

'Well, quit it.'

Jones snorted loudly. 'You're touchy this morning. Nervous about your date with the stripper tonight?'

'No.'

'Then what's your problem?'

Aimee bit her lip again and abruptly stopped when Jones set his dark eyes on her. That look of his was dangerous and they both knew it. Aimee gave him a stern glance as she turned to leave.

'My spare key is under the plant pot on the side,' she said as she walked away.

'Now look who's dodging questions … and you're wrong, it's not there.'

Aimee turned to see Jones holding up the plant pot. 'That's weird,' she said with a frown.

'Maybe Dot or Cindy took it?'

'No, they have their own.'

'Both of them have spare keys? Why?'

'They're my friends. I have keys to their places.'

Jones replaced the pot and sighed. 'Well, looks like you have yet another mystery on your hands … The mystery of the missing spare key.'

Aimee dumped her bag and jacket in the office and waited for her friend to turn up. She was most likely off somewhere procuring gossip. Aimee was frustrated, in more ways than one. Jones was still hiding something from her. What could he possibly need to run errands for? Why was he constantly avoiding her questions?

'Babe!' Cindy screamed when she saw her. 'Oh my god, thank fuck you're here. Have you heard?'

'Heard what?'

'Tony arrested someone yesterday.'

Aimee's stomach lurched, as if she'd taken a punch to the stomach. 'H-He did? Why didn't you tell me?'

'I've only just found out myself.'

'Who's he arrested? I didn't see it on the news.'

'It's not been released to the media or the public yet, but I don't know who's been arrested. It's not your homeless man, is it?'

'No, I saw him this morning.'

'Naked, I hope?'

'Don't you start.'

Cindy held her hands up in surrender. 'Hey, I'm just saying ... when a tall glass of water is available for drinking and your mouth is dry then don't blame me if ... you ... can't ...'

'You had no idea where you were going with that, did you?'

'It seemed like a good analogy in my head.'

Aimee and Cindy burst out laughing. 'Will you tell me if you hear anything about the arrest?'

'Of course. So, since you're not seeing your homeless man naked ... what about the stripper? You excited about your date?'

'Yeah. Sure.'

Cindy picked up her bag and slung it across her shoulder. 'Yeesh, I was more enthusiastic about my recent Hollywood wax.'

'Sorry ... just got a lot on my mind.'

'Well, unless he stuffs his package you're in for a treat.'

'I don't sleep with guys on the first date.'

'There's a first time for everything.'

Aimee and Cindy had just reached the doors leading to the outside when a familiar shout stopped them.

Aimee turned and smiled. 'Hello, Detective.'

'Hello, yourself. Having a good weekend?'

'Um ... yeah, it's going fine, thanks.'

'Haven't managed to snoop around any other crime scenes then?'

'Nope, just the one.'

'Good to know. I assume Cindy has filled you in on the latest news involving the case?'

'Only that someone's been arrested. Am I allowed to know who? Is it Adam?'

'Who's Adam?' interrupted Cindy.

'James's twin brother.'

Cindy's mouth fell open, but DI Fields shook his head and spoke before she could get her words out, 'I'm afraid I cannot confirm or deny who has been arrested. I just wanted to let you know that you can tell Tom Jones his services are no longer required so feel free to kick him out onto the streets whenever you like.'

'Great, thanks, Detective.'

Cindy stepped forwards, twirling a strand of pink hair around her fingers. 'Say ... Detective ... you've never thought about becoming a stripper, have you? I mean, you have the uniform already ...'

DI Fields glanced at Cindy for a brief moment, looking as if he wanted to say something, but in the end he merely smiled slightly and walked away.

'One of these days you're going to get done for sexual harassment,' said Aimee.

'Oh, please ... I have pictures that I could have sent to HR years ago.'

Aimee grabbed Cindy's shoulder and pulled her back. 'Explain. What pictures?'

'Oh geez, look at the time. We must be getting to lunch otherwise I'll be late getting back.'

'Cindy?' Aimee warned, using a sterner voice. 'What pictures?'

Cindy leaned in close and whispered in Aimee's ear, 'Pictures of a certain nine-inch cock.'

Aimee gasped so loudly that she startled a nearby police officer, who glared at her. Aimee kept her voice low as she replied, 'He's sent you pictures of his … of his …'

'Cock.'

'Yes, thank you …'

'Do you want to see?'

'I'll pass. I can barely look him in the face as it is. Why didn't you ever tell me this before?'

Cindy shrugged. 'Some things I like to keep private.'

'Since when?'

'Can we go to lunch now?'

'Only if you promise to tell me why you have pictures of Tony's—'

'Cock.'

'—On your phone. You told me you haven't slept with him.'

'Who said anything about sleeping with him?'

Aimee stared open-mouthed at her friend as she waltzed out the door, flipping her hair casually over her shoulder like it was no big deal.

Chapter Fifty-Nine
Then

Maynard's Place, March 2010

Thank god that's over because getting up in front of hundreds of people and accepting a medal was, quite possibly, the worst experience of my life, even worse than the time I wet myself on stage during a Year 3 performance of *A Christmas Carol*. I'd wanted to back out of the awards ceremony, but my mum had basically forced me to go because if I didn't then I wouldn't receive the medal. Even my therapist had said it perhaps wasn't a great idea for me to attend because of how messed up my head was (not that she said those exact words). I'd practically overdosed myself on anti-anxiety and anti-depressant medication just to get through the day and now I'm feeling the woozy after-effects, probably not helped by the four tequila shots I've downed in the past half an hour.

The stool I'm perched on doesn't feel very stable, or maybe it's me that's swaying from side to side. I lean against the bar and order another shot. I told my mum I was going for a walk three hours ago, but the truth is that my legs carried me into the nearest watering hole and now I can't seem to make them leave. All I want to do is drink until my body feels numb and then I might throw myself off the nearest bridge or step out in front of a car. Yes, I'm back here again; despite my best efforts my brain is telling me to end it all because it will be easier than trying to fix my tattered life. These ups and downs are driving me insane; no one day is the same.

The Military Cross is lying on the bar in front of me, a small stream of spilled alcohol slowly inching its way closer and closer to it. The medal is smaller than I imagined. Not that I assumed it would be a giant medal, but the small silver cross engraved with imperial crowns with the Royal Cypher in the centre seems extremely ... I don't know ... *simple*. The purple and white vertical striped ribbon is nice enough. It doesn't even have my name engraved on it, so it could belong to anyone. The medal's nothing special, not to me. This medal is proof that my life is over. It's proof that I aborted my child in order to progress in my career. It's proof that I got blown up and saved a man, destroying his life and future in the process. It's even proof that I was kicked out of the Army and now have no job or career aspects. It's proof of my failings ... and it makes me feel sick just looking at it.

'Oooh, that's pretty,' says a high-pitched voice beside me.

I slide the medal across the bar towards the woman next to me, not even glancing up at her. 'Here. You have it. Congratulations.' My boozy buzz is giving my voice a slurred edge.

The woman laughs. 'Na, babe, I can't accept that. It looks important. What is it?'

'It's a Military Cross medal, awarded for bravery or something or other.'

'Is it yours?'

'Unfortunately.'

'Are you a soldier?'

'Not anymore.'

'Hey, Dot! Come and meet ... I'm sorry ... what's your name?'

'Aimee.'

'I'm Cindy. Nice to meet you.' She scans the bar and shouts again. 'Dot, come and meet Aimee. She's like a real hero or something.'

'I'm no hero.'

I finally take a look at her. Cindy's pretty and her skin is a lovely dark brown, so flawless that I automatically assume she must be a model. Her ears are studded with numerous earrings of varying shapes and sizes that sparkle even in the dim light of the bar, and her hair is bright blonde, a shocking contrast against her dark skin, but the whole look is quite stunning.

'Maybe you don't think you're a hero, but I reckon you're a hero to someone,' she says. She leans across the bar, her enormous breasts almost bursting out of her low-cut green tank top. 'Three tequila shots!'

Another woman appears next to her. She has short black hair and a gold nose ring. 'Ooh, cool medal. I'm Dot.' She extends her hand.

I shake it. 'Aimee.'

Dot smiles at me. 'You look like you could use a drink.'

'I'm on it!' Cindy starts handing out the shot glasses, spilling a few drops over my lap. She holds up her glass. 'Here's to Aimee ... our new best friend!'

'Cheers!' shouts Dot.

I can't help but smile. I've never had a best friend before, unless you count my mum and sister. Something tells me that these two girls may have just saved my life tonight without realising it.

Chapter Sixty
Now

Aimee and Cindy settled into their usual corner table by the window of the coffee shop around the corner from the station; their normal Sunday routine. Cindy ordered a chicken and mayo sandwich, crisps and a large coffee and Aimee went for a tuna wrap and a large mocha.

'So, come on ... tell me the story, but please leave out any gross details. I'll lose my appetite,' said Aimee as she unwrapped her tuna wrap.

'Okay, so this was way before you started working at the station. I've basically worked there my whole working life. Started when I was eighteen. One day this new guy joins the force and we hit it off. He was a DC back then, or a PC ... I forget. Anyway, he flirts. I flirt. We laugh—'

'Wait ... are you talking about Tony? Because the Tony I know doesn't flirt, nor does he laugh or fraternise with women at work.'

'Yeah, but you didn't know him before *it* happened.'

'Before what happened?' Aimee leaned forwards in her chair automatically.

'Before he got his partner killed.'

Aimee stopped mid-chew. 'He *what*?'

'After that he wasn't the same. It was like his soul got sucked out of his body or something. Anyway, before that happened we used to sext back and forth a lot, but it never went any further. It might have done had he not got his partner killed.'

Aimee continued chewing slowly as she stared out of the window. She'd never considered that there was a reason for Tony's cold exterior. Now that she knew it made him more human, more ... understandable. She cast her mind back to when he'd complimented her, telling her that he doubted he'd have been brave enough to save a man's life ... It made sense now.

'Do you know the details of what happened?'

'Not really. He never talks about it.'

'I can't believe you've kept this from me for eleven years. If you like him so much why don't you try and rekindle the romance?'

Cindy scoffed. 'I'd hardly call what we had *romance*. He sent me pictures of his cock.'

Aimee coughed loudly in an attempt to cover up the word as a waitress walked past, but she must have heard because her eyes flicked over to their table briefly. 'Did you send him pictures too?'

'Maybe.'

Aimee laughed. 'I can't believe this!'

'What's the big deal?'

'The big deal is that you've been swooning over him for as long as I've known you, always joking and saying you'd never sleep with him or whatever and I find out that both of you clearly have some sort of feelings for each other, but are too stubborn or scared to act on it.'

Cindy slurped her coffee loudly. 'I could say the exact same thing about you, babe ... That homeless guy still living with you?' Aimee was impressed at her ability to smoothly switch the conversation over to her within a matter of seconds.

'Yeah,' said Aimee with a nod, 'but now someone, possibly Adam, has been arrested he's not a person of interest anymore so I guess he can leave whenever he wants.'

'You really think it's this Adam guy?'

'The last time I saw Tony he was going to speak to Adam, so yeah ... it's a possibility.'

'So what will happen to the homeless guy? You think he'll go back to living on the streets?'

Aimee took another bite out of her wrap and chewed for several seconds before swallowing. 'I don't think he's actually homeless.'

'No?'

'He's hiding something from me.'

'Why do you care so much?' Cindy took a sip of coffee.

'I don't ... not really.'

'It sounds like you care a little.'

Aimee leaned back in her chair and glanced out of the window and onto the street. She watched as a few people walked past, their heads bowed over their phones and then spoke. 'Jones has never been a nice guy. In fact, he made me think that I'd ruined his life by saving him. He could have reached out to me whenever he wanted over the years, but he hasn't. Now he's suddenly in my life and although he's still just as annoying as ever, he's also ... changed. But he's constantly avoiding answering my questions. I need to—' Aimee squinted against the bright sunshine, leaning forwards to get a better view. She'd seen someone walking on the other side of the street. It was definitely him. 'Look ... there he is. Quick, let's follow him.' Without waiting for Cindy to answer Aimee grabbed her bag, leaving her mocha untouched on the table and sprinted out the door.

Cindy caught up with her outside, breathing heavily. 'Babe, what the fuck? I didn't get to finish my lunch.'

'Come on, follow me.'

Aimee set off across the road, stepping in front of a car without looking both ways. The driver beeped his horn furiously, waving a rude hand gesture in her direction. Aimee ignored it completely as she scurried across the road and stopped by the side of the next building, peering around the corner.

Jones was walking down the street with his hands in his pockets. Unlike everyone else he wasn't glued to his phone. In fact, Aimee was sure she hadn't even seen him with one. What kind of person didn't own a phone? Aimee and Cindy kept their distance as they followed him, ducking into doorways and down side alleys when necessary to avoid his line of vision. Eventually he reached a tall building and went inside.

'Woking Homeless Shelter,' read Cindy. The words were printed on a piece of paper stuck to the door. 'He looks homeless to me.'

Aimee screwed up her nose. 'I'm going in.'

'No! You can't. He'll see you and I have to be back to work in ten minutes.'

'Then you go back.'

'I can't leave you here alone.'

'Then come with me. Please, I have to know what he's up to.'

'Babe, I love you, you know that, but you're acting like a crazy person. Leave the poor guy alone to go and get some lunch or something.'

'There was food at my place!' shouted Aimee a little louder than she intended.

Cindy tilted her head. 'How about we come back here another time when he's not in there and ask around about him?'

Aimee shook her head. 'You stay here, I'm going to talk to him now.'

'You're impossible, you know that?'

Aimee pushed the double doors open and entered the small hallway. She heard voices and smelled hot spicy food cooking. Cindy crept along behind her as she entered the main hall, keeping back a few paces. A dozen or so long tables were laid out in rows with benches running along each side, which were full of people who were eating and drinking hot beverages. Every person had a smile on their face and were talking amongst themselves, swapping stories. Most of their clothes were over-sized and tatty. Some even had dogs by their side who were being fed scraps of food from the tables. She scanned the hall for Jones, but she couldn't see him.

'Can I help you?' asked a polite voice from behind them.

Aimee spun around as if she'd been caught out doing something naughty. A friendly looking man of about thirty smiled at her. He was wearing a blue tracksuit with a small white badge that said *volunteer*.

'Um, sorry ... I was just looking for someone.' Aimee glanced around, her eyes darting back and forth. 'Is Thomas Jones here?'

'Tommy? Yeah, he's just helping to unload the van out the back. Is he a friend of yours?'

'Sort of.'

The volunteer smiled again. 'I can go and get him if you like.'

'Um ... no, that's okay. I was just wondering what his ... situation is.'

'His situation?'

'Is he really homeless?' Aimee gave herself a mental slap. What was she doing? She knew she was being rude, but she relaxed slightly when the volunteer started laughing.

'Oh god no, Tommy's not one of the homeless. He might dress like one, but he's a volunteer. I think he dresses like that to blend in, to appear more approachable. In fact, he actually only arrived here a few days ago, but he's given the shelter a very generous donation to help with food and supplies. He's a big hit here, although he probably wouldn't approve of me telling you that, but since you already know him ...' The man tailed off when he saw Aimee's mouth drop open. Cindy elbowed her in the ribs.

'Right, um ... thanks. Please don't tell him I dropped by,' said Aimee as she started backing out the way she'd come.

The volunteer frowned. 'Are you sure? I can run and grab him if you need to talk—'

'That won't be necessary!' Aimee was already out the door. She slammed it shut behind her as she attempted to catch her breath.

'Well, I guess that answers that mystery,' said Cindy.

'So that's what he does with his money ... travels from place to place volunteering at homeless shelters and giving them money. Why the hell wouldn't he tell me that?'

Cindy shrugged her bag higher up on her shoulder. 'Maybe he doesn't want you to think he's a decent person.'

Aimee groaned and covered her face with her hands. 'I've been calling him a dickhead and everything. Now I can't even say that I know because then he'll know I followed him. Fuck!'

Aimee stepped out of the steaming shower and wiped the condensation off the mirror with her left hand. She pulled her towel tighter around her chest as she stared at her reflection. Her date with Nathan was in an hour, yet all she could think about was Jones and what she had found out earlier. She desperately wanted to apologise to him and confront him about the situation, but she knew she'd overstepped a line by following him and now was overcome with gnawing guilt.

'Price!'

Aimee jumped at the sound of his voice from outside the bathroom door. She hadn't heard him come in.

'Yeah, just stepped out of the shower. Be out in a bit.'

'I need to talk to you.'

'Give me five minutes.'

'It's important.'

Aimee sighed as she clutched her towel tighter and opened the door. Jones stood in the hallway wearing new clothes, which Aimee hadn't seen before. Had be bought new ones? The casual jeans and blue shirt looked good on him, highlighting his physique. He grinned as he looked her up and down, taking in her wet hair and towel.

'What's up?' she asked timidly.

'Nothing, just fancied seeing you wearing nothing but a towel.'

Aimee clenched her jaw and slammed the door in his face. She heard him laughing as he walked away. Aimee fought back a smile as she leaned against the door.

Ten minutes later Aimee walked into the lounge where Jones was watching television. He had his feet up on the coffee table again, but she kept quiet as she picked up her bag, checking to ensure she had everything she needed. She'd chosen to wear a simple black mid-length dress which emphasised her curves with a long-sleeved white jacket over the top to cover the scars on her arms. She was an expert at dressing to hide them. Her hair was still wet, but she often let it dry naturally, especially in the summer. Her makeup was minimal, but elegant.

'You look nice,' said Jones after giving her the briefest of glances and then returning his eyes to the screen.

'Thanks.'

At her one-word answer he looked up. 'No snarky comment?'

'You gave me a compliment so I said thank you.'

Jones frowned at her. 'No sarcastic comment and you haven't mentioned the fact that I have my feet up on the coffee table … What's going on?'

'Nothing.' Aimee turned away before he could see her face turn red.

'You wouldn't be being nice to me because you feel guilty for following me today, would you?' Aimee silently swore as she turned around to face him, but before she could answer him, he said, 'Mark told me that two women stopped by looking for me. I made an educated guess that one of them was you. I'm guessing the other was Cindy or Dot.'

'I'm really sorry, I ... didn't ... I mean I didn't ... Why the hell didn't you tell me that that's what you were doing? Why wouldn't you want me to know?'

Jones switched the television off and stood up, stepping closer to her. She shuddered as all the hairs on her arms and neck stood to attention.

'I like to keep a low profile. Is that so bad?'

'But what you're doing is incredibly generous and selfless.'

'So because of that you now think I'm a better and nicer person than I was before?'

'No, I ... what I mean is ... Look, I'm coming across like a real dickhead right now, but you made me believe that you were homeless and that you refused to spend your compensation money. What was I supposed to think?'

Jones smiled as he leaned in closer. She felt the warmth from his body seeping into hers, all of her nerve endings tingly with apprehension. 'Maybe you shouldn't automatically assume the worst of people, Price.'

'And maybe you should stop playing games and just give me straight answers for once.'

'Fine. Ask away.'

Aimee straightened up, attempting to look and act serious. 'Are you *actually* homeless?'

'No, my permanent address is in Milton Keynes, but I don't spend a lot of time there.'

'What do you do for a job?'

'I used some of my compensation money to set up a charity for homeless veterans, which I now run solo. I also spend my time volunteering at other homeless shelters in various towns and cities. Maybe it's not classed as a proper job, but I get by. I move around from place to place, city to city, chatting to them and helping where I can.'

'Did you know I lived here when you decided to come with James and Adam?'

'Yes.'

With every answer Jones moved closer, their bodies now barely an inch apart. Aimee asked her last question in a whispered voice. 'Do you like me?' She cringed at how *high-school* her question sounded.

'Yes, I do.'

Aimee couldn't look away as he moved his lips in line with hers. His warm breath tickled her face. He wasn't touching her, but she sensed his hands all over her body, wanting them to explore her. She gulped and opened her mouth, licking her lips.

'Bad move, Price—'

A loud knock on the front door caused Aimee to jump away from Jones as if she'd been electrocuted. She backed away, attempting to steady her heart rate, clutching at her chest.

'That's Nathan,' she stuttered.

Jones locked his eyes on hers. 'Have a good evening. I'll make myself scarce in case you want to bring Loverboy back here.'

'No, I ... no, that's okay. Stay. Here. Please.'

Jones nodded as he slumped back down on the sofa and switched the television on again, propping his feet up on the coffee table. Aimee ran to the door, yanking it open, plastering a fake smile across her face.

'Hi, Nathan.'

'Hey, Aimee. You ready?'

'Sure.'

Chapter Sixty-One
Then

Maynard's Place, March 2010

The air in the bar is stuffy and warm, despite the cool temperature outside. I sit with Cindy and Dot for hours, talking and laughing — actually laughing. Dot, I find out, is training to be a hairdresser and tells me I never have to pay for a haircut ever again. Cindy works at a local police station as an administrator, but says she wants to work her way up to be an Evidential Property Officer, and she's also a pole dancing instructor, newly qualified, so she has plans to open up her own studio one day.

'Hey, you know, you should try pole dancing sometime. It's great fun and gets you really fit,' she says as she turns her empty shot glass around and around on the table, causing a watermark.

'Dancing's not really my thing. I'm very uncoordinated,' I say, slurring my words slightly. I have slowed down with my drinking now, but the previous shots are catching up with me fast.

'Maybe something like kick-boxing then,' suggests Dot.

My minds drifts to my dodgy leg. The muscles are slowly healing, but I still have some long-term damage that will no doubt prevent me from using my legs to kick.

'It's good to have a hobby, or something you can use to take your mind off everyday life stuff,' says Cindy.

'Yeah, life stuff sucks,' adds Dot.

I smile and sigh. 'Yeah, maybe you're right.'

'What do you do now you're not a soldier?' asks Dot.

'Nothing. I'm ... still recovering from ... what happened.' I haven't divulged all the details to my new friends yet, but I'm sure I will eventually. They're very easy to talk to and never seem to judge or disrespect me.

'There's an opening for an admin assistant at the police station where I work. I could put in a good word for you. They'll surely snap you up if they know you're an ex-soldier. Hey, maybe you can become a cop one day!'

The idea lights up my mind for a moment before being snuffed out by my dark thoughts. 'I'm not good enough to be a cop. I'd jump at any loud noise or gunshot.'

'Maybe start as an admin assistant and work your way up.' Cindy certainly is persistent and I can't fault her for that. She has a good point though; even through my alcohol-fuelled haze, working in a police station does sound more appealing than stacking shelves at Tesco (my mum's suggestion the other day).

I nod my head slowly. 'Yeah. Sounds good.'

'Great! I'll speak to my boss on Monday.'

'But I don't want anyone knowing that I'm an ex-soldier.'

'Why not?'

I stare at my empty shot glass for a few seconds. 'It's a part of my life I'd rather forget.'

I watch as Cindy and Dot exchange glances, but even if they disagree with me, they don't question it any further. Maybe they will later on down the line when we all get to know each other a bit better, but tonight they seem happy to go along with whatever I say.

Chapter Sixty-Two
Now

Nathan had certainly dressed for the occasion because as Aimee walked down the street next to him she felt a little under-dressed in her plain black dress. Nathan had donned a pair of fitted, smart jeans and a black shirt, which was open at the collar and had the sleeves rolled up due to the warm evening. His black leather shoes were impeccably clean and shiny, his hair freshly washed and styled to perfection, and Aimee caught a whiff of tangy aftershave whenever the wind blew in her direction. Next to him she felt extremely average. Why would he be interested in her?

'I thought I'd take you to that new Thai restaurant. Do you like Thai food?'

'I like any food,' replied Aimee with a smile. Her stomach grumbled in response. She was regretting not finishing her lunch earlier with Cindy. A pang of shame still lingered in her chest from following Jones earlier and butting into something that was none of her business. Luckily, he'd taken it well ... too well. Her heart jumped as she recalled how close they'd been only moments before Nathan had arrived at her door.

'Great, then afterwards we'll go to The Teacup Lounge, that place I told you about. They do amazing cocktails.'

'In the little teacups?'

Nathan laughed. 'Yeah, the name gives it away, right?' Aimee laughed, relieved at how easy it was to talk to Nathan. He was, thankfully, quelling the tightness in her chest from earlier. 'How's your brother?' he asked as they turned a corner.

'My brother? Oh, damn, I forgot to give you back your clothes.'

'No worries. I can grab them any time.'

Aimee tensed slightly. She honestly didn't want Nathan and Jones coming face to face again if she could help it. Jones was bound to say something awkward and reveal that he wasn't actually her brother.

The restaurant was filling up with hungry customers when they arrived, all smiling and smartly dressed for an evening out. The atmosphere was romantic and calm, not too noisy and hectic. Violin music played softly over the speakers and candles in large, ornate holders adorned every table, flickering whenever the front door opened. Nathan stepped to the side to allow her to walk inside first; the perfect gentleman. He even pulled her seat out for her.

'Thank you,' said Aimee as she lowered herself onto it. 'This is a beautiful place.'

'It only opened a month or two ago and has already won a tonne of awards.' Nathan sounded impressed with himself as he picked up the drinks menu and scanned it. 'Do you like white wine?' he asked.

'Yes.'

'Would you like to share a bottle?'

'Absolutely.'

'Any preference?'

'You choose.'

'Great.' Nathan lowered his eyes to the menu, scanning it back and forth as a waiter appeared beside them.

'Good evening. My name's Oliver. I'll be your waiter this evening. What can I get you to drink?'

Aimee watched intently as Nathan discussed the wine menu with the waiter. He pronounced every name fluently and genuinely appeared to know what he was talking about when it came to wine. Finally, he settled on a bottle and the waiter hurried away to fulfil the order after giving them a short nod of the head.

A flutter of nerves made Aimee feel uneasy. Now they were sat down the pressure to hold a conversation loomed like a dark shadow. She wasn't used to dating or speaking with someone on a one-to-one basis, apart from her girlfriends. Did she actually want this to go somewhere? Dating seemed like such a normal thing to do, yet it filled her with dread; the exact reason why she'd avoided doing it for so long.

'So,' said Nathan, leaning back in his chair, 'I can't believe I finally convinced you to go out with me.'

Aimee thought that was an odd thing to say, considering he'd only asked her out for the first time a couple of days ago. 'Yes, well … I don't always have time to go on dates.' It was a small lie, but he didn't need to know that.

'Does your job at the police station keep you busy?'

'Sort of.'

'Do you get to hear all the juicy gossip before it's released to the media?'

Aimee laughed softly. 'Sometimes, but it's usually my best friend who tells me. She seems to always know what's going on before anyone else.'

'Cool. This murder that happened … awful, right?'

Aimee gulped. *Awful* wouldn't have been the word she'd have used. More like … horrific and gut-wrenching. 'Yeah,' she said at a loss for words, 'but I guess it happens … even in Woking.'

'True. I saw him, you know.' The way Nathan said it was so casual, like it didn't mean anything to him, but why would it?

The waiter appeared with their drink order just as Aimee was about to question him further. He saw him? Who? James? When? Why hadn't he come forward as a potential witness? Aimee frowned as she secretly willed the waiter to hurry up, place the glasses and bottle down on the table and go away. Nathan picked up the wine bottle and uncorked it, giving it a sniff.

'You saw the victim?' she whispered loudly as she leaned across the table towards him. 'When?'

Nathan poured wine into her glass. 'The day he was killed.'

'Why didn't you tell the police?'

'Um ... I don't think this is appropriate dinner-and-date conversation, Aimee.'

Aimee bit her lip, quietly annoyed. 'How long before he was killed did you see him?' She refused to let it go. After all, he'd brought it up.

Nathan poured his wine and set the bottle on the table with a sigh. 'I accidentally bumped into him outside our building, but I didn't think anything of it. In fact, it took me a while to recognise him when he turned up on the news.'

Aimee gripped the edges of the table with her hands, her fingers turning white from the strain. 'Wait ... he was coming *out* of our building?'

'Yeah. Weird, right? Maybe he was visiting someone.'

Aimee's stomach lurched. 'Excuse me,' she said as she scrambled to her feet and headed towards the toilets, which were situated at the back of the restaurant. She barely made it to the nearest toilet bowl before heaving, but nothing came up; her stomach was empty.

He had been in her flat. Had James taken the photograph? But why would he have done that when he had a copy of his own? Aimee trembled from a sudden chill, but there were no open windows in the toilets. She angled herself so she was sitting next to the bowl and stared at the door to the cubicle. Her date with Nathan was now the last thing on her mind. All she wanted to do was retreat into her mind, a place that was warm and dark and familiar. Maybe she'd try and make it through dinner, then excuse herself afterwards, saying she felt unwell.

Nathan stood as she approached the table. She'd splashed her face with water and taken a few sips from the tap, which calmed her stomach, but it still ached.

'Are you okay?' he asked.

'Yes, sorry … I'm fine.' She took a seat; Nathan followed. He picked up his wine glass.

'Cheers,' he said.

Aimee begrudgingly lifted hers and clinked his glass. 'Cheers,' she echoed. The cool, crisp flavours of the wine danced on her tongue. It was delicious. Nathan had certainly chosen well. 'It's lovely.'

'I thought you might like it. Here's the menu.'

Aimee took the food menu and sipped her wine as she scanned the words on the laminated page, but she could barely make her eyes focus. Every word was wavy and fuzzy. She could recognise the early signs of a panic attack.

Not here, not now.

Why did this have to keep happening to her? Her panic attacks had been sporadic for the past few months, but within the last three days she'd suffered one major attack and several instances of mild symptoms. It was like she was back at square one again.

'Everything looks great,' she said with a smile, although her stomach was still gurgling, a clear sign that while she may have been hungry, it was not settled enough to digest food. The wine was going down fast, maybe too fast. She placed her glass on the table. As she did her phone vibrated in her bag. She quickly checked it under the table. It was her mum.

'I'm sorry,' said Aimee as she rose to her feet, 'do you mind if I take this? It's my mum. If I don't answer she'll just keep calling.'

'Of course,' answered Nathan, sipping his own drink. 'Shall I order for both of us?'

'Yeah, sure, I'll eat anything.'

'Great.'

Aimee pressed the answer button as she hurriedly walked away from the table in search of a more secluded area in which to talk. 'Mum?'

'Oh, darling, thank goodness you answered. Zoe's not come home. I'm really worried about her.'

'What do you mean she hasn't come home?'

'She finished work four hours ago and told me this morning that she was coming straight home from work, but she's not here and she's not answering her phone. Should I call the police?'

'Mum, Zoe's nearly twenty-four. She's an adult. I'm sure she's just out with some friends and forgot to tell you.'

'But it's so unlike her.'

'Try not to worry.'

'But—'

'Mum, I'm sure she's fine. Call me again in an hour if she hasn't turned up, okay? I'll try her phone now and leave her a message.'

'Okay, thank you, darling.'

'Bye, Mum.'

'Bye, darling.'

Aimee hung up and leaned against the wall. Her head was spinning fast and she could barely see the screen in front of her. She called Zoe, but it went straight to voicemail. She wasn't worried. As she'd told her mum, Zoe was an adult, and, although she still lived at home, she clearly wanted to be more independent. She'd been saving up for a deposit on a flat for the past year so she could move out. Aimee didn't blame her for wanting some space from their mum. Zoe had gone to university to study law, but had dropped out within a year and switched to art, but then dropped that too. Eventually, she'd decided not to go to university at all and had started working in the local council offices doing a mundane office job. Aimee had always wanted the best for her little sister, but Zoe was a free spirit, always had been. As long as she was happy then Aimee was happy with whatever she chose to do in life, and if that meant bouncing around from job to job then so be it.

Aimee saw Nathan ordering their food from the waiter, so she reluctantly put her phone away and started walking back to the table.

'Everything okay?' asked Nathan.

'Yeah, everything's—'

She never finished her sentence.

Her legs collapsed underneath her as she stumbled forwards into the table.

She lashed out her hand to grab the back of her chair, but it didn't help.

Her head bounced off it and everything went black.

Chapter Sixty-Three
Then

Aimee's Mother's House, March 2010

I don't remember how I got home last night, but clearly, somehow, I did, because I wake up with the worst hangover known to man, but at least I'm tucked up in my bed, all warm and cosy. I'm still wearing the same clothes I had on last night and when I peer out from underneath the covers I see my medal on the bedside table. I gingerly reach out a hand and brush it swiftly to the floor, out of sight, then slowly roll onto my back. Cindy and Dot must have brought me home. There is no way I'd been in a position to get myself back. I don't even know how to get in contact with them to thank them.

My phone starts vibrating, which sounds exactly like an electronic drill. I groan, quickly picking it up, and check the text message which has just come through.

Hey babe! Hope your head isn't too sore. We managed to get your address out of you and dropped you home about 3 a.m. this morning. Your mum wasn't too impressed, but she seems cool. If you feel up for it, how bout meeting us for lunch later in town? Cindy xx

I smile, sit up and swing my legs over the edge of the bed as I begin typing my reply.

Thanks so much. Feel like death. You girls saved me last night. I'd love to meet you for lunch. Text me where and when. Aimee xx

The journey from my bedroom to the kitchen where my mum and Zoe are sitting takes me longer than usual due to the fact that the whole world is spinning.

'Ha! You look like shit.'

'Language, Zoe!'

'Sorry, Mum, about last night,' I say as I gingerly take a seat at the kitchen table.

'You left without barely a word after we got back from the awards ceremony. I was worried.'

'I went to a bar.'

Zoe laughs. 'You think? You smell like you've been bathing in something funky.'

'That would be the tequila shots. Zoe, I'm going to give you some big sister advice … Never do shots.'

'Too late.'

Mum wheels round, a look of horror across her face as her mouth drops open. '*When* have you done shots, young lady?'

Zoe looks at me for backup, a sad puppy-dog expression on her face. 'Um …'

'She hasn't, Mum. She's kidding, right?'

'Right. I'm kidding. I've never done shots.' Zoe fake laughs.

Mum nods and goes back to drying a plate. Zoe and I exchange smiles.

'You want a coffee?' she asks me.

'Yes, please.'

Zoe leans forwards and gives me a kiss on the cheek. 'I'll make it extra strong.'

'Thank you. Love you.'

'Love you too.'

I watch Mum and Zoe move around the kitchen with smiles on their faces and it suddenly dawns on me how selfish I'd been last night. Thinking about suicide again is ridiculous. How could I even think about doing that to my family? I'm determined to change, to get better, to make something of myself.

'Mum, I've decided what I want to do with the main bulk of my compensation money.'

Zoe turns to me. 'I still get a new phone and we can go on holiday, right?'

'Right, yes, we'll still do all that. I want to buy a place in Woking. Maybe a small flat, and I want to get a job, possibly in a police station.'

'A police station?' My mum sounds horrified. 'Why?'

'I'm not saying I want to be a police officer, not right now. Maybe in a few years' time, but I want to keep working in the services.'

'If you're sure, darling. Of course I'll support you, but I would like you to start seeing a therapist for your mental health.'

I nod. 'Sure. I'll do that. Also, I want to start up a new hobby, something to focus on and something I'll enjoy.'

'Like what?' asks Zoe as she places a full cup of coffee in front of me, spilling a few drops onto the table runner.

'I don't know. My leg is still healing and I have limited mobility at the moment, but maybe something like boxing?'

'Why can't you be like a normal girl and do something safe, like dancing?'

I immediately pull a face. 'Mum ... I've never been a girly girl, have I?'

'But boxing? It's so ... dangerous.'

'Mum, I've already had the worst possible thing happen to me. A few punches in the face isn't going to bother me, nor should it bother you.'

My mum frowns. 'If you're sure.'

'I am.'

'Then let's get looking for properties. It will be so lovely to have you living nearby.'

Chapter Sixty-Four
Now

Something was tapping softly directly in front of Aimee, but she couldn't see what was causing the noise. It was irritating, like a dripping tap, but louder, more solid than water hitting a surface. Perhaps a hard object tapping a soft surface?

Aimee tried to open her eyes, but something was pushing down on her eyelids, something soft: a blindfold. Why was she blindfolded? Her arms were held above her head; her feet barely touching the ground. She wriggled her fingers, attempting to wake them, but she couldn't; something was restricting the blood flow to her hands. A tight, burning sensation bit at her wrists: a rope. The back of her neck ached from where her head had been hanging forwards during her time of unconsciousness, but how long had she been in this position, hanging from the ceiling like a carcass? Where the hell was she and what had happened?

'Hello?' she called out softly.

Her throat hurt and she coughed violently as her brain searched frantically for some sort of memory as to why she was here. The last thing she remembered was the restaurant and Nathan's worried expression as she'd tumbled to the ground in front of him. Had she hit her head on the way down? That might explain why she had a pounding headache, as if she'd consumed one too many tequila shots, but this wasn't a hangover. She hadn't drunk that much wine at dinner. In fact, she'd never even got as far as eating dinner. How long had she been unconscious? Where were her shoes? Aimee clenched her toes, finding that they were cold against the hard ground.

Her legs ached deeply, but she forced them to remain upright, otherwise the pain in her arms and wrists became unbearable.

Aimee lifted her head, inwardly groaning at the pain in the back of her neck. That damn tapping noise was grinding on her nerves, sending shivers down her spine, causing every hair to spring to attention. Someone was nearby, someone was making that noise.

'Who's there?' she tried again. Her heartbeat jumped when a gargled groan responded. It sounded weak, like the recipient was in pain or uncomfortable, as she was. 'Hello?'

'A-Aimeeee?' The voice was low and small, but instantly recognisable.

'Zoe? Oh my god ... Zoe ... are you okay? I can't see you.'

'A-Aimee?'

'I'm here. I'm here. Are you hurt?'

An ear-piercing scream filled her ears as something thrashed about in front of her, a piece of metal scraping against something else hard.

'Zoe! It's okay. Calm down. I'm here. Are you hurt?'

'Aimee! What's going on? Where am I? Oh god ...'

'Try and stay calm. Save your energy. Please just tell me if you're hurt?'

'I ... I don't think so. My arms ache. I think I'm tied to the ceiling. I can't feel my arms. I can't see anything.'

'What's the last thing you remember?'

'I ... I don't know.'

'Think! Try and remember.'

There was a short pause and then, 'I was walking home from work. I was on my phone ... flicking through Instagram.'

'And then?'

'I can't remember … I think there were footsteps behind me … and then nothing. Everything went dark and then I woke up here just now.'

'Mum called me while I was at dinner saying you hadn't come home. I just assumed that you'd gone off with friends somewhere and forgotten to tell her.'

'What time was that?'

Aimee searched her foggy memory. 'Eight, I think. It was about four hours after you were supposed to have come home from work.'

'Shit … Mum must be going mental right now.'

'I told her to call me in an hour if you hadn't turned up. I don't know how long it's been, but I expect it must have been that long by now. She's probably called the police—'

'Actually, she hasn't. I've texted her, pretending to be you, saying that you and Zoe are fine.'

Aimee froze at the sound of a man's voice cutting through the darkness. Zoe screamed again. Aimee knew exactly who the voice belonged to because it had been the last voice she'd heard before blacking out.

'Nathan?'

'I hope your head doesn't hurt too much. You weren't supposed to hit it when you passed out.'

'What the hell is going on? Did you drug me?'

'I slipped a little something into your wine when you went to the toilet at the restaurant. It took effect quicker than I imagined. Are you on any medication I don't know about?'

Aimee craned her neck from side to side; it was cramping up. Her legs were barely able to hold her up; most of her weight was being supported by the restraints around her wrists, the rough rope digging into her tender flesh.

'What the hell!' she shouted, which made her head pound even more. Anti-anxiety and anti-depressant medication, combined with wine and whatever drug he'd used on her was not making her headache any better, not to mention the thump she'd endured on the way down to the floor.

'Calm down. You'll hurt yourself.'

'What's Zoe doing here?' Aimee demanded.

'She's collateral.'

'Collateral for what?'

'You'll see.'

A low growl escaped her lips. 'Nathan!' she shrieked. 'Take off this blindfold and tell me why you've kidnapped me and my sister!'

Aimee flinched as a strong hand grabbed her arm and held her still as the blindfold was yanked down her face. It was still tied together at the back of her neck, so the material hung around her throat like a noose. She gasped as she stared into the eyes of the man she'd been on a date with merely hours before. He looked exactly the same, still charming and handsome, his hair still perfectly styled, yet there was something behind his eyes she hadn't noticed before; pure rage and hatred.

Aimee wanted to keep screaming at him, but she knew she had to be sensible about this. She'd been taught how to survive being kidnapped and tortured in the Army. It had been part of her basic survival training she'd received before she'd been deployed. She needed to save her energy, keep him talking, stay calm and not blurt out the first thing that came to mind. She had to think about her answers, learn who she was dealing with and, most important of all, not antagonise him or Zoe was at risk of being hurt. She had to keep both herself and Zoe alive for as long as possible in the hope that they would be rescued; but who would rescue her? No one knew where she was. Hell, *she* didn't know where she was. The dark, small room appeared to be a basement. There were no windows and the only door she could see was on the opposite side of the room, no light peering through the cracks.

Nathan circled her like a predator surrounding a scared and wounded prey, but Aimee held her nerve, willing her body not to fail her, to give away the fact that she was petrified.

'I don't understand,' she said quietly, 'what have I done to you to deserve this?'

Nathan clicked his tongue. 'That's not the question you should be asking right now, Aimee. The question you should be asking is what *haven't* you done?'

Aimee shook her head. 'I haven't done anything.'

'Leave us alone you freak!' Zoe's panicked voice echoed across the room. She was still suspended from the ceiling, blindfolded. Aimee blinked back tears as she saw her sister, the dark stain of dried urine on her jeans, the raw skin abrasions around her wrists where the rope was digging into her. How long had she been tied up like that?

Nathan whipped his head round in her direction and began to slowly approach her.

'No!' shouted Aimee. 'Leave her alone. She's got nothing to do with any of this. She's done nothing wrong.'

'Ah, that's very true, Aimee. She's done nothing wrong ... but neither had my sister and look how she ended up.'

333

Aimee coughed, blinking rapidly. 'Your sister? I don't even know your sister. I thought you said you were on only child?'

'I am ... *now.*'

Aimee stopped coughing. 'Nathan ... you're not making any sense.'

'Oh, come on, Aimee. I thought you were supposed to be smart. You want to be a cop, right? Let's see those wannabe detective skills at work. You know the answer. I want *you* to tell me and you have five minutes to work it out or your sister is going to start losing blood.'

Zoe squeaked and cried as Nathan ran a finger gently along her cheek.

'Don't touch her!'

'The five minutes have already started, so I suggest you hurry up.'

Aimee bit her lip, thinking. Her brain was cloudy, nothing in focus. The room slowly span, round and round and round, but she couldn't make it stop. Her stomach groaned and rolled.

Hold it together, she thought, *remember your training ... think!*

Aimee reached into the far corners of her mind for any sort of detail, anything she could remember and then, exactly like a light-bulb moment, she knew.

'Jennifer Lincoln,' she said, raising her head, 'your sister's name was Jennifer Lincoln.'

Nathan raised his eyebrows, a smirk across his face. 'Keep going. Tell me what happened to her.'

'She was hit by a drunk driver and killed eleven years ago.'

'And?'

'And James Daniels was driving ... oh my god, it was you ... *you* killed James!'

'We'll get onto him later. I want you to tell me why *you're* here and why your sister is here.'

Tears streamed out of Aimee's eyes, but she had no way of wiping them away so they trickled into her mouth. She licked her lips, tasting salt. 'I had nothing to do with the accident. James got drunk because—'

'There it is.'

'—Because I broke up with him. Wait ... You blame me for what happened to your sister?' *If I hadn't broken up with James then he wouldn't have got drunk and hit her with his car.*

'See, I bet you could make a decent detective after all. You're doing really well, but you're missing something.'

Aimee gulped. 'It wasn't really James, was it?'

'Bingo.'

'It was Adam.'

Nathan growled as he clenched his jaw. 'I had everything planned out ... *everything*. It took me a long time to formulate it and put all the pieces together. Like the police and everyone else, I believed that it was James who killed my sister. Hell, even he believed it. He confessed after all. James went to jail, so I had to bide my time. I started to do some research on him, to get to know him, to get to know the monster who took my sister away from me. He was a respected Army doctor, never stepped a toe out of line, always followed the rules, not a single mark against his name while he was serving. Why on earth would he suddenly go on a drinking binge and ruin his entire career by killing an innocent young woman? There had to be something I was missing. I hate myself for not seeing it sooner because, you see, there was nothing online about him having an identical twin brother. I didn't know that gem of a detail until James got out of jail and I saw them together, with that homeless guy who's staying with you. Did you really expect me to believe he was your brother, Aimee?'

Aimee's legs wobbled, so she quickly regained her footing. 'Nathan, I'm so sorry about what happened to your sister, but Adam has been arrested now. It's all over, but James didn't deserve to die. He was innocent.'

Nathan stroked Zoe's arm as he spoke softly, 'Yes, yes he was, wasn't he? I killed him – my mistake. I watched them all talking at the bar. James had on a black jacket, but then he must have given it to his brother to wear or something because I killed the wrong fucking brother. All those years of planning, of waiting ... ruined.'

Tears filled Aimee's eyes as it suddenly dawned on her. 'James came to see me. You basically told me as much at dinner. He was at my flat. He must have broken in and taken the picture of us and that's why he had it on him when you killed him.'

Nathan shook his head. 'You were so close on that one, but you're wrong.' Without pausing Nathan reached into his pocket, drew out a small penknife and flicked it expertly across Zoe's pale skin on her upper arm, slicing it as smoothly as butter. Zoe screamed as a trickle of blood oozed out, small at first, but then the cut began to open wider and the blood ran out of her body and dripped onto the floor.

'Noooo!' Aimee fought against her bindings, but the rope only bit into her wrists further. 'Stop it!'

'Then make sure you answer correctly next time. *Why* did James have the picture on him?'

Aimee attempted to control her breathing as adrenaline surged through her body. She couldn't concentrate. 'I don't … I don't … Wait, it was you … *you* broke into my flat and took the picture. You're the one who's been moving things about. I've been thinking that I've been going crazy or blacking out, but it was you.'

Nathan nodded. 'The first time I picked the lock, but then I found your spare key. I know your flat very well. I've looked through every drawer, every cupboard. Your hamster is a bit of a dick, the bloody thing bit me when I tried to pick him up the first time.'

'Actually, it's a girl.'

'My mistake. So you see, Aimee … the reason you're here is I believed that James got drunk for a reason. Because of *you* my sister is dead, but I couldn't just kill you like I killed James.'

'But James didn't kill her,' Aimee whimpered.

'Maybe not, but it still all comes back to you, doesn't it? If it hadn't been for you then James and Adam wouldn't have gone out that night and got shit-faced drunk. I don't know the exact details of what happened of course, I can only assume. The point is that you started it all, so first, I had to punish you. Killing you straight away was too good for you. You've been enjoying life for the past eleven years, completely unaware of how many lives you've ruined.'

Now it was Aimee's turn to laugh. 'You think I've been enjoying my life? You have no fucking idea of what I've been through, of the torture I endure on a daily basis because you're so wrapped up in your own pathetic life, determined to blame everyone but yourself. It was a goddamn accident, Nathan. It's horrible, but it's true. People die every fucking day because of stupid mistakes. I think it's about time you realised that and stop blaming everyone for what happened. Clearly Adam isn't a good guy, but he'll be in jail soon, so your stupid vendetta plan is over.' As soon as the words tumbled from her mouth she regretted them, having forgotten her training.

Nathan raised the knife and pointed it at Zoe's neck, pushing gently. Zoe shook violently, whimpering. 'I'd be careful what you say to me, Aimee, or you'll find out just how much a person can bleed.'

'I've already seen how much a person can bleed. I don't need a reminder.' Aimee closed her eyes briefly as a flash of red appeared in her vision; her blood-soaked hands, trembling, trying to stop the blood flowing from the mangled limb in front of her.

'Then I suggest you do as you're told.'

'Nathan, it doesn't have to end like this. Jennifer wouldn't have wanted this—'

'Don't you dare say her name! You killed her. You killed my little sister and now I'm going to kill yours so you know exactly how it feels.'

'No! Stop! Please!' Aimee's voice faltered as Nathan twirled the knife around his fingers, circling Zoe. Zoe still had her blindfold on; at least she wouldn't be able to see what was about to happen.

A loud bang followed by shouts erupted.

It all happened so fast …

Chapter Sixty-Five
Then

Aimee's New Flat, Woking, April 2010

I fling my bag on the kitchen counter and sigh with pure relief and pleasure. Here I am, standing in my very own kitchen, in my own flat, completely alone. Mum and Zoe left about ten minutes ago. I told them I didn't need help with unpacking, that I was going to take it slow and enjoy the time to myself. It's completely surreal to be standing here now. I never, not in my wildest dreams, thought I'd be in this position.

During the past month so many things have happened. I bought this flat, for a start. It's brand new, so I didn't have to worry about a chain. I got accepted for a mortgage pretty much straight away and I used a big chunk of my compensation money for the deposit with enough left over to treat us all to a holiday to Spain next month.

I started my new job as an administrative assistant at the Golding Police Station two weeks ago and it's going very well. I've settled in and picked up the demands of the job quickly. I left out my previous job as a soldier from my application and, so far, no one has found out. I can't see how they ever will either.

Cindy and Dot are now my best friends and we chat every day. Cindy is my work wife and is notorious for spreading gossip around the station. It's a slightly dull job at times, I won't lie, but there is plenty of prospect to work my way up in the years to come. Who knows, maybe one day I'll be stable enough to apply to become a police officer. It's crossed my mind more than once, but I'm not ready to take the plunge yet. I have a lot of healing to do and my new therapist is helping with that. She's actually pretty decent as far as therapists go. I'm still not sure if I'll ever fully recover. After all, mental illness isn't something that's treatable indefinitely; it's something I'll have to learn to live with. I'll always have the scar on my wrist to remind myself just how dangerous the dark path is and I'll do my best to steer clear and stay in the light, and with my new best friends by my side, I have no doubt I'll succeed.

Tomorrow night I'm attending my first boxing class. Dot is coming with me for moral support and said she'll stand at the side and cheer me on. I'm beyond terrified, but I'm looking forward to starting a hobby and doing something that's considered normal, for a change. I want to continue to get fitter and healthier and my physiotherapy is still ongoing for the time being. They said that, physically, I should have no problem in making an almost complete recovery.

I often think of James, but I know it was the right decision to end things with him. I didn't want to be responsible for ruining his life, his chance of being happy, his chance of having children that are biologically his. My hand sometimes hovers over my phone, itching to call him, to check if he's okay, but something always stops me. Maybe one day I'll see him again, but a part of me hopes I don't. I knew him during one of the lowest phases of my life and, although he was a glimmering spark of hope for a while, I'd rather not go back down that road. He's better off without me.

The last person I think about every night is Jones. I wonder how he is and if he'll ever be happy in life. I hope so. Despite him being a complete dickhead I do care about him, but I don't even know where he is now, so I can't contact him.

Maybe he's better off without me too. I'd only be afraid of hurting him even more.

It's time to start focussing on myself and I really think I'll be happy here.

The first thing I need to do now, at this precise moment … is find the kettle. A cup of NATO tea is in order.

Chapter Sixty-Six
Now

Loud male voices echoed, vibrating around the room as the door in front of her burst off its hinges and clattered to the floor. Half a dozen armed police officers trampled the door, forcing their way into the room, shouting and pointing their weapons at Nathan. Zoe screamed amidst the chaos, still completely unaware of what was happening all around her. Nathan flung himself at the nearest officer, hurling abuse and wielding the penknife, but he was easily taken down by two others, who shoved him to the floor and pulled his arms behind his back, kicking the knife away.

Aimee attempted to control her breathing as an officer approached her. Another was sweeping the room for any further danger while another began to untie Zoe, who was whimpering, but at least she was alive.

'Please, just make sure Zoe's okay,' said Aimee, shaking her head. At that moment Jones ran into the room, almost tripping up on the discarded door. 'Jones!' cried Aimee.

Jones hurried up to her and nodded at the officer, a silent acknowledgement that he would take care of her now. 'Looks like now I'm the one saving your life,' he said as he reached up to untie the ropes binding her wrists.

'You did more than save my life. You saved Zoe's life too. How did you find us?'

'I'll tell you later. You scared the crap out of me, Price.'

Aimee groaned with relief as her arms were freed. Blood rushed to her upper limbs and her legs crumpled beneath her, too weak to support her weight, but before she hit the floor Jones caught her and held her up. They held eye contact, neither blinking, their bodies pressed against each other.

'I bet when you saved me it wasn't quite so romantic.'

Aimee let out a snort of laughter. 'I think you need a refresher course on what's considered romantic, Jones.'

'Maybe you could teach me sometime.'

Aimee just smiled. Jones ensured she was able to stand on her own before he let her go and then they both turned to Nathan, who had been handcuffed and was in the process of being read his rights. Aimee allowed the officer handling him to finish and then approached him.

'Nathan ... for what it's worth ... I truly am sorry about Jennifer and about what Adam did and for the part I played, albeit unknowingly, but you deserve to go to jail for what you did to James.'

Nathan bared his teeth in an evil grin. 'I hope you rot in hell, bitch.' He spat at her, barely missing her face. Aimee grimaced, but before she could properly react Jones lunged forwards and punched him square in the face. Nathan's nose cracked, blood spurting onto his face, and he screamed.

DI Fields approached the commotion, his arms folded, but his face grinning. 'As much as I agree with what just happened I suggest you not assault my suspect any further.'

Jones smiled and took a step back. 'He's all yours, Detective Dimwit.'

DI Fields sighed. 'Really? You're still going with Detective Dimwit?'

'Hey, I'm the one who found Aimee and basically told you how to do your job.'

Aimee glanced at DI Fields and shrugged, while he rolled his eyes. 'We'll discuss this later. Aimee, there's an ambulance outside waiting to take you and your sister to the hospital. I'll meet you there and get one of my DCs to take a statement from you both later. Your mother has been called and she's meeting you there. She may need a sedative or something because apparently DC Forman said she was hysterical when he told her what was going on.'

Aimee nodded. 'Thanks for handling everything, Detective. What are you even doing here? I thought you preferred to stay behind a desk.'

'Yes, well ... usually I do, but when Tom Jones here called me and told me his concerns about you going missing I couldn't just sit behind a desk and wait. Cindy would kill me if anything happened to you.'

Aimee raised her eyebrows. 'Cindy?'

DI Fields's face reddened as he scratched himself behind his ear, avoiding her eye contact. 'Let's discuss this another time, shall we?'

'Sure thing, Detective.' Aimee grinned. As soon as everything was sorted out she knew she'd be calling Cindy to find out what on earth was going on to make Tony blush like that, although she had a vague idea already.

DI Fields patted her on the shoulder. 'You good?'

'I'm good. Has Adam been arrested?'

DI Fields nodded briefly, but wasn't able to respond any further because Zoe hurled herself into Aimee's arms, crying and shaking. Aimee cradled her sister, like she used to do when she was a child, and kissed the top of her head.

'It's okay, Zoe. It's okay.'

'Oh my god, I was so scared. I thought I was going to die. I thought he was going to kill us both.' Her voice broke and she began crying again. Her tears dripped onto Aimee's shoulder. 'What the hell is wrong with that guy?'

'He just needed someone to take the blame for his sister's death.'

'But it wasn't your fault.'

Aimee merely smiled, keeping her thoughts to herself. It was true that she didn't think she was directly responsible for Jennifer's death, but Aimee knew that her actions all those years ago had, in part, eventually led to her death. She could, had she been inclined, have contacted James after she'd broken up with him and checked he was okay, but she hadn't. Her mind had been elsewhere, solely intent on getting out of the situation she'd found herself in. Had she spoken with him further, not been so impulsive, she may have saved Jennifer's life. For every action there was a consequence and Aimee now had far too many real examples within her own life to prove that.

'Hey.' Jones's voice interrupted her thoughts. 'You okay?'

Aimee nodded as Zoe slowly lifted her head off her shoulder. 'Yeah.'

'Let's get you two checked over then.'

Apart from the deep gash in Zoe's upper arm she was otherwise not physically injured. She was, however, suffering from shock, but the colour started returning to her cheeks by the time they arrived at the hospital and she'd drunk the sweet tea that was offered. Aimee was relieved that Jones and DI Fields had found them before Nathan could have caused any further damage. She was glad she'd kept him talking and had been able to bide enough time to be rescued, even though she hadn't known that they would be.

Aimee's mum was in floods of hysterical tears as she embraced her girls, kissing them both over and over. Aimee didn't attempt to pull away. In fact, she clung to her mum as tight as she could, closing her eyes. Someone cleared their throat behind her, so she glanced over and saw Jones hovering awkwardly nearby.

'Mum, Zoe ... I'd like you to meet someone ... this is Thomas Jones. This is the man who saved me and Zoe today. Jones, this is my mum and my sister, Zoe.'

Her mum gasped loudly, covering her mouth. Zoe smiled shyly.

'It's a pleasure to meet you both,' said Jones, nodding at each of them.

Aimee's mum reached out, took his hand and squeezed it. 'I can't thank you enough, Thomas, for saving my girls. I owe you everything.'

Jones shook his head. 'No, Mrs Price, it's *I* who should be thanking *you*. Your daughter saved my life twelve years ago in Afghanistan. I owe *her* everything.'

Aimee's mum gasped again, too stunned to respond directly, but she turned to Aimee. 'You didn't tell me the man you saved was so handsome.'

Aimee rolled her eyes. 'Thanks, Mum, for ruining the moment.'

Jones chuckled. 'Can we talk?' He gestured behind him.

Aimee nodded. 'Mum, Zoe, I'll come and find you in a bit.'

They both nodded as they hugged each other again.

Aimee followed Jones down the hospital corridor, taking care to avoid a gurney that was parked to the side. They walked in silence, their shoulders barely touching, until they found a secluded spot and stopped.

'Your mum and sister are cool.'

Aimee laughed. 'Zoe is cool. My mum is most definitely *not* cool.'

Jones leaned against the wall. 'So ...'

'So ... how did you find us? If we'd been there any longer Zoe could have been seriously hurt, or worse. He was so unpredictable. I didn't know what he was going to do from one moment to the next.'

'When you left for your date I felt ... weird.'

'Weird?'

'I was jealous. I didn't want you to go out with him. I should have told you that before you left, but you know me, I'm not one to share my feelings.' Aimee raised her eyebrows in response, but said nothing as he continued. 'Anyway, I decided I wanted to tell you how I felt, so I went to the restaurant.'

Aimee held up her hand. 'Hang on, how did you know which restaurant we were going to? Even I didn't know until he told me.'

'I didn't. I knew you guys were walking there and that your reservation was at seven and he picked you up at ten minutes to seven, so the place you were going to had to be within a ten-minute walking distance.'

'Are you telling me you actually searched every restaurant within a ten-minute walking distance of my building?'

'Pretty much, yeah.'

'How many did you search until you found me?'

'Twelve, but I didn't find you. Not exactly. I found a restaurant with an ambulance outside and a confused-looking first-aider who'd been called out because a woman had collapsed, but then had disappeared. I spoke to one of the waiters and he said that the man the woman was with had taken her home and that she had merely fainted.'

Aimee held her breath for a moment as she took in his words. 'I don't remember anything. All I remember is passing out and then waking up in that room.'

'I knew it was you. I just had this feeling, so I went back to your building and knocked on Nathan's door, but there was no answer. That's when I knew something was wrong, so I called Detective Dimwit and explained the situation. He said he and his cronies were on the way, so while I waited for backup I had a look around Nathan's flat.'

'You broke in, you mean?'

'I wasn't exactly thinking clearly at the time, Price. I just needed answers. I needed to find you and as soon as I entered his flat I knew exactly what was going on. He actually had a shrine dedicated to his sister set up in the lounge. I recognised her from the online article you showed me. By the time DD showed up I knew where Nathan worked, thanks to a random business card he had lying around. We didn't know for sure that that's where he'd be holding you, but it was all we had to go on ... and I guess you know the rest. You were being held in the one of the basement rooms. Sorry it took me so long.'

'Are you kidding! If you hadn't finally realised that you have feelings for me and continued to be a stubborn dickhead then Zoe and I could have been dead by now.'

Jones straightened his posture, fidgeting slightly. 'Hey, I never said I had feelings for you.'

'Yes, you did, you said that you were jealous and you didn't want me to go out with him.'

'No, you're wrong, what I actually said was—'

'There you go, being a stubborn dickhead again. Just admit it, Jones.'

'Admit what?'

Aimee huffed loudly. 'For fuck's sake, you're such a—' She never finished her sentence. Jones reached his hand around the back of her neck and pulled her against his body, pressing his lips roughly against hers. Aimee gasped, realising that her whole body had forgotten how to breathe as she tasted his lips. Her muscles turned to jelly as she sank into his hard chest. Finally, he pushed her harshly away from him.

'Let's not get carried away. This is a public place, Price.'

'You started it … and if I recall it never stopped you before.'

They grinned at each other, both remembering the quick shag they'd had at the nightclub in a random back room, not even a door separating them from the masses of the club all those years ago.

'So,' said Aimee as she straightened her dress, 'now what?'

'Now I expect DD will be looking for you so you can give a statement and he can explain what's going on with Adam.'

'We're at DD now?'

'Detective Dimwit is too much of an effort to say.'

'Right …' Aimee lowered her eyes to the floor. 'What did happen with Adam? Was he really the one driving that night?'

Jones nodded. 'Apparently James was unconscious the whole time. From what he told me and from what he could remember he woke up strapped into the driver's seat, but was adamant that he would never have driven in that state. Adam must have crashed the car and put James in the driving seat and then left the scene, framing him and letting him take the fall.'

Aimee shook her head. 'I can't believe he would do that to his own twin brother.'

Jones shrugged his shoulders. 'Some people are just born bad. It's just a shame that a decent, innocent man landed up dead.'

Aimee allowed her eyes to drop to the floor. 'I can't believe he's really dead and this is all over.'

'Yeah … it's over, but now that it is I think you and I need to talk.'

'I hope alcohol will be involved because talking to you is like slamming my head against a brick wall sometimes.'

'Alcohol will definitely be involved … although maybe just for me because you look as if one shot would knock you out.'

Aimee grinned. 'Sounds like a challenge to me. I guess … I'll see you later back at mine then.'

Jones's eyes grew dark and serious. 'See you later, Price.'

It was nearly seven in the morning by the time Aimee was allowed to leave the hospital and after she'd given her statement to DC Forman. DI Fields also told her that HR had discussed her application to join the police force and had granted her permission to carry on with the process if she still desired. She was pleasantly surprised when she found herself turning the opportunity to progress to the next stage down. DI Fields said that they could talk more in a week when she returned to work, but Aimee had already made up her mind. She no longer wanted to become a police officer. It wasn't what was going to make her happy. She had something else in mind.

Jones was asleep on the sofa when she walked into her flat. She smiled as she watched him for several seconds, his breathing shallow, and then flicked the kettle on. Jones stirred.

'Sorry,' she said. 'I didn't mean to wake you.'

Jones yawned and stretched, his t-shirt riding up slightly. 'What time is it?'

'Seven.'

'You okay?'

'I could do with a coffee.'

'I'll make you one.' Jones stood up and joined her in the kitchen area and began to make the brews. They both reached for the sugar pot at the same time, their fingers overlapping.

'Jones ... can I ask you something?'

'Depends what it is.'

'It was you, wasn't it?'

Jones found her eyes and held her gaze. 'What was me, Price?'

'That day when I took the knife from the mess hall ... you saw me, didn't you? You knew what I was going to do and you alerted the staff. You saved my life.'

Jones took the sugar pot and opened the lid. 'I can neither confirm nor deny that fact.'

'And you recommended me for a medal, didn't you? It wasn't James after all.'

Jones placed two heaped spoonfuls of sugar in each cup. 'I have no idea what you're talking about.'

Aimee sighed angrily. 'Why won't you just admit that you're a decent guy?'

'Because I'm not.'

'Yes, you are. You live and work with the homeless using your compensation money and you helped out James when he—'

'Am I going to have to kiss you again to get you to shut the hell up?'

'Yep.'

Jones dropped the spoon he was holding and pulled Aimee against him. He leaned in close, their lips barely touching as he said, 'I hope you know what you're doing, Price.'

'I do,' she replied with a smile. 'You don't happen to have a job going at your charity, do you?'

'Depends.'

'On what?'

Jones traced his fingers down the side of her body. 'You can come and work for me ... *if* ... you apply to compete in the Invictus Games.'

'Why do you care? Boxing is just a hobby.'

'It makes you happy and, after what we've both been through, I think we deserve to be happy, don't you? By the way, I have something for you.' Jones pulled away and reached into the pocket of his trousers.

Aimee clasped both her hands over her mouth as she laid eyes on the set of dog tags Daffy had given to her all those years ago; the ones she'd lost on that fateful day.

'B-But how? How did you ...' Aimee blinked back streams of tears as she took the tags from Jones. They were a little worn around the edges and slightly blackened, but it was them. She squeezed them tight in her palm.

'I don't care how you found them, but thank you.' She kissed him on the lips. 'You have no idea how much these mean to me. Now I don't feel as if I'm jinxed anymore.'

'Oh, Price ... only an idiot would believe in jinxes.'

Aimee bit her lip. 'So what now? What about us?'

Jones stared at her lips and lightly brushed them with his. 'I tell you what ... after the count of three we each have to say yes or no. Yes means we want to give whatever this is between us a chance and no means ... no.'

Aimee leaned away from Jones and raised her eyebrows. 'Okay ... on the count of three ... one ... two ... three ...'

'Yes,' they both said quietly.

'Jinx,' they both replied with a laugh.

Author's Note

While the characters in this book are purely fictional, some of the situations, conversations and experiences are based loosely on true events.

I was a British soldier from 2007 until 2011. Whilst serving, I experienced sexual harassment and bullying, and it affected me so much at one point that I became severely depressed in 2008. I did not experience the horrors of war or any form of PTSD, but each story that Aimee flashes back to throughout the book does have some true roots, including the fact she broke her hip in training. That being said, I did experience some fantastic times in the Army and am proud to have served my country. Unfortunately, bullying and sexual harassment does happen, but it doesn't just happen in the Army, and it doesn't just happen to women, so I don't want readers to think I'm causing offence to only male serving soldiers.

Aimee's hamster, Darth, was actually a real hamster belonging to my best friend, Katie, whose three children named him after Darth Vader. Sadly, Darth passed away peacefully in his sleep on the 13th of January 2023. RIP Darth.

I originally wrote Jinx when I was a teenager, but the plot has changed massively since then (with the added inclusion of the Army story). The characters, however, are all relatively the same and I wanted to bring an old story of mine to life, and I'm really pleased with how it's turned out.

Leave a Review

I hope you've enjoyed reading Jinx.

If you have, please consider leaving me a review on Amazon and Goodreads, share a review on your social media pages and tag me, share my book to any book clubs you may be a part of or recommend my book to friends and family.

Reviews are massively important, especially to self-published authors. They help find other readers who may enjoy the book and spread the word to a wider audience.

Connect with Jessica Huntley

Find and connect with me online via the following platforms.

Sign up to my email list via my website to be notified of future books and receive a twice-monthly author newsletter www.jessicahuntleyauthor.com

Follow me on Facebook: Jessica Huntley - Author - @jessica.reading.writing

Follow me on Instagram: @jessica_reading_writing

Follow me on Twitter: @jess_read_write

Follow me on TikTok: @jessica_reading_writing

Follow me on Goodreads: jessica_reading_writing

Lightning Source UK Ltd.
Milton Keynes UK
UKHW042244020323
417954UK00001B/105